Old Cravings

A Scary Good Romance

Joy Jarrett

Literary Wanderlust | Denver, Colorado

Published in the United States by Literary Wanderlust LLC, Denver, Colorado.

https//www.LiteraryWanderlust.com

ISBN Print: 978-1-942856-72-6
ISBN Digital: 978-1-942856-78-8
Cover design: Pozu Mitsuma

Printed in the United States of America

Dedication

To my mother, Sherrie, who first took me to the library and my father, David—I miss you every day.

1

Piper pulled her phone from the pocket of her white coat, glanced at the screen, and in her shock, dropped it onto the floor of the exam room. Part of the case popped off and her patient, on account of being an Irish setter, lunged for it with an audible *snap*. The owner yanked back the dog and shot Piper a disapproving look.

Piper bent to pick up the phone and reattached the case. She used the moment to blink back the tears that came as unexpected as the phone call had.

"Sorry about that," she said with a brightness she didn't feel and straightened up, trying to put the phone call from her mind. She patted the setter, feeling kinship with a fellow redhead. "Rusty is definitely an eat-first-and-ask-questions-later kind of dog, isn't he? You said you're worried he's been eating gravel?"

After ten minutes of repeated reassurances that Rusty showed no signs of an intestinal blockage, Piper was relieved at the knock on the exam room door.

"Dr. Mitchell?" Her receptionist poked her head in, and

Piper smiled as she always did when her best friend had to address her in such a manner. "Hate to bother you, but you have an emergency call."

Something about the way her best friend smiled back tightly made Piper wonder about her earlier phone call. She told Rusty's owner they were free to go and slipped back to her office.

The red light blinked on her desk phone, indicating someone was holding. She sank into the chair and drew a deep breath, allowing herself a moment. Just in case.

She stared out the window at the ski lifts hanging still and empty on the brown mountainside. The calendar on her bulletin board might say November, but the sun shone warm and bright. The entire town of Crested Butte was waiting anxiously for the flakes to fall and the tourists to blow in with the cold.

Piper's vet practice didn't rely on ski tourism, but she too couldn't shake the distinct feeling she waited for the cold as well. Waited for it with an odd sense of dread she didn't understand.

With a sigh, she picked up the phone. "Hello, this is Dr. Mitchell."

"Piper."

Just like that, his voice sliced open one year, two months, and nine days' worth of healing. She heard so many things packed into two syllables when he said her name—pain, relief, longing.

No, not longing.

"Dylan," she whispered. Then cleared her throat. "What's going on?"

"It's one of the horses."

"Maybe you should call Dr. Rodriguez."

"Piper."

She wished he'd stop using her name. His voice was thick like he was fighting off tears, and Dylan wasn't a man who cried. Ever. Something was wrong.

"Piper, it's Lightning." She caught a rustling sound, so faint she might have imagined it and could picture him sitting at his desk in the barn office, taking off the black cowboy hat that had won her heart, and running a hand through his thick, dark curls before shoving it back on. "He needs to be put down." His voice grew even thicker. "I thought you'd want to come."

Damn him. He couldn't have spared her this? Lightning had been her horse for seven years. She'd sat astride him when Dylan got off his own mount and proposed to her one beautiful spring day five years ago. He wanted her to euthanize him?

She wasn't even a large animal vet.

"I'll do it," Dylan said, with that uncanny ability of his to somehow read her thoughts. "But I thought you'd want to come and say good-bye."

Damn him twice. He knew her too well. If ever there was something to make her set foot on that ranch again with all its painful memories, this was it.

"Okay."

"Piper? Hurry, all right? He's hurting bad."

"What happened?"

The faint rustle came again. "That's just it. I have no idea, but something tore him up real good. I was hoping—"

A screaming whinny cut through his words—and her heart.

"I gotta go. Hurry, Piper."

The line went dead.

—

The Crazy K Ranch lay only fifteen minutes away from town, but Piper hadn't driven this road since the night she found Dylan kissing Holly behind the horse barn.

Or, if what he'd said was true, when Holly had been kissing Dylan. Regardless, he'd appeared to be enjoying the kiss. At any rate, their marriage was already almost through by the time she discovered her husband locking lips with the young wrangler in the tight jeans.

She shoved the memory from her mind only to have it replaced with the unpleasant situation at present.

Lightning. The lump in her throat grew as she guided the silver Honda down the dusty, red-tinged dirt road. Leaves rattled across the hood in warm gusts, and she turned up the air in the car.

She crested the hill that afforded the full view of the two-story, log ranch house below, nestled in a broad mountain meadow. The new red horse barn stood a short distance off to the north and behind that, the East River winked in the afternoon light. The elk pen—more the reason for their divorce than Holly—lay to the east, where a few large brown bodies could be seen resting on the hillside. Gunnison National Forest, dark and green, stretched behind the elk pen.

Various outbuildings—trailers for the ranch employees, sheds, a few cabins, even an old schoolhouse—lay scattered across the three-hundred-acre spread. No cars were parked outside the cabins, which was strange. It was the middle of hunting season, after all.

Piper put down her window and smelled hay and dust and sagebrush. Crazy K, even during a dry spell that rendered it brown and dull, still looked beautiful. Beautiful and dangerous as a rattlesnake.

A gunshot made her jump. It sounded close, rolling like terrible thunder over the surrounding mountains.

She was too late.

"Oh, Lightning." She gripped the steering wheel so hard that her fingers hurt, an echo of the ache in her heart.

She stopped the car and put it in park, trying to figure out where the sound came from. Not the new horse barn below. Past the elk pen maybe. Tears spattered the front of her shirt. She could turn the car around and head back into town. Dylan didn't need her anymore. She'd call him later and tell him she heard the gunshot and thought it best to leave him in peace.

She could. She'd sound like a coward though if she did. Piper wiped her face and put the car in gear. The road curved past the elk pen and a little ways off, Dylan's white Chevy sat in the grass, a rifle propped against the front bumper.

And then she saw him. She'd seen him around town many times since the divorce. How could she not when the place was so small? But they'd managed to avoid speaking or coming into closer contact than a glimpse across a street for over a year.

The last time she'd spoken in person to this man, he'd still been her husband. Now he was . . . just Dylan.

She didn't know if she could handle interacting with him in the best of situations, and the scene before her showed it was the worst.

Dylan, his broad back to her, crouched beside the body of Lightning. A crimson patch, horrifying in its size, surrounded the palomino. A wide trail of blood headed from the forest. At her car's approach, Dylan turned to look over his shoulder, but she couldn't see his face under the cowboy hat.

Her pulse thundered in her ears at the sight of him. At the sight of her dead horse.

By the time she'd pulled off the road and climbed out of the car, he was standing, hat in hand, beside Lightning. It unnerved her, the way he watched her walk toward him. She'd seen him give that same look to others over the years before he hired hunting guides or entered a business dealing with someone.

He was taking the measure of her.

She squared her shoulders and strode over to the body of the horse she'd loved. Flies rose and fell in clouds over the mess that had been Lightning. The smell of offal hit her like a punch to the gut.

At the sight of him, she gasped with shock. As a vet, she was well-versed in dealing with dead animals. Indeed, death was often an old friend, called upon by her own hands to administer mercy.

There was nothing merciful about this.

Lightning lay on his side. His stomach had been slashed open to release glistening loops of intestine, strewn ten feet away. Four long slashes ripped open his back. The cuts were so deep she could see the bluish-white glimpse of vertebrae and ribs. A large hunk of his hindquarters was missing to reveal a mass of red muscle too reminiscent of ground beef for Piper's comfort.

Something was very wrong here. The cream-colored skin on three of his legs had been stripped back from the bone like a peeled apple. It was unnatural.

The only part of the scene that made sense was the blood streaked down his white blaze from forelock to nose from the bullet hole. The first sob escaped her when she noticed one of his eyes had been ripped out. She turned away and found herself enfolded in Dylan's arms.

He led the horse out of the barn with that wide grin of his, and she swore he and the horse sauntered over with identical cocky steps.

"Lightning and I had a talk," he said.

"Oh, yeah?"

"Yeah. Said he'd much rather have you as his rider from now on. He said you're awful pretty."

"Really. I didn't know you spoke horse."

"I've always had a way with different tongues." He raised his eyebrows and she rolled her eyes. Then Dylan's mouth pressed against hers in a kiss both sweet and hot as he showed her just how good he was with that tongue of his.

When Piper finally came up for air, it was to bury her face in Lightning's mane to breathe in the smell of horse. He nickered softly in approval.

"I've never had a horse before," she said.

"Yeah? Seems we're both having new experiences because I've never loved a woman like I love you, Piper Mitchell."

And he'd pulled her back into his arms much as he was doing now in circumstances that couldn't be any more different.

Dylan held her tight against his chest as she cried. His scent— his deodorant and sweat and leather and something uniquely Dylan—hurt more than the smell of death overpowering it all.

"I know," he said, his deep voice rumbling under her ear.

She stiffened in his arms, but he felt so familiar and good, she let him pull her in tighter.

"He must have suffered so much," she said.

"I shouldn't have tried to wait for you. So stupid." His voice caught, and a tear fell from above to slide down her hair and over her jawline.

He hadn't cried on their wedding day. He hadn't cried when she told him they wanted different things in life. He hadn't cried when she asked for the divorce.

But he was crying over a horse. Irritation flared inside her, despite her sorrow for Lightning.

Dylan's tears on her skin were too intimate anyway, and she eased away. A glance at his face was all she could stand. His hazel eyes were red-rimmed, and he had a day's worth of stubble, but he looked as good as ever.

He turned away and spun his hat in his hands. "Two months ago, one of my mares foaled Lightning's colt." His mouth curved, not quite a smile. "Looks just like him."

Part of Lightning would live on. She wished she could see the colt. "What'd you name him?"

Now he really did smile. "Thunder, what else?" The smile vanished. "I think I'll bury Lightning right here. He always liked being up near the forest."

Piper looked up at the tree line where the national forest began. What secrets did it hide? She and Dylan stood for a bit in a silence only interrupted by the flies and the occasional raucous cawing of some ravens sitting in a nearby tree. They waited for their chance to start in on Lightning, and she tried not to hate them for it.

Dylan cleared his throat, once more reading her thoughts. "What do you think did that? I thought maybe a cougar. But Lightning's torn to shreds. Big cats strangle their prey."

"Yeah." She made herself look back at the body, and the impression of wrongness returned. "Mountain lions eat neatly.

They don't start at the hindquarters or spread around the intestines. And something had to be strong enough to drag him from there." She pointed at the forest. What had he been doing up there?

"Agreed. A bear?"

"Not unless we suddenly have grizzlies in Colorado. When did you find him?"

"A minute before I called you. I think it might have happened earlier this morning."

"You didn't hear anything?"

"Don't you think I'd have mentioned it if I had?"

She experienced another flash of irritation.

"I looked around for tracks, but I couldn't find anything," he added. "Ground's pretty dry. It's covered in leaves."

Piper followed the blood, climbing up the hill and into the steep forest where the trail ended in a patch of wet, crimson leaves. She studied the ground, but she was no tracker. Other than the smears of blood, there was no sign of anything unusual. She didn't see any animal prints. Dylan was right. Too many leaves everywhere.

The forest was still and quiet. The base of her skull prickled. She hurried back from the tree line and returned to Lightning's body. The cloud of flies buzzed higher. "I'm going to take some photos."

Dylan hung his hands on his hips. "What for?"

"Just in case."

"In case what?"

"You make any enemies lately?"

His tongue went to the inside of his lower cheek, despite giving up chewing when they started dating years ago. Or maybe he'd taken it up again. None of her business now. "You think a person—"

"I don't know, Dylan. I just can't imagine what animal could inflict this kind of damage. It seems—cruel."

"Nature is." He shook his head. "Hell, I know better than

anyone, right?"

"Domestic elk aren't exactly natural." She regretted the words as soon as they slipped out her big, fat mouth. Her ex-father-in-law had been very unlucky, becoming one of a handful of people ever killed by an elk. But if the Kincaid men hadn't run this stupid operation that counted as canned hunting in her book, he'd still be alive today. "I shouldn't have said that," she said. "That was—"

"Low, yeah." His mouth tightened. "Last week made four years he's been gone."

She'd forgotten. She hung her head. Dylan crying over a horse made more sense now. Most likely those tears weren't just for Lightning. They were for Dylan's father. And she didn't think she flattered herself to believe her presence brought up as many painful memories for him as it did her. He was probably feeling, like her, all alone. His mom died of a rare form of bone cancer when Dylan was eight, and his older brother had moved to his wife's ranch in Idaho. His mom, his dad, his brother. Piper. Lightning. All gone.

"I—I'm sorry."

Dylan squeezed the bridge of his nose. "Um, as far as enemies, I had to let one of the hands go last month. Caught him stealing liquor from the house. But he was a pathetic mess from his wife and kids leaving him, not some kind of psychopath. He wasn't even that mad about losing his job."

"Anyone else?"

He leveled a look at her. "I'm sure as hell not Holly's favorite person."

Piper's stomach clenched. She didn't want to hear this. She had to hear this. How many nights had she imagined her husband tangling legs and sheets with that twenty-year-old? Veronica said she'd seen them down at the Black Diamond bar shortly after Piper moved out.

Had he slept with her? She took a deep breath. Did it matter? Dylan was a good-looking man. If it wasn't Holly, there'd surely been other women. He wouldn't have stayed celibate over a year.

"You think Holly did this?" she said, not asking the question she really wanted answered.

"Course not. But you asked me about enemies. I wanted to be clear she doesn't like me much now." He waited a couple of beats, but she refused to give him the satisfaction of asking why. "When she kissed me, I had no choice but to terminate her employment. It was completely inappropriate. I was her boss. She's more than ten years younger than me. And most important, I was married." His gaze dropped to the ground. "I liked being married."

"Yeah." Her heart beat harder, and her throat closed on what was meant to be a snort. "Just not to me."

A muscle in his jaw twitched. "You believe what you want. You always did."

"I'll just take some pictures and then I'll be on my way."

"That's probably a good idea."

Whether he meant the photos or her leaving, she wasn't sure. Maybe both.

Careful to avoid stepping in the mess, she held her phone high over the scene and took several pictures from different angles.

Dylan leaned against the bumper of his truck and studied her studying Lightning. She did her best to ignore him. She moved around behind the horse and wondered what wounds might be hidden on the side he lay on. She bent to examine the slashes closer when she caught sight of something black protruding from the wound over the spine.

"What is it?" Dylan asked, pushing off the bumper in that sexy way he had of moving.

"Let's find out." She took a pair of latex gloves from the back pocket of her jeans and snapped them on.

She poked inside the wound and glanced at Dylan, who'd moved nearer. His top lip curled in disgust. Piper's stomach curdled, but she was determined not to let Dylan see how sick this made her. She was a professional after all.

Her fingers curled around something hard and cold, about as thick as her thumb. Whatever it was, it had stuck into Lightning's backbone. Piper fought off her disgust as she wiggled it back and forth until it gave. Then, with a terrible *squelch,* she slid the bloody thing out and stood to show it to Dylan.

"What the hell is that?" he breathed.

2

Piper's hand shook a little as she held up what appeared to be a glossy black claw, at least seven or eight inches long.

"So, it was a bear," Dylan said.

She took it between her fingers to mimic a bear's paw. "You know any kind of bear with claws this long?"

"A grizzly—"

"Dylan."

He opened his mouth and shut it again. "Yeah, all right." He turned in a slow circle, stopping to face the national forest.

The wind whipped through the trees, rattling the skeletal branches of the aspens where a few straggling yellow leaves remained. The branches of the evergreens, of the firs and pines, undulated in waves as if some large, unseen creature moved through them.

A cold finger of dread traced down Piper's scalp and raised the hairs on the back of her neck. She took a step closer to her car, then another.

"Just the wind, Piper." But when she looked at Dylan, he

had his hand on the door of his truck. His foot rested on the running board in an attempt to look casual. Or maybe cocky in his case. Regardless of what he was attempting, he looked like he wanted to dive into his truck and tear out of there as badly as she did.

No wonder, with the bloodbath of Lightning lying on the ground behind them, the wicked talon gripped in her hand still.

She held it up, resisting the urge to fling it as far from her as possible. "If you don't mind, I'm going to take this with me. I know this guy. He's a wildlife biologist at Western State." At the mention of Nate to her ex-husband, Piper's face blazed hot. She and Nate went on two dates after being introduced by a mutual friend. The second date with the biologist went well right up to the make-out session, which ended when Nate slid a hand up her shirt. Piper broke down into sobs and jumped out of the car. Fortunately, Nate had gone through a divorce himself and understood well. They became friends instead of lovers.

Dylan frowned at her. No doubt because she was glowing like a hot coal. "I was gonna call Parks and Wildlife to send out an officer to confirm the kill," he said.

"Get reimbursed for Lightning?" There were programs that paid farmers and ranchers for livestock killed by certain predators like bears, cougars, or wolves.

"Is that so bad? If it's a bear, might as well take advantage of the government, right?"

"I can give the claw back to you later if you need it. Or Nate can send a report to Parks and Wildlife for you." She babbled on. "He's smart. Knows his stuff. He can help us out. Super nice guy." Why couldn't she shut up?

Dylan raised an eyebrow. "You sleeping with him or something?"

She lifted her chin. "It's none of your concern if I am."

He held up his hands—palms out. "True." He smirked at her though, a smug look showing he thought nothing of the sort was going on.

God, he irritated her so much.

"You take this Nate guy that claw and if Wildlife wants it, you can give it back later," he said.

Another gust of wind ruffled her hair, blowing red-gold strands across her face, and she shivered. Was it her imagination, or was the wind getting colder?

Dylan rummaged around in the bed of his truck and pulled out a blue tarp.

She watched for a moment as he unfolded it, and then helped him cover Lightning's body. Together, they worked in silence to put some rocks on the corners of the sheet.

He pulled off his hat and held it in front of him. They stood side-by-side a few moments and looked at the shapeless mass under the tarp, which didn't quite cover all the bloodstained grass. The rapidly chilling wind clawed at the edges of the tarp with a rustling that set Piper's teeth on edge.

Dylan put his black hat back on and scratched a finger down his jaw, making a rasping noise on his stubble. "I'll come back later this afternoon with the backhoe and some help, but I didn't want to leave him like that."

"Be careful," she said suddenly. It hit her hard. Irritating or not, if anything ever happened to Dylan, it would kill her. Since she had no control over what the man did anymore, it put her in a vulnerable position. "There's either the world's biggest bear running around or some twisted sicko."

He gestured at the talon she clutched. "I'm putting my money on a velociraptor."

"Real velociraptors were the size of a turkey. You mean a Utah raptor."

Dylan rolled his eyes. "Some things never change. You always were such a nerd."

For some reason, the words stung. Maybe because they cut to the heart of their problems. Piper, the city girl, the book-smart, bleeding-heart liberal versus the rough-around-the-edges, good-with-his-hands, gun-toting cowboy that was Dylan.

"Well, when I hear back from my fellow nerd about this claw, I'll let you know."

He nodded a few times. "All right."

An awkward pause followed where neither knew what to say next, but several conversations of unspoken words pressed down between them.

Giving up on speaking altogether, Piper turned and walked to her car. When she opened the door, she faced Dylan. "Thank you."

His face screwed up in puzzlement. "For?"

"For Lightning. For calling me about him." Her throat clogged with tears again. "For giving him to me in the first place."

"Piper."

"Yeah?"

"You be careful, too."

—

Piper polished off the bottle of wine knowing she would regret it in the morning. With her luck, she'd be dealing with some dog's abscessed anal glands to go with a nasty hangover. She shut off the old rerun of *Sex and the City*.

God, what a cliché she was.

Osiris, her black cat, jumped onto the blue plaid couch beside her and purred.

"I'm pathetic, aren't I, O?" She stroked a hand down his sleek back, grateful he offered no judgment.

The wine bottle, along with an empty bag of chips and a container of hummus, sat on the coffee table in silent reproach.

Piper sighed and forced her butt off the couch. One of the things she liked about living alone was she could keep things neat and tidy.

Dylan was a consummate slob. With gorgeous eyes and washboard abs that wouldn't quit.

Total. Slob.

She gathered up her trash and carried it through to the tiny kitchen. Everything about her apartment was tiny. Attached to the back of her vet practice, it was located at the end of an old green Victorian building that was divided into several businesses on the town's main drag.

The trashcan under her sink was overflowing, and she sighed again. Dylan had at least been good at gender-stereotyped roles like taking out the garbage. She shoved the trash down and gathered up the bag in a movement made clumsy by the wine.

When she opened the back door, a cold gust of wind whipped it out of her hand. The weather was changing. Leaves rattled down the alleyway. She clicked on the light over her back stoop and stepped onto it to pause a moment. The streetlight over the dumpster had gone out leaving a thick pool of darkness.

She should just put the trash on the stoop and take it out in the morning. But if Cynthia, the owner of the art gallery next door, spotted it, she'd put in a complaint to the management of their building. She hated Piper's vet practice, with its barking dogs and "animal smell" located next to her upscale gallery.

"Come on, Mitchell, woman up," she said. Piper considered leaving the back door open before deciding against it. Osiris liked being an indoor cat, but it wasn't worth the risk.

The trash clinked as she went down the two steps and crossed the alley. A loud cawing startled Piper as a couple of crows rose off the fence and flapped away into the night. She approached the dumpster, and though it always stunk, tonight it was far worse than usual. It didn't smell like garbage. Instead, a putrid, rotting smell reminiscent of the scene earlier in the day slapped her in the face.

Stories of bodies left in dumpsters filled her mind as she lifted the lid. She threw in her trash bag, and the glass shattered—a loud reproach that she hadn't recycled her wine bottle. The dumpster was empty.

The stench worsened on a gust of cold air. She pulled her shirt up over her nose and tucked her elbows in to ward off the chill.

A heavy feeling of dread filled her. Turning her back on the dark dumpster area felt very wrong. At the same time, she couldn't bring herself to turn around and look behind her. She hurried toward her back porch and its welcoming glow of yellow light.

The light blinked out, plunging the entire alleyway into darkness.

Behind her, something sharp scraped over metal. She couldn't look, but she couldn't *not* look either. Slowly, she turned around.

The sound was coming from the dumpster, like someone softly running fingernails on a chalkboard. That curved claw came to mind. She'd stopped by Nate's office to give it to him this afternoon, and he'd been just as puzzled as her when she'd put it on his desk. She'd handed it over with a sense of relief to be rid of the thing.

The noise screeched a little louder. Claws. That was what it sounded like—something running its claws along the metal inside the dumpster. Goosebumps rose on her arms, and she ran.

What if it *was* claws? It could be a cat or a dog stuck inside. A few months ago, a woman had brought in a litter of kittens she'd found in a pile of garbage outside her condo.

Piper couldn't leave an animal in need. It took a Herculean effort, but she made herself turn back around. And stumbled at the sight.

The black plastic lid of the dumpster was slowly rising.

Giddy terror swirled in her stomach.

She knew, without a doubt, no dog or cat was inside there. She knew it as surely as she did that, whatever it was, she didn't want to see it.

Her feet remained stuck to the ground.

The lid rose higher.

3

Dylan stood on the wrap-around deck and took a long pull of his beer. He frowned at the sweetness.

Running a ranch took blood, sweat, and tears that filled every second of his waking hours. But when Piper left, he stopped sleeping much. His waking hours suddenly stretched out, and he found himself trying to kill time. Brewing beer seemed as good a hobby as any.

He took another sip. Too much sugar left. He tipped the bottle so Waylon could try it.

The dog lapped greedily at the beer, but the Catahoula hound also ate horse shit so he wasn't exactly a good judge of taste.

"That's enough, buddy."

The dog, a speckled brown and gray, looked up at him in disappointment with one blue eye and one gold, as if to say he'd have happily drunk the whole thing.

Dylan dumped the beer out over the deck railing. Just add this latest batch of homebrew to his long list of failures. He resisted the urge to lob the bottle as far as he could. It would be a melodramatic gesture, and as a rule, he avoided those. Not to mention it was his ranch, and he took pride in its orderliness.

Piper called him a slob because he left his breakfast dishes in the sink and his socks on the floor. Big deal. That stuff was easily cleaned up. If she'd ever considered the state of his ranch, she'd never have called him a slob.

You wouldn't find broken-down tractors and rusted cars lying around his property. No, sir. The fences were in good repair, the hay stacked neatly in the barn, his patch of front lawn was weed-free.

Hell, he'd given the hunters' cabins a fresh coat of paint last month. No, not hunters' cabins. He had to stop calling them that. They were just cabins now. His dad must be rolling over in his grave about the changes—and his bank account wasn't thanking him. But Piper had gotten her way in the end.

What was that expression? Closing the barn door behind the horse? Maybe he was an idiot to give in to Piper's wishes *after* their divorce. That was how his life felt these days. A constant bid to win the approval of his ex-wife, as if she stood behind him watching every move he made.

Which showed what a fool he was. The ink had long since dried on their divorce papers. The fact that she had no idea he'd shut down the hunting operation showed how much she'd completely cut him out of her thoughts.

Or if she did think of him, it was only to assume the worst. He could always see everything she was thinking on that freckled face of hers and this afternoon, he hadn't missed what she wondered about him and Holly.

Did she think so little of him she imagined he'd been banging someone barely more than a child? Since she thought he'd been the one kissing Holly that night, Piper *must* think so little of him.

How many times since Piper left had he wanted to call her up and demand she come over? *See? No dishes in the sink. No more hunting on the ranch.* Never mind his finances were taking a nosedive. He'd even started reading things that weren't hunting magazines to make himself more interesting to her. And he'd never liked reading before. Hemingway, Dickens, Tolstoy, and more every week. He found he enjoyed the classics, would have liked to discuss them with Piper.

But no. If she could drive off this ranch and never look back, he wasn't about to go begging. If she thought he was gonna go running after her, she was mistaken. A man had his pride.

So he'd let her go. He'd signed those damn divorce papers. Hadn't spoken to her in person in over a year.

Until today.

He'd never have wished something as bad as Lightning's death as a reason to see Piper again, but God, it had been good holding her. And that made him pissed as hell at her all over again that she'd deny him something that felt so right.

Even if everything else about the scene had been so wrong.

He hated to admit it, but it had taken a huge dose of courage to return to Lightning later in the day to bury him. The Parks and Wildlife officer had come out, taken one look at the body, and declared it a bear kill. Rubber stamped the whole thing through and couldn't get off the Crazy K fast enough.

Something on the ranch didn't feel right. Well, nothing felt right since Piper left last year.

But this was different.

Off in the distance, an elk bugled from the pen. It was high-pitched and haunting, like the screaming of a rusted, ancient gate. Full of sadness and longing, the sound carried far on the still night air. Oddly still, now he thought of it.

Waylon leaned against his leg, and Dylan reached down and scratched the dog behind the ear.

Dylan narrowed his eyes and surveyed the ranch spread around him, the mountains stretching up beyond. For the first time in his life, the forest was menacing. He'd loved exploring there as a kid. He'd fished, hunted, and camped in that forest more times than he could count. He and his older brother had scared each other silly with stories of ghosts and the man with the hook and sasquatches. Every once in a while, they'd even mention their great-grandmother's story of the witherling, a terrible beast that lived among the trees. The story was so scary, his brother and him agreed not to bring that one up too often. But the forest itself? It was an old friend.

Tonight, it seemed to hide some secret threat from him. Like it wasn't only Piper that was betraying him lately. Even the forest had turned on him.

"Idiot," he said to himself.

A cold wind whipped up and rustled the bushes demarcating his yard from the open space of the ranch. So cold. He'd rolled up the sleeves of his flannel, and goosebumps broke out on his forearms. All of a sudden, he wanted to go back in the house. He glanced at the sliding door. Inside, a lamp on the end table glowed. The rest of the house was dark and empty. Lonely as usual.

But an empty house sure beat standing around outside creeping himself out like a kid with an overactive imagination.

At his side, Waylon stiffened, and Dylan dropped a hand on the dog's head. An elk bugled again. Then the sound cut off.

Dylan sucked in a breath, waiting for a scream. Only heavy silence. He was ashamed at his relief because he knew full well if the animal had screamed, he didn't have the nerve to go investigate just now.

Then Waylon growled low in his throat. Dylan felt the reverberations travel up the dog's skull. "What is it?"

Waylon's growl deepened. In the dim light from the slider, Dylan could see his hackles rise all the way down Waylon's back. The wind soughed through the bushes again.

Waylon gave two staccato barks and backed up toward the house with a whimper. His dog might not have taste in beer, but Dylan trusted his judgment about danger. Dylan followed him across the deck.

That's when the vibrations moved up through his boots. A

deep scratching came from underneath the deck, a long scraping across the underside of the boards.

Dylan raced to the door, slid it open, and he and Waylon launched themselves into the living room.

"What the hell was that?" he said to Waylon.

In answer, the dog shot under the kitchen table, shaking and whining. Dylan didn't blame the dog. Right about now, he wanted to run upstairs, jump in his bed, and hide under the blankets.

He imagined it. A grown man cowering under the covers like a little kid.

"Screw that, Waylon." He strode into the laundry room and rummaged in a cupboard to pull out a big Maglite. Then, for good measure, he opened his gun cabinet in the front entry. He ignored the rifles and the tranquilizer guns for knocking down elk and selected his favorite handgun—a .357. Dylan returned to the sliding door, braver now.

For his part, Waylon remained shivering under the table.

"Coward," he said to the dog, but only because his behavior unnerved Dylan more than he cared to admit. Waylon had never acted like this before.

He flipped on the back light and opened the door. The wind blowing in was downright icy now. His boots thudded hollowly as he stepped out on the deck.

"I got Mr. Smith and Mr. Wesson with me now," he said into the waiting night. "So, yeah. Get the hell off my property, whoever you are."

Somewhere off to his left, a crow or a raven cawed. No other sound but the rustling wind.

His great-granny had been dead for many years, but he heard her voice as clear as the night she'd tucked him up with a terrible bedtime story. *The witherlings are rotting beasts with sharp teeth and long claws. They live in the woods and call to themselves all of Mother Nature's hunters to hunt for the flesh of men.*

He ignored the chill sliding down the back of his neck and shook his head in self-reproach.

Knock it off, Dylan.

He shone his flashlight down through the deck boards, but the gaps between them were too narrow to see anything down below. He and his brother had made this deck, after all, so the craftsmanship was solid.

If he really wanted to investigate, he should go down the stairs and look under the deck. That struck him as a bad idea. He ran his hand over his head and shone his flashlight over the yard.

"Aagh!" he shouted. In the bushes, a pair of luminous green eyes stared back. He blinked and laughed. "Stupid raccoons."

That's what he must have heard. Raccoons under his deck. He let out a long, slow breath, shut off his flashlight, and went back into the house feeling stupid, but relieved as anything. Lightning's grisly death had him on edge, that was all. What did he think? Some giant bear with red eyes was lurking under his deck?

"Idiot," he said to himself for the second time that night.

He settled himself on the couch and switched on the TV to catch the sports.

"Come here, Waylon." He patted the cushion beside him, but the dog stayed under the table. "Come here, boy. It was just a raccoon, buddy."

The dog slunk out from under the table, jumped on the couch, and pressed himself against Dylan. A gust of wind howled around the windows, and Waylon whined.

"What's the matter with you? Weather's changing, that's all. And it's high time it did." Waylon loved the snow, loved bounding along in it after Dylan on his snowshoes, tongue lolling with snow on his muzzle. The thought cheered Dylan. "We'll be out playing in the snow before you know it, Way."

He stroked his hand down the dog, who was trembling still, and a less cheerful thought struck him.

Waylon was brave. So brave, he'd chased coyotes out of the yard on multiple occasions. Hell, Piper once had to stitch up his leg after he'd scrapped with a raccoon, and that hadn't stopped the dumb dog from chasing one off the deck not a month later.

So why would a raccoon spook him so much now?

Because maybe it wasn't a raccoon out there, Dylan, said the voice in his head.

"Aw, shut up," he told it and turned up the TV until it drowned out the howling wind.

4

Piper stared in horror as the lid of the dumpster rose inch by inch. A soft, sucking sound issued forth, like something large inhaling. Two glowing green eyes, the size of golf balls, appeared under the lid.

"Oh, God." All at once, the fear rooting her to the spot turned into a terror that freed her to move.

She ran across the alley, stumbled up the porch steps, and threw herself against her back door. The jarring impact threatened to shake her teeth loose. She turned the knob and almost fell into her kitchen. She slammed the door and locked the deadbolt, backing away.

Her breathing came as hard as if she'd run a mile.

Osiris stood on the kitchen counter staring at the door. His back arched like a Halloween cat, and he emitted a low, warning growl.

Piper ran into the living room and snatched her cell phone from the coffee table. In the kitchen, Osiris hissed.

"Oh no, no, no." Piper wondered what her plan was, as she

held the phone like a weapon. *Like* a weapon, but not one.

All of a sudden, she wished she hadn't climbed up on her liberal high horse and refused Dylan's offer to buy her the handgun of her choice when they'd married. She wouldn't have minded the weight of something like his .357 in her hand right about now.

The phone was all she had though. She could call 9-1-1. And tell them what? A creature with glowing eyes was climbing out the dumpster?

Why, yes, I have been drinking. How much? Well, a whole bottle of wine, as a matter of fact. And yes, of course, there could be another explanation besides the Creature from the Black Dumpster. Thank you so much, 9-1-1 Dispatcher Person. You're so right. I do sound like a drunken fool. What's that? It sounds like a wild animal got in the dumpster? Like what? Oh, a—

A raccoon. She'd seen them several times before in the alley, even feeling a certain level of glee it was Cynthia's trash can, closed improperly, that hosted a veritable raccoon rave one night.

She sank onto the sofa and slapped a hand to her forehead.

Osiris jumped off the counter in the kitchen with a jingle of the bell on his collar and trotted into the living room, back to normal.

She must have scared him with her own crazy behavior.

And who could blame her for getting scared? After what she'd seen today with Lightning, anyone would have freaked out over scratching noises in a dumpster and glowing, creepy, green eyes.

Stupid raccoons. She let out a deep sigh. Sleep was definitely in order. Tomorrow, with all its challenges and anal glands, would come all too fast.

Piper dragged herself into an old pair of flannel pajamas and slid into bed. She'd tried to put off thoughts of this horrible day with wine. It had worked. With any luck, she could continue to push them away with sleep.

—

The wind shrieked so hard, it rattled her bedroom window in its frame. Piper opened her eyes and glanced at the clock.

3:52 a.m.

Her mouth was dry from the wine. Guilt and remorse filled her. She hadn't drunk so much in years. It might have been tempting after the divorce to go crazy, hit the bars and drown her sorrows in booze, or crawl into bed with strangers like so many in her shoes often did. Instead, she'd been principled and controlled—like it would counteract the spiraling *un*controlled feelings she'd had ever since leaving her husband. *Ex*-husband.

Why had she drunk so much tonight?

It wasn't just Lightning's death, as upsetting as that had been. It wasn't just seeing Dylan again, as hard as that was too.

It was standing there with Dylan, looking at Lightning's torn-up body—the horse she'd been on when she got engaged—and not missing the symbolism there for one second. Her pride and stubbornness and *convictions* had turned their marriage into a torn-up, bloody mess every bit as ugly as Lightning.

Dylan wasn't innocent. No way. When they'd married, she'd been honest with him that she wasn't sure she wanted kids. But a year after their wedding, he'd started pressuring her to begin a family right when her career was beginning to take off. As for her vet career, he wanted her to focus on the ranch animals, the elk, and horses. Even suggested she respecialize in large animal medicine and give up small animals. Take care of the elk to make sure they had a shot at growing a trophy rack? Never.

She hated the elk hunts on his family's ranch. Where was the sport in it? She'd gone to vet school to save animals, not help some numb nut with an overpowered rifle blow an elk away once it set one hoof outside its pen.

He'd been furious when she'd bought the small animal clinic in town with her grandmother's inheritance.

Then there was the small matter of all the times she'd seen him flirting with the wranglers or that woman who worked at the feed store.

So, yeah. Dylan was to blame.

But a year later, Piper could see she took at least half the fault. Maybe more than half.

The wind moaned at the window, like a hungry animal demanding to be fed. Piper pulled the covers up a little higher as her thoughts churned.

She'd been scared of how different she and Dylan were, that he might change that bright-eyed beach girl from San Diego into someone she wouldn't recognize if she listened to country music or handled guns.

So what did she do? Before he could get to her, she'd tried to change Dylan first. Listen to my music, drive this car, vote for that candidate, read this book, eat that food. She'd criticized everything he said and did until he couldn't do anything right. Until he perversely did the exact opposite of what she wanted.

The clock now read 4:03 a.m. Fat chance getting back to sleep with nothing but these painful thoughts of her failed marriage for company.

Over the last few months with Dylan, as she'd become impossible to please, she'd convinced herself she could never please *him*. Even as she feared her high-strung demands would drive him into the arms of another woman, she couldn't stop herself. Somehow, she let herself believe he didn't want her anymore, that it was his fault their marriage was falling apart.

But that wasn't true.

She knew it in her heart. She knew it in the way his strong arms closed so instinctively around her yesterday, the way it had felt so right—he hadn't stopped wanting her. *She'd* pushed *him* away. And now, thanks to her, a chasm yawned between them she couldn't ever see them crossing.

How could she think just because her vet practice was busier than ever and her bank account growing that she was happy?

She'd messed everything up. One look at him crouched by his truck today, and she knew the truth in an instant. She didn't love him any less than the day of their wedding. She'd never stop loving him, all their differences be damned. In fact, most of those differences were what made her love him so much because, at his core, Dylan was a good man. A rare man. She'd been a fool to push him away.

Her stomach roiled with nausea.

She threw back the covers and Osiris, who'd been curled in a ball on her legs, jumped off the bed. She instantly missed the heat of him. It was so cold. The hardwood floors were icy under her feet. She should've worn socks to bed.

She flipped on the light in the bathroom and barely got to the toilet in time to be sick. Gut-wrenching was an expression she now understood quite literally. She might have curled up on the floor in front of the toilet if the tiles weren't so freezing. Shivering, she splashed cold water on her cheeks and rinsed out her mouth. As punishment for all her bad choices leading right up to that bottle of wine, she made herself look in the mirror. Her face was pale under her freckles, and above dark circles, her blue eyes gleamed in an anguished, crazed way.

"Fool," she whispered at her reflection.

Osiris rubbed against the backs of her legs and looked up as if to say, *Back to our warm bed, human.*

"You're right, O."

She shut off the light and returned to her bedroom. Osiris leaped onto the bed, and she started to climb in herself when—

Squeeeeeeeeeeeeeak. Something scraped against the window's glass.

Osiris growled, and her heart galloped in her chest. Piper dove under her covers and stared at her bedroom window. Those white net curtains she liked because they let in the morning light turned out to be just about the dumbest window covering for a bedroom ever. They left her exposed.

Screeeeeeeeeeeeeeech, came the noise again. Like the

clawing inside the dumpster earlier. Only no raccoon could reach up and scrape its little claws on her window.

Her heart thudded so hard, she worried her sternum would crack. Or her heart would explode. Whichever came first, it wasn't going to be good.

Osiris continued to growl. She licked her lips and, on a deep breath, sat up with the covers clutched to her eyebrows.

Squeeeeeeeeeeeeeeeeeeeeeeeeeeeak. The sound unhinged her, but she screwed up her courage and lowered the blanket enough to see the window.

Puzzled, she lowered the blanket further.

A side-view silhouette of spiked, branching antlers was visible against the sheer curtains. An elk must be standing under her window, rubbing its antlers against the glass. The rack was huge, a 7x7. Piper knew, all too well from all those hunters hanging around the Crazy K, that a 7-point bull elk was called an Imperial.

It was so weird. Elk came into Crested Butte from time to time and walked down the main drag, to the delight of tourists. There was even an Elk Avenue in town. But it struck Piper as a little too odd after the incident with the dumpster earlier in the night. Two unusual and terrifying brushes with local wildlife? An elk had chosen this same night to come up to her building and scrape its antlers on her window? Seriously?

What made it even weirder was *why* the elk was rubbing its antlers on her window. The shadowed outline of tattered strips of velvet hanging off the forked antlers was enough to send a cold dread pouring over her body.

Elk shed their velvet to leave their bony antlers ready for fighting off other males during mating season. Bloody ropes of the soft velvet would hang off their antlers in a shredded, disgusting mess. Piper always hated seeing the elk in such a state on the ranch. She knew it didn't hurt the animals, but it always looked like it should.

The last time she'd been living on the ranch when the elk

were due to shed their velvet—in *August*—she'd avoided the elk pens as much as possible. It started in the summer. Not at the beginning of November.

Maybe this guy was an outlier, an anomaly. There was no reason for the cold tongue of fear lapping up her spine.

But Piper couldn't shake the feeling something was very off. It was creepy.

The antlers outside the window shifted so they faced the window head-on. Like the elk was trying to look at her.

Osiris stood up on the bed, arched his back, and hissed much as he had in the kitchen earlier.

Screeeeeeeeech. The aptly named dagger point, the longest prong on the antler, scraped again over the glass.

Piper reached up and turned on her bedside lamp and regretted it immediately. The view outside turned black in comparison to her bright room, and she could no longer see out well. It occurred to her the elk could now see her a whole lot better.

Which was a ridiculous thing to worry about. It was an elk, for crying out loud, not a werewolf.

And yet, she didn't think she'd feel any more scared of a werewolf as she was of this creepy elk standing outside her window. She switched off the light to return to the safety of darkness.

She scooped up Osiris, who hissed before he realized it was her. Then she grabbed her pillow and comforter off her bed so they could go sleep in the windowless interior of her living room. Clutching the cat like he could protect her, she glanced at the window again. The silhouette of antlers had disappeared. Part of her thought she should go look out the window to see where the elk had gone.

The other part of her decided to go into the living room with Osiris and shut her bedroom door without looking back. She didn't set foot in her bedroom again for the rest of the night.

5

Piper woke to a knocking on the door between her apartment and the clinic.

"Piper?" came Veronica's voice.

She sat up and rubbed her face. "Yeah?"

"Hooray. You're still alive. Open up."

Piper opened the door and Veronica bustled in. Bustling was the only way she ever moved.

"You all right, *chica?*" Veronica shoved a cup into her hand. "Here. Macchiato. You oversleep? Why you on the couch? You kick yourself out of your own bed?"

"Yeah, I couldn't stand my company." Piper took the cup and pulled her into a hug. "Thank you."

"You look like—not so great." Veronica never swore, which meant she didn't say the word Piper knew she was thinking.

Veronica, as usual, looked amazing with her scads of wavy black hair and makeup to highlight her huge, dark eyes. She was short, where Piper was tall and lanky. Veronica's small frame carried non-stop curves while Piper was built like a twelve-year-old boy.

"You sick or something?" her friend asked.

"Or something."

"Hmm."

Piper had already told Veronica about Lightning and seeing Dylan again, minus all the complicated and painful feelings that reunion brought up. Veronica probably knew what Piper was feeling better than she did.

"Well," Veronica said, "your first appointment is here already, so you better get your rear in gear."

"Abscessed anal glands?"

Veronica's huge eyes widened in surprise. "You never check the schedule. How'd you know?" Then she threw back her head and laughed. "You should see your face. It's just an annual with a Schnauzer."

"Let me throw some clothes on."

"All right, I'll buy you some time being my usual charming self. And then maybe later you can tell me why you didn't call me last night to help you earn that hangover."

"Is it that obvious?"

"Only to your best friend."

"That's a lie, but that's why you're my best friend."

Veronica started to close the door. "Oh, and there was a voicemail from that Nate guy." She waggled her eyebrows. "Wants you to call him as soon as you can."

—

The man with the Schnauzer, with salt-and-pepper hair similar to his dog's, waited in an exam room. He was bundled in a wool coat and red scarf.

"Isn't it great?" he said. "They're talking snow on the news this morning. Maybe by the end of tonight. Temperature shift of thirty degrees from yesterday's high."

"Colorado for you." Piper's head pounded as she placed the stethoscope in her ears.

"The snow can't come soon enough for me," he continued, as Piper tried to listen to his dog's heart. "I run a coffee shop next to the resort. I need the skiers. Snow, baby, snow."

The wind shrieked at the high transom window. Piper glanced at it and saw dark clouds gathering in the skies above. She tried to muster the same enthusiasm as this man, but couldn't. Normally, she loved the snow. She might be a beach girl, but the mountains won her heart as surely as the Pacific, and even after ten years in Colorado, the snow was still a novelty that filled her with child-like wonder.

The weather, though, like Lightning's body, like the eyes in the dumpster, like the elk at her window—it felt wrong.

Which is dumb, Piper. It's high time for snow.

—

She wanted to call Nate between appointments, but she couldn't catch a breath between patients after her late start this morning. The darker the sky grew outside the clinic, the harder her head pounded. It got so gloomy, it looked like early evening. If only. Then this day would be over.

Finally, at eleven-thirty, she had an hour break for lunch and slipped back into her apartment. She made a grilled cheese sandwich and downed some painkillers with a cup of peppermint tea.

Girded, she called Nate.

"Hey, Piper!" She winced and pulled the phone from her ear. "How's it going?"

"Fine," she lied. "You?"

"Fine, fine. Just calling about that claw you found. It's caused a big flap around here. People are getting all worked up with their own theories, but I think I might be on to something."

"And?"

"Don't you want to hear all the theories first?"

Piper certainly did not, but Nate loved to spin out a story, and he was impossible to stop. "Sure."

"One biologist thinks it's from the alien. As in the movie *Alien*. You know, the one with Ripley?"

"Ha. Yeah. Okay." Piper tried to keep the strain from her voice. "What do you think?"

"There's a woman here who's certain that claw came from a chupacabra. She was pretty excited about it."

"A chupacabra?" Piper almost, but not quite smiled as she stretched out on the couch. Lying down was heaven. "I hate to disappoint her, but Dylan called last night to say the Wildlife department declared it a bear kill. Filed his claim already."

"Well, that means Wildlife came up with something closer to my theory."

"Which is what, exactly?" Osiris jumped on her stomach, knocking the air out of her.

Nate's sigh traveled over the line, all playfulness gone. "It's going to sound insane, Piper. But there's another guy in my department that did some graduate work in paleontology. He happens to agree with me."

"Paleontology? Don't tell me Dylan's right, and it's a raptor?"

"No, definitely mammalian. But every bit as crazy."

"What is it, Nate? Just tell me."

"That claw is preserved so well. It's not fossilized or anything, it's still keratin, like it was merely frozen."

"Fossilized?" What the hell was he talking about?

"It matches perfectly with the size and shape of some claws found from an *Arctodus simus*."

"And that is?"

"The short-faced bear. A true monster. Ten feet high, two thousand pounds, with massive canines and claws like the one you found. And if my buddy and I are right, seeing as *Arctodus* went extinct over ten thousand years ago—thank God—then you still have a big problem on your hands. Because it means—"

"A person must have put it in Lightning's back," Piper finished. She closed her eyes, picturing the claw stuck in the horse's spine. Why someone would do that was a real mystery.

But it might also be their undoing. There could only be a limited number of people with access to such an unusual item. "You're positive the claw was from this prehistoric bear?"

"Confident, but not certain. If it's a black bear, then great. If it's a short-faced bear, then a human put it at the scene. And if a person did to that horse what you described, you need to call the police."

That was what frightened Piper at the scene yesterday. She couldn't imagine any animal doing to Lightning what she'd seen. The way his legs had been peeled like a hard-boiled egg? It made her queasy. Finding the claw had both terrified her and reassured her that at least Dylan didn't have any enemies of the two-legged variety.

"Lightning's body had been dragged quite a ways," she said at last. "How could a person drag a horse? Even several people couldn't pull a dead horse that far."

"Could've used a truck with a winch, right? Or maybe there was some scavenging after the fact. Something like a bear, ironically, could've dragged the horse after the person hurt him."

Piper shuddered thinking how Lightning was still alive when Dylan found him. Poor horse. "Bear or human, then. Or bear *and* human. How can we know for sure?" she asked.

"Do whatever anyone does in a crisis. Call a paleontologist."

Piper laughed, but it was short-lived. Thinking a monster bear was running around Dylan's ranch was scary enough. A sick human was far more terrifying.

6

Two men tromped up Dylan's front porch. Willis, his gruff and bearded foreman of sixty, looked like a giant next to the ranch hand. Raymond was a small family man with a quick smile and a big gap between his front teeth. He wasn't smiling now. Both men were blowing on their hands and stomping their feet and wearing grim expressions that made Dylan's stomach clench.

A blizzard warning is in effect for all of Gunnison county beginning tonight after midnight, said the weatherman on TV.

Dylan opened the door and waved the men in. "Come in, I'm catching the weather."

Waylon launched his brown and gray speckled body at the foreman, ecstatic, as always, to see him.

"Found a dead elk," Willis said. He pulled his graying ponytail from out his red-and-black checked coat.

"A sick one?"

Raymond shook his head with a bleak look.

"Something killed it in the pens?"

We're expecting upwards of three feet of snow in the next thirty-six hours and wind gusts of fifty miles an hour as conditions are lining up for a perfect winter storm.

"Not exactly."

"So he was outside the pen?"

"Uh, no.'"

"Willis." It wasn't like the man to play games. "Was it inside or outside the pen?"

"Neither. More like *on* the pen. The body was slung over the fence."

"What?" The fences around the elk pen were eight feet high.

"Yeah, it's a head-scratcher, all right."

Raymond kept stroking his hand over his thick mustache and Willis kept stroking his beard, his fingers trembling. Willis had worked on the Crazy K ever since Dylan's dad took over from Dylan's grandfather. He'd grown up around the foreman and even though Dylan was technically his boss, Willis felt more like an uncle. Maybe even more like a father now his dad was gone. The man was rock-solid. Nothing fazed him. But he sure looked fazed now.

"Hey, listen, you got any beer or anything?"

Willis didn't normally drink beer at noon on a weekday either.

"Yeah, sure. Hang on. Raymond?"

Raymond shook his head.

Dylan opened the fridge. Rejecting his homebrew for Willis, he reached in and pulled out a Heineken. He started to close the door, then thought, *What the hell,* and pulled out a second for himself. "So, tell me what's going on."

Our forecast models show an unprecedented second storm lining up behind this one, which promises to be even bigger. It's a real doozy, folks, so you'll want to be prepared.

Dylan glanced at the TV. The suited meteorologist looked as shaken as Willis.

These conditions developed with little warning to our

meteorology team. The handsome news anchor with the fake tan perhaps remembered the weather should be a cheerful segment and turned on a hundred-watt smile. *The ski resorts should be in good shape for the Thanksgiving holiday in a few weeks. Stay tuned for more updates.* His smile wavered. *And be careful out there, folks.*

Willis slowly lowered himself to the couch in the way of older men until he was about halfway down, at which point, he collapsed with a groan. Raymond perched at the other end, eyes darting around the room. Dylan took the recliner across from them and waited while Willis gulped a couple of loud swallows of beer.

"Whew, Dylan. Some strange shit is going on around here. Lightning. Now, this. I don't like it. I do not like it."

"Tell me how you found the elk."

Raymond spoke. "Willis and I were filling the feeders—you know—giving 'em extra grain with this weather." He trailed off into silence, seemingly haunted by what would come next.

Willis picked up the story. "So anyway, we're pulling up on the north side of the pen where that gate is, and we both just see it. This elk hanging over the fence." He screwed up his face. "Ugly business, D."

"A bull?" Dylan remembered the bugling last night, the way it suddenly cut off.

"Yeah. His guts were spilling out and get this—they'd been pulled through the wire fence. Pink guts just hanging through the squares in the fence."

"A mountain lion?" Dylan asked hopefully.

"A mountain lion?" Willis looked at him like he'd suggested Bigfoot himself had done it. "Son, you think a cougar pulled a seven-hundred-pound elk up on that fence and looped his guts through the holes like some kind of chicken wire parade float?" He took another long gulp of beer. "We got all those lights up anyway. No, I think you know what we're dealing with here."

"A poacher?"

"Hell of a lot of effort for a poacher. Why pull the elk up there? But here's the kicker that tells me *no*. The antlers were still there. Not on the elk, mind you. This is where it gets a little strange." Willis flashed a wry smile, the man knowing full well it was already plenty strange. "The antlers were ripped out of the elk's skull and left in front of the gate in a letter X."

"Ripped out? *Ripped* out? No person could rip antlers from a skull."

"And here's where it goes from strange to crazy. I would've sworn I saw a dark blur or shape or something zip past me out the elk pen. I blinked, and it was gone. But I swear I felt something brush past me." Willis rubbed his right hand down his left arm with a dazed look. "Like evil itself touched me."

That did sound crazy. But Willis was not a crazy man. "What do you think it was then?"

"Something real bad," Raymond said in a hush.

Dylan's phone buzzed in his shirt pocket. He pulled the pocket forward to see the screen. "Piper."

Willis frowned. He didn't bother hiding his dislike of the woman. Well, to be fair, he'd liked her fine before the divorce. More than fine. He'd had a soft spot for Piper. Called her the daughter he'd never had. Sometimes Dylan thought Willis felt more betrayed than he did when Piper left.

"What is it?" Dylan answered, too stressed to care he sounded harsh.

She didn't even react to his rudeness and sounded every bit as stressed as he did as she told him about Nate's assessment of the claw.

"A prehistoric short-faced bear?" he said slowly, and Willis's furry eyebrows shot up. He spoke to the man. "Her scientist buddy says that claw we found belonged to some giant extinct bear."

Willis made a scoffing noise but then nodded in thought as if agreeing. Like a giant short-faced bear was the *only* thing that made sense.

Dylan, in turn, told Piper about the elk Willis and Raymond found.

Willis raised his finger to get Dylan's attention. "There's something else." Judging by the foreman's face, Dylan didn't want to hear it. "Tell Piper Thunder went off his creep feed today." He held up his hands. "Now don't go off in a panic, son. I thought it might be worth mentioning. Just tell her."

"I heard him," Piper said in his ear. "He showing any other symptoms?"

"Anything else?" Dylan asked Willis.

He waggled his head side to side. "Uh, maybe a little less jumping around like a nut in his paddock today."

"Pooping okay?" Piper asked.

"Here." Dylan shoved the phone at Willis. "You talk to her."

Dylan enjoyed the way the man's beady blue eyes widened in alarm. Willis batted it away, but Dylan kept pushing the phone at him.

Finally, Willis took it with an evil glare at Dylan. "Hello. Yeah, hey, Piper." His voice was guarded, but as he discussed Thunder—he told her everything else with the colt was normal—he loosened up some. At the end of the conversation, Piper must have been talking a lot. Whatever she said made Willis grow very still, and when he answered, his voice was gruffer than normal. "You take care, too." He hung up and handed the phone back to Dylan.

"What was that all about?"

"She said to keep an eye on Thunder for colic."

Dylan narrowed his eyes. "No, at the end there."

Willis watched him for a couple of beats and then shook his head. "You two are some of the most ornery, pigheaded jackasses I've ever had the misfortune of meeting."

"So in other words, you're not gonna tell me what she said."

"If you wanna know so bad, you call her up and ask her yourself. In the meantime, we got bigger fish to fry. Like Moby Dick-sized fish."

"Moby Dick was a whale, not a fish." Dylan realized who he sounded like and shook his head in annoyance.

Raymond watched the exchange, his dark eyes darting between Dylan and Willis so nervously, it made Dylan nervous too.

Willis scowled. "Some psycho's out there killing our animals, Dylan."

His shoulders rose and fell on a mighty sigh, and he scrubbed a hand down his face. "I know. I'll call the sheriff."

"I think you'd better. Only a matter of time before it's a person gets killed."

7

Piper stood in the waiting room late Thursday afternoon and stared out the front windows of the clinic. Leaves, a plastic bag, and papers tumbled down the street. Up and down the sidewalks, people were hurrying about, anxious to be out of the cold. Her last two appointments had already canceled. One said he needed to go grocery shopping ahead of the storm and the other person said she had to get all her goats inside.

She'd sent home her two technicians a half an hour ago.

She paced the waiting room and clutched her phone, thinking about what she'd found on it while doing some impromptu research. After what happened last night, with those antlers scraping at her window, she couldn't stop obsessing over the idea that the elk was something unnatural. Which left her with the word *supernatural*. She was uncomfortable with that word, uncomfortable letting her mind go down that dark road. But those antlers. They reminded her of some stories she'd heard in her college class—Folklore and Mythology. There were no shortage of horned creatures in myths around the world. She'd looked up some on her phone. After what she'd found, she wished she hadn't.

She rubbed her hands over her upper arms. The stories weren't real, of course. That's why they were called *myths*.

On impulse, she slipped into an empty exam room and called Dylan.

"Yeah?" he answered, sounding grumpy.

Losing her nerve, she said, "So, I, uh, wondered how Thunder's doing?"

"You mean since you spoke to Willis just four hours ago?"

It was her turn to sound grumpy. "A young foal can turn fast."

"Look, I'll check on him later. Right now, I've got my hands full getting the ranch ready for this blizzard."

Piper closed her eyes and gathered her courage. Dylan would think she was crazy, but it didn't matter. "Hey, did you get rid of any of the books I left behind?"

"Uh, nope. Still in the bookcase in the living room."

"Could you do me a big favor and find me an old college book? It was real thin. It's called *Spine-Tingling Myths from Around the World*. I think it's wedged between a chemistry textbook and—"

"Did you not hear me say I've got my hands full?"

"Dylan."

He sighed. "I'm not at the house. I'll look for it later."

"Please. It's important."

Was it? Or was Piper losing her mind even going down this line of thinking? She could *not* stop thinking of those antlers. "Will you call me when you find it?"

"Fine. Gotta go."

They hung up, and Piper sat holding the phone until Veronica stuck her head in the room, breaking into her creepy thoughts.

"Want me to reschedule tomorrow's appointments?" Veronica asked. "I doubt we'll be open Monday either. What do you think? It's going to be a lot of snow."

"Three feet." She shook her head. "Seems crazy. It was sixty degrees yesterday. It's just—it's weird."

"It's not that weird, Piper. It's Colorado. Should we at least reschedule tomorrow?"

Colorado for you. That was what she'd told the man with the Schnauzer earlier. So why didn't it make her feel any better about this blizzard?

Veronica put a hand on Piper's arm. "You look freaked out. And you didn't answer my question."

"Um, yeah. Reschedule. Tell them I'll be available tomorrow for any emergencies."

"Okay, but I doubt anyone would be able to get to us. Well, not *us*. You. I'm not coming in."

Veronica lived half an hour outside town in a trailer with her construction-worker boyfriend. It was a nice trailer home, actually, and an even nicer boyfriend. Piper figured they'd get married soon. Gilbert was already planning to build them a house on his land in the spring.

"You wouldn't have to worry about driving into town tomorrow if you stayed with me tonight." Piper batted her eyelashes and clasped her hands in front of her chest.

"And get stuck here for the next week? No, thanks."

"Come on. It'll be fun! We can eat lots of junk food, drink hot chocolate, watch funny movies."

Veronica cocked an eyebrow. "I don't think Gilbert would be happy with me. I kind of saw us climbing into bed and not getting out for a few days."

"Please, Ronnie, stay with me." Piper sounded pathetic, begging like this. But every time she thought of those eyes in the dumpster, the shrieking of the antlers on her window, her blood ran cold. No one else lived in the other businesses in her building. She was alone every night in this old Victorian place at the end of the street, at the end of the town. Only highway and mountain views lay off to the west of her bedroom window. And if this storm—and the second one coming right on its heels—were as big as they'd predicted, she'd also be alone in this building day after snowy day. "It'll be like a sleepover. A mini-vacation."

"Sweetie, what's the matter with you? This isn't like you. I mean, the whole girlie sleepover thing. And being afraid. I've never seen you scared like this. Not even right after your divorce."

Piper told her about what happened last night, all the strange things she'd seen, the elk on Dylan's ranch.

"Oh, Piper, you know we aren't in California anymore."

Veronica had been one of Piper's five roommates crammed into an apartment when Piper was going to UC Davis. Veronica, a waitress, was the only one in their apartment going to a community college instead of the university. The other girls had been snobby about it, but Piper loved how real Veronica was, and they'd become fast friends.

They'd stayed in touch when Piper came to Colorado to go to vet school at CSU. When Piper bought the clinic in Crested Butte, she needed a new receptionist and called up Veronica. She couldn't get out here fast enough. Her friend had been in Colorado two years to Piper's ten, but she loved to act like a native.

"Piper, you know there are wild animals here," she continued. "We're in the mountains surrounded by wilderness. It's not exactly weird an elk was outside your window, or some animal got in the dumpster in back. And hello, did I mention mountains? That means snow and lots of it sometimes. Chill out, girl."

"What about Lightning? Something killed Lightning. And the elk."

"Some*one,* not something. Which is super scary, yeah? But it's Dylan's problem out on the ranch. Not yours. You're safe here."

To Piper's horror, tears sprang to her eyes. She hugged her arms across her chest. "You're right. I know you're right. I just don't want to be here alone."

"Hey, hey." Veronica came and wrapped her arm around Piper's shoulders. "Why don't you come stay with Gilbert and me instead."

Piper sniffed. "In your love trailer?"

"Mobile home. And hey, we got enough love for everybody."

She laughed and let herself consider it for half a second. It was sorely tempting, but—"No, Ronnie. I appreciate the offer, I do. But three's a crowd in a trailer."

"Mobile home," Veronica corrected again with a laugh.

Piper heard the relief and couldn't blame her. If she had a man she loved to keep her warm during back-to-back blizzards, she wouldn't want Veronica crashing at her place either.

"If you change your mind, they say the snow's not gonna start till after midnight."

"I'll be all right. Really." Piper tried her hardest not to sound sad. As much as she might want to take up Veronica on her offer, she couldn't get stuck away from her clinic. What if someone had an emergency and managed to reach her?

Piper said, "Why don't you go home and I'll call our clients to reschedule. There's no reason for you to stick around."

"If we do it together and split up the calls, it'll take us half the time. And we can hit the King Soopers for groceries before I leave. Make sure both of us got plenty of hot chocolate."

—

A person would think ten people lived with Piper, judging by the amount of food she'd bought. To her dismay, all the hot chocolate had been cleaned off the shelves at the store, but she'd made up for it with copious amounts of coffee, onion bagels, popcorn, Oreos, M&M's, and boxes of macaroni and cheese.

Veronica didn't say anything but piled her cart with fresh produce and whole-grain pasta. Piper was one of those lucky people who could eat whatever she wanted and not gain a pound, but it didn't mean she didn't feel like crap when she ate nothing but junk. Veronica was always trying to get her to eat healthier. Piper added some bananas to her cart.

They hugged good-bye in the parking lot of the grocery store.

"You sure you don't want to come home with me?" Veronica said.

"Nope."

"Well, call if you get scared or need anything."

"And what would you do if I did?"

"Call the cops for you. The station's just down the street from you."

Piper laughed. "I guess we'll see each other again whenever this weather clears out. There's supposed to be a lull between the storms, but that's Saturday. By Saturday afternoon, even more snow's coming, so maybe I'll see you Tuesday or Wednesday."

Veronica hugged her one more time and got into her car to drive off to her boyfriend and home-cooked dinner. Piper couldn't help but feel forlorn as she climbed into her Honda. She started the engine, and the radio came on, too.

" . . . to be one for the record books," the DJ was saying. "Get yourself home tonight and prepare to hunker down for the next few days, everyone." A car dealership ad came on next.

Piper drove through town toward home. A few flakes blew across her windshield. The main street was picturesque, like a Christmas village, complete with old-fashioned street lamps. They glowed yellow in the ever-darkening evening. A thin stripe of setting sun, about to slip from sight, hovered between the mountains and the heavy storm clouds. It filled her with a sense of deep foreboding.

No, sun. Don't leave me. The night was coming, and there wasn't anything she could do to stop it.

"Geez, Piper, get a grip," she said out loud. She turned into the alleyway behind her building, noting with relief that all the streetlights were on, including her back porch light, which appeared to be working again. There must have been a short of some kind. She maneuvered her Honda backward into the parking space beside her porch so she could unload the groceries easier.

She turned off the engine, and the cheerful radio jingle for honey-smoked salmon cut out to leave her in silence.

A sinister sort of silence.

Piper got out and was overwhelmed by the urge to hurry inside, but her car was full of groceries. She popped the trunk and jogged up the steps to unlock the back door with her arms full of groceries. Two ravens sat on her back porch railing like they'd flown off the pages of a collection of Poe to come and personally haunt her.

"Shoo!" She waved a hand at the pair. One rose into the air, the other uselessly beating its ebony wings.

Almost ebony. The bird displayed leucism. Two white feathers punctuated the sleek black plumage of one wing. Unlike albinism, which left an entire body lacking pigment, leucism only occurred in one part, affecting just a couple of feathers on this animal.

"What's that? Hey, hey, shhh." She set her groceries on the porch and approached the frantic animal. A fishhook was embedded in the raven's wing, wrapped in fishing line. Probably the unlucky victim of some fly fisher on the East River.

Piper peeled off her mustard yellow coat and spoke to the animal in a soothing voice. The raven gave a raucous caw, fixing her with a bright, black eye as she lifted her coat over it.

Without warning, she dropped her jacket onto the bird. She wished she had a tech or two to help, but it was only her, and she couldn't leave the animal in this state. She scooped up the bird and her jacket in one bundle and carried it into her kitchen.

As carefully as she could, she adjusted her coat to pin the uninjured wing against her side and fan out the injured one in front of her. Ravens could be feisty when threatened. She had no idea how she'd avoid the creature's beak, but corvids possessed keen intelligence. She got the impression this one knew she was trying to help. It didn't try to bite and instead, stilled as she unwrapped the knot of line tangled around its wing. Holding the raven snug against her, she yanked open the kitchen junk drawer and located some pliers. Her heart pounded hard while she struggled to cut the barbed end of the fishhook.

At last, the silver hook slipped free. Piper flung open her back door to release the impatient raven. It flew clumsily off her porch to land in the back alley. The bird spread its wings and flapped them a few times, as if experimenting, the two white feathers gleaming in the darkness. Then it cocked its head at Piper and took to the sky, flying off into the night.

Piper let out a slow breath. Feeling like a hero, she returned to unloading her groceries from the car.

She propped open the door with an old flower pot and shuttled the bags inside as quickly as possible. When she slammed the trunk closed, it rang in the quiet evening.

The wind had died down. Everything waited in a heavy stillness. Piper rushed inside and turned on every light in her apartment along with the television. She opened a can of corn chowder and heated it on the little stove as she put away the groceries.

When she ran out of room in her kitchen cupboards, she went into the laundry room and piled boxes and cans on her dryer. She carried her bowl of soup into the living room and ate in front of the local news.

Not surprising, every story related to the two monster blizzards ready to take aim at the Rockies, with Crested Butte in the middle of the bullseye. She turned up the volume when the forecast came on.

A blonde weatherwoman came on screen. *Our weather map is covered in winter warnings.* Maniacal delight gleamed in her eyes. *I guarantee you'll never have seen anything like these two back-to-back storms. Not only are we expecting snow totals topping out at seven to eight feet—yes, you heard me right!—but the wind and cold temps are going to be the real showstoppers here, folks. Sustained winds in the forty-*

to-fifty miles-per-hour range with occasional gusts as high as seventy to eighty. Those are wind speeds you'd get with a Category 1 hurricane. Dressed in a skin-tight black dress with brown fur at the collar and cuffs, she moved in front of the map where numbers popped up. *Overnight lows will be in the single digits as this moisture-filled stream from the Pacific meets an arctic blast. We at News 5 cannot stress enough the need to prepare for this storm. After midnight tonight, you will not want to be out on the roads. And it goes without saying that animals—and that includes livestock wherever possible with these conditions—need to be brought into sheltered areas.*

Speaking of animals—Piper paused with her spoon between her bowl and mouth. "Osiris? Where are you, big kitty?"

He often came to greet her when she came home, but not always if he was feeling lazy. He probably took one look at Piper helping that raven in the kitchen and ran away to hide.

She set her bowl on the coffee table and went into her bedroom. Sometimes Osiris napped in the laundry basket in her closet. A look inside showed only a reminder to do laundry. Just to be sure, she plunged her hand in the basket and fished around.

No cat.

She stuck her head in the bathroom and pulled back the shower curtain to make sure the tub was empty.

"Here, kitty, kitty, kitty."

Piper got down on her hands and knees and checked under her bed to find nothing but dust bunnies.

She sat back on her heels, trying to think where else Osiris might hide in her small apartment. Then she remembered.

"Stupid!" Why had she left the door open when she brought in the groceries?

Fighting back a rising tide of panic, she unlocked the connecting door to her clinic and called for Osiris. The cat hated the clinic with its barking dogs and medicine smell, but she wanted to check every possibility before admitting he could be outside.

Everything in the clinic was silent and still. The surgery suite, the two exam rooms, her office, the little waiting area. She stood at the front window and peered through the blinds at the street. The wind hadn't picked up again, and it was eerie. Some teenagers walked by across the street, laughing as they came out of the pizza place at the end of the block with a big pizza.

This storm must feel like one huge party for them. No school, getting stuck at each other's houses.

The sight of those happy teenagers cheered her. Osiris was probably out back of the building, cowering in the bushes. Maybe he was even waiting for her on the porch. She hurried back through the clinic, locked the apartment door behind her, and walked straight to the porch.

Once more, the porch light was out. She flipped the switch several times, and when nothing happened, she noticed the streetlights in the alleyway weren't on either. The alley was dark and empty, and it felt like 2:00 a.m. instead of 6:00 p.m. No one else was parked back here. She was at the end of the street, at the end of the town, in an alleyway of businesses shut up tight, their owners all tucked in their own homes elsewhere.

With her cat gone, Piper felt truly alone. If she didn't find him before the snow hit, he'd never survive the night.

"Osiris? Kitty, kitty?" She saw and heard nothing.

She rushed back into her apartment, pulled on her boots, her coat and gloves, and grabbed the bag of kitty kibble from the laundry room.

Once outside again, she shook the bag. "O! Osiris! Kitty, kitty, kitty!"

She took a deep breath and plunged down her porch steps into the alley, into the last place she wanted to be after last night's scare. She got Osiris after her divorce—Dylan didn't like cats—and the animal had seen her through some long and tear-filled nights. He'd come into her clinic abused and half-starved after someone found him in this very alley. She wasn't about to abandon him out here again.

Using her phone as a flashlight to check in the bushes, she marched down the alley, pausing every dozen feet or so to shake the bag of food and call his name. She made it all the way along the line of businesses and saw no sign of him. It had only been half an hour since she left the door open. How far could he have gone?

With every step she took, the temperature seemed to drop a degree or two. She kept going though, walking up the front of her street. When she couldn't find him there, she walked back a block to search the street behind her with the realtor and quilt shop.

Another half an hour went by and then another as she widened her search to include every block of the heart of downtown Crested Butte. The business district had emptied of cars. She'd never seen the streets so empty. To her amazement, a handful of hardcore people were still eating in restaurants and drinking in bars. Not many, but a few.

Piper couldn't help but wonder if they had homes as lonely as hers to return to. She couldn't feel her cheeks, and her hands and feet had gone numb despite the gloves and boots. Time to stop in at the appropriately named Wind Chill Distillery and Bar for a quick hot drink to warm up.

A couple of hipster men stood at the bar sampling premier vodkas. Clear glass bottles with brightly colored labels lined the backlit wall in a pyramid behind the bar. Piper pushed in beside the men and asked the barman for a coffee.

"To go, please."

One hipster, with chunky black glasses and a scraggly goatee, gestured at the bag of cat food she carried in one hand.

"Brought your own snacks?"

She managed an anemic smile.

When the barman brought her the Styrofoam cup a minute later, her numb hands refused to cooperate, and she spilled half the hot liquid down the front of her coat.

"Ow, ow, ow." She pulled the coat away from her chest and then burst into tears.

"Hey, you all right?" asked the hipster in skinny jeans and a flannel shirt.

"Uh, yeah. Burned myself a little."

She mopped at her chest with the napkins the barman handed her. He took the cup from her and refilled it as the hipster continued to stare.

"You sure you're okay?"

"Yeah. I just—my cat's got out and I can't find him and I'm worried I won't find him before the storm hits."

"You want some help looking?"

Piper was touched at his kindness. "No, it's all right. I've searched most of town already."

"Hope he turns up soon," the man said. "I live in a house that way"—he pointed in the direction of Piper's building—"and I kept hearing something last night making the most God-awful noises. Like a mountain lion or something."

"Don't tell her that, you idiot," the barman said. "Here. Careful now." He handed her the coffee cup again. "Most likely, your cat's waiting back at your place. Animals have a sense of bad weather coming. Cats in particular. You go on home. I bet your kitty's there."

Piper smiled and took a sip of coffee. The brew was bitter but hot.

The barman glared at the men. "And you two knuckleheads finish up your vodka. Looks like the storm's coming earlier than they said." He lifted his chin at the window. The wind had picked up again.

"You're right," she said. "Time to go home."

Piper thanked the barman and left the light and warmth and company to head out into the cold street. Small flakes fell, picking up a bit from earlier. By the time she reached her block, her feet were numb again, but at least the coffee kept her belly warm.

She considered walking along the front of her street instead of through the back alley, but if Osiris were anywhere, the alley was the most likely place.

"Kitty, kitty," she called again.

The wind gusted. Behind her, a bottle shattered on the asphalt. Piper whirled around but saw nothing but an overflowing garbage can. As proof the wind was responsible for the breaking glass, a plastic cup flew off the pile and tumbled down the alley.

Something stunk, turning her mouth dry. Rotting, putrid. Like a dead animal left decomposing somewhere damp. Her heart tripped, remembering the same smell from last night.

And then she heard it, carried by the whipping wind.

Mew. Mew. Feeble and pathetic, it came from behind the garbage pile.

Her heart caught in her throat. "Osiris?" Piper ran toward the sound and pushed aside the trashcan.

There, in a pool of blood, Osiris lay on his side. His big golden eyes looked up at her, pleading.

"O! What happened to you?" She reached down and felt along his body. He was so cold. Even the blood leaking all over his black fur had cooled.

She turned on her phone's light. Long slashes ripped up his side to reveal pink muscle. It reminded her of wounds she'd seen on a Chihuahua injured by a bobcat.

First her horse Lightning. Then the elk Dylan had described. Now, this. But of course, this was unrelated. Did she think somebody was terrorizing both her and Dylan?

The thought provided the opposite of reassurance. Maybe someone was. Could Holly be so angry with Dylan she had killed Lightning, killed that elk? And what? Just happened to be walking by in the alley behind her place when her cat got out the open door and slashed him up to look like a bobcat attacked him? That made *total* sense.

Osiris let out a weak mew like a kitten.

"Oh, no, buddy. Let's get you back to the clinic." Her mind already raced with what she'd need to do to stitch him up on her own.

She peeled off her jacket to help a second animal this evening and wrapped Osiris in it.

"Hang on, O." His eyes shut as she carried him down the alleyway. Without her coat, she was freezing. The wind clawed at her hair like a personal affront.

She'd almost reached the end of her building when the light on her back porch came on.

She suddenly didn't want to go into her apartment. Which was silly. It was just a short in a fuse somewhere. And what choice did she have? Osiris needed her clinic and neither one of them could stay out in this cold much longer.

As further motivation, behind her, something growled, deep and low.

8

Dylan, with Willis and the other ranch hands, did all they could to prepare the animals and ranch for the coming blizzard, working hard until sunset. The hands were tense and grouchy with each other. Finally, Dylan sent them all home to their trailers. Willis stayed longer to help Dylan attach the snowplow to his truck, but in the end, Willis gave into the cold and went home too, muttering under his breath about the stubbornness of some men when Dylan announced his plans to check over his property.

He couldn't ignore the gnawing feeling in his chest that something wasn't right on his ranch. Who would want to kill Lightning? Or hang a gutted elk like a disgusting *piñata?* He was compelled to look over his ranch one more time before dark, like doing so would protect it and everyone who lived on it from harm.

He saddled up Juniper and headed out. He'd miscalculated though and somehow, while he'd been doing his final once-over, the sun had slipped behind the mountains. Dylan cursed himself for living a lifetime here and still getting caught by surprise at the speed of the setting sun.

In the gathering darkness, he closed the gate on the elk pen and mounted his horse tethered outside. He loosened the reins and let Juniper have his head, knowing the gelding couldn't be happier to be returning to the horse barn below. Dylan didn't blame him. The wind had been strengthening noticeably over the past half hour. The temperature dropped with every passing minute. Small snowflakes began to fall.

As they moved back past the pen, he wished the elk well.

Dylan wasn't worried about the snow. Elk were built for snowy conditions. It was this damned wind. If these gusts clawing at his hat were any taste of what was to come, add in some snow, and he had no idea how he'd get to his animals to feed them in the coming days.

The twilight, in a matter of minutes, had given way to full dark. A small sliver of moon hung in the night sky. The red anti-predator lights came on, startling him for a second. They blinked on and off around the elk pen, and while they might deter predators, they didn't provide enough light to see by. Juniper didn't have any trouble though, negotiating his way down the hillside.

Below, the anti-predator lights turned on and off on the barn as well. Tonight, they unsettled Dylan. The sight was like the eyes of unseen creatures watching him from the darkness. He preferred to look at the lights glowing in the five scattered trailers where Willis and the other hands lived, some with families. He imagined meals being prepared there, the noises and smells of cooking, the kids laughing in Raymond's place. Uncharacteristically, Dylan had left a few lamps on at his own house, and lights blazed at his windows, too. But it was with false cheer. No one waited at home for him.

Dylan shook off the melancholy thought like Juniper shook off flies in the summer and instead, took stock of his day. Had he done everything he needed to prepare for this storm? He'd been irritated at first when he'd called the sheriff's department, and nobody was concerned enough to come out and talk to him about his dead animals. But it turned out to be a good thing because he'd needed every minute of today to tend to his livestock.

The deputy he'd spoken to said to take photos of the slaughtered elk on the fence and suggested after the blizzards blew over, he come in and make a report. Dylan needed to call Piper and ask for those photos she'd taken of Lightning. When he found that book she wanted.

He regretted being so short with her earlier and realized the prospect of calling his ex-wife filled him with warmth. Which was a dangerous thing to feel.

Another gust of cold wind blew past, and Juniper sidestepped under him with a nervous whinny.

Dylan smelled something bad. "Oh, God." He covered his mouth and nose with a gloved hand. Real bad.

Once, he'd had the misfortune of coming across a dead skunk on a hot summer's day. This was worse. This was worse than the time, on another hot summer day, he'd had to follow a truck from a rendering plant, full of offal from a nearby cattle ranch.

What the hell would smell like that?

It was from a short-faced bear, Piper had said and the thought, out here in the dark, scared him. Not for a prehistoric giant bear, of course, but the good old-fashioned black bear.

He'd smelled them, too, in his time. A little musky and stinky, like a wet dog.

This smelled more like dead things. Something dead must be nearby. His gut clenched thinking someone might have killed another one of his animals. But he'd counted all his elk and horses. Maybe something had died in the forest? It lay behind him, dark and vast.

The prickling sensation of being watched itched him between the shoulder blades.

Juniper reared up under him with a scream and broke into a gallop.

"Whoa, whoa!" The stupid horse was liable to break a leg running through the dark like this down a hill. Dylan pulled on the reins, fighting to bring his horse to a walk.

Once they reached level ground, he let him run. Dylan kept checking over his shoulder, half-expecting to find something chased them, but saw only the unnerving flash of the anti-predator lights on the elk pen. He could see nothing out of the ordinary on the Crazy K. He heard only the wind and the soft thudding of Juniper's hooves on the ground. Juniper didn't slow until they made it through the gate into the barnyard. Dylan would have sworn the horse sighed in relief.

He and the other men had brought all eighteen horses into the barn earlier. Dylan dismounted and led Juniper inside. The horses' collective body warmth and familiar horse smell were a welcome respite from the cold and the memory of the stench on the hillside.

"Easy, Juniper, easy, boy." He brushed down his horse, taking pleasure in the simple, rote task. It calmed Juniper as well.

When he was finished, he put Juniper in his stall. Nothing for it. Time to head back to the house and hunker down.

He stuck his head in Thunder's stall to check on him one last time. The two-month-old colt stood tucked against his mother. Dylan didn't like the way his head hung a little lower than usual. Maybe he just sensed the coming storm. Now that he thought of it, all the animals were subdued. Still, he didn't like the look of the colt enough that he decided he better check on him later before he went to bed.

The last thing he needed was a sick foal in a blizzard.

Dylan shut off the lights in the barn and closed the doors with a heavy rumble. A motion-activated light came on so he could see. He left the safety created by the pool of fluorescent light to make the short walk back to the house.

Tonight, however, the walk felt much longer than usual. As he approached his house, he couldn't help but think about last night and the clawing under the deck. In the dark, out here alone, it wasn't so easy to convince himself it had only been a raccoon.

He resisted running up the porch steps. Okay, he might have broken into a fast trot. The important thing was he didn't *run* into the house like some kind of scared kid. Waylon greeted him at the door, but he didn't miss how quiet his dog was too. He'd been acting weird ever since last night.

It was the blizzards putting everyone on edge. Dylan felt it, too. Like they were all waiting for something and somehow, they all knew it was gonna be bad.

"Batten down the hatches, Kincaid," he whispered and, feeling foolish, but doing it anyway, he double-checked his locks and patted his gun cabinet twice for good luck.

He heated himself a can of stew and found the book Piper was talking about. Dylan flipped through it, wondering why she'd taken a sudden interest in it.

As he read, the hot stew did nothing to stave off the chill spreading in his gut.

9

Something growled behind Piper. She ran with Osiris up the steps, not bothering to turn around until she was pulling open the back door. She stared in disbelief. It had to be the weather.

A mountain lion crouched, snarling in the alleyway, watching her with golden eyes like the housecat's in her arms. Piper, for the second night in a row, threw herself inside the apartment and slammed the door shut. She peeked out the kitchen window while her legs trembled.

She'd been out in that alley for who knew how long with a mountain lion. A mountain lion! The creature wasn't living up to the *ghost cat* nickname tonight. It stood there, bold as could be, staring back. Its long tail twitched like Osiris's did when he was irritated. Then, without warning, it turned and slunk away, toward the edge of town. She leaned to see out the window and follow its departure. It melted into the darkness in the open space at the end of the street.

A moment later, the mountain lion let out one of its signature unearthly screams. The hairs on the back of her neck lifted. That was happening a lot lately.

A raccoon, an elk, and a mountain lion. What would Veronica say to this latest animal sighting? But there wasn't any time to ponder it. With the immediate danger for herself passed, Piper turned her attention to her mangled cat. The mountain lion must have attacked Osiris, but why it hadn't eaten her cat or finished the job, Piper couldn't explain. Maybe Osiris was tougher than he looked.

She hoped and prayed he was as she carried him into the clinic to begin the worrying work of putting her cat back together.

—

Osiris pulled through the surgery. It had been a nerve-wracking business to repair the lacerations alone, with no one to monitor his anesthesia. The wounds had been deep. Doing so many sutures had taken longer than she'd expected. He was alive, but Piper worried about blood loss and infection. Exhausted, she settled Osiris in a crate in her bedroom, careful not to lay him on the drain in his side. She picked up his IV bag from her bed and hung it on the curtain rod.

About an inch of snow had already fallen, but the real teeth of the storm hadn't arrived yet. She turned up the thermostat in her cold apartment and decided a shower was in order.

Piper stood under the spray of hot water. The heavenly sensation was ruined by the cold feeling she got every time she thought of that mountain lion. It was so bizarre. No. Her first instinct was right. The storm was making the animal act against its normally secretive nature. Some people went their whole lives never seeing a mountain lion. She should feel lucky, she told herself, as she pulled on flannel pajamas and brushed her teeth.

But all Piper felt was scared. It wasn't just that her cat had been attacked by that creature. It was the feeling she'd had watching it watching her.

Veronica would tell her she was being silly, tell her to chill out. But Piper knew. Something about the mountain lion had been unnatural.

Piper checked on her cat one last time and climbed into bed with that unpleasant thought. But her tiredness was such she fell into a deep sleep, which was interrupted a mere several hours later.

—

Piper fumbled for her cell phone on the nightstand where the clock read 1:24 on the unbearably bright screen. It displayed Dylan's number.

She sat up in bed. "Hello?"

"Piper? Oh, thank God you answered."

The wind shrieked at her window. "What's the matter?"

As Dylan described how sick Thunder had grown, she peered out her bedroom window. Not that there was much to see beyond swirling gusts of white. It was like being trapped in a snow globe shaken by an angry giant. The snow came from every direction.

"Did you call Dr. Rodriguez?" she asked.

"He's stuck with a case at another ranch almost an hour from here."

"A couple of problems, Dylan. First, I'm not a horse vet."

"Piper, you helped with our horses for years—"

"Second, my cat got hurt tonight and I can't leave him."

"How did he get hurt? No, wait. Tell me later. Bring him with you."

Piper glanced at the crate where Osiris lay sleeping. "You hate cats."

"I never said I hated them."

"Third, how am I supposed to get to you?"

"You're not. Not in that stupid, little Honda. I'll come get you in my truck. I've got the plow on."

"Dylan, that's—"

"The wind makes it sound worse than it is."

"Really? Because I'm looking out my window and I can't see a damn thing."

But then, for a brief moment, she did. The dark figure of a person stood out in the storm, facing her direction. It filled her with an ominous feeling of evil she couldn't explain. It was hard to judge distance in the whiteout, but the person looked to be twenty or so yards away. She blinked and in the swirling snow, she would've sworn she saw the silhouette of giant antlers atop the person's head. She blinked again and the figure disappeared. The storm must be playing tricks on her eyes. After what she'd researched on her phone today, it must have planted suggestions in her subconscious, made her see things that weren't there. Her imagination was getting the better of her. That was all.

And yet, she couldn't shake the feeling of evil waiting outside.

Piper swallowed hard, her decision made. "If you come get me, I don't know how much I can help, but I'll try."

"Thank you." He cleared his throat. "I appreciate it."

"You know I'll be stuck with you for the storm, right? Assuming we make it back to the ranch alive?"

It sounded quite a lot like he was smiling when he said, "Yeah. I already realized you'll be socked in here for the blizzard." He sounded pleased.

But then again, her mind was playing tricks on her tonight, wasn't it?

10

Piper returned to her clinic and packed a medical bag with everything she could imagine to care for the foal. There would be no coming back anytime soon. Her eyes kept straying to the windows, searching for the figure in the snow, at the same time she tried not to look. Concentrating on the task at hand took a huge effort.

Surgery packs, bags of fluid, stethoscope, otoscope. All of these went into her bag. She stared in the cupboards of drugs and with a sigh, scooped handfuls of medications into another bag. A small animal clinic didn't have the supplies for equestrian medicine. She'd have to make do with what she had. Pain meds, antibiotics, sedatives. Bottle after bottle went into the bag.

The wind gusted and then dropped to nothing for periods of time that made Piper nervous. When the wind died, the snow stopped swirling around to fall in thick, fat flakes visible in the light of the streetlamps. Piper refused to look too hard, afraid she'd see someone standing out there staring in.

Her medical bags bulged and she went back to her apartment

to pack for herself. So much for staying in pajamas for the next few days. She reached into her dresser drawer and didn't think too long about why she fished around for her best underwear and bras. During a big gust of wind, the lamp on her nightstand flickered. She held her breath, waiting, but the power stayed on.

When she was packed and changed into jeans and a sweater, she sat on her couch surrounded by her bags and Osiris's crate, the IV bag on top. She'd shut her bedroom door so she could sit in the windowless living room. Why did she feel relieved in here, like she was finally somewhere she could be unseen?

She waited. And waited. A fifteen-minute drive in nice weather was taking an hour in the storm. The television was playing a rerun of *Friends* she didn't bother watching. Anything to drown out the wind.

Piper paced the five steps it took to cross her living room and back again when she snapped her head around.

There! From the other side of the door to her clinic came a low, scraping sound.

She turned off the TV to leave a thick silence.

Her heart leaped into her throat. She stepped back toward her kitchen.

Another noise, a long, long scratching. It grew louder as if whatever made the noise was moving down the clinic hall toward her apartment door. Then it stopped. Piper's breath quickened. She had the uncanny sense somebody listened and waited on the other side.

Bam! Bam! Bam!

Piper let out a muffled scream and whirled to the back door. On a burst of adrenaline, she ran into the kitchen and peered out the window over her sink. Dylan stood on the porch, hunkered against the wind. Already, snow was collecting on the brim of his cowboy hat.

She'd never been happier to see him. She yanked open the door and barely resisted dragging him into the house.

"Dylan! I think someone's in my clinic."

"What?" His snow-crusted eyebrows rose. "You think a burglar's out in this weather?"

"I keep hearing noises in there."

Dylan pressed his lips together and without a word, reached inside the left side of his coat and withdrew his handgun from a shoulder holster.

"You always carry that around?"

"I bet you're glad I am tonight, aren't you?" He cocked his head at her, but she didn't bother answering.

He strode to the adjoining door, flipped the deadbolt, and said, "I'll go check it out. You stay here."

Piper was too scared to bristle at that. "Be careful."

He opened the door and stepped into the clinic. She stood in the living room, hands clenched at her chest, and watched as he went from room to room, flipping on the lights. It was a small clinic and didn't take long to search.

"There's nobody here," he called from the front waiting room. "But come look at this."

His voice sounded funny.

Piper lowered her hands and joined him.

"What do you make of that?" Dylan pointed, gun still in hand, at the welcome mat in front of the door.

Bloody chunks were strewn all over the mat with the clinic's logo of a cat and dog inside a heart. She bent down to get a closer look and picked up one of the pieces between her thumb and finger.

Dylan grimaced. "Aw, why do you always have to touch the gross stuff?"

The feeling of evil returned like a cannonball to her gut as she recognized what it was. She turned and held it up for Dylan.

He squinted, his nose scrunched up. "That looks like velvet."

Piper grabbed a tissue from the reception desk and wiped off the bloody bits of velvet strips, the kind antlers shed. Her voice shook when she answered. "Yeah."

"Why?" Dylan looked as horrified as she felt.

"Something weird's going on around here. And at the ranch. You feel it, too, right? Something . . . bad?"

Normally, Dylan never would have gone in for any nonsense about bad feelings. But tonight, standing there looking at the pile of bloody velvet with the wind moaning at the windows, he just gave a curt nod.

That scared Piper more than anything. She crossed to the clinic's front door. "It's unlocked. I definitely locked it this afternoon. But my alarm didn't go off."

Dylan opened it and went onto the sidewalk. He pointed at the ground. "Some kind of footprints."

Piper came out beside him. A series of indentations stretched down the sidewalk toward the highway, but any details had been covered by falling snow.

They returned inside.

Dylan took his black cowboy hat off and brushed the snow from the brim in a nervous gesture. "I think it's about time you and me compared notes. We can talk on the drive, but for now, let's get the hell out of here."

The wind gusted again, slamming snow against the clinic windows.

"Oh, good," she said. "I was worried the ride might be boring."

11

As the truck passed by where he crouched under a tree, he could smell the flesh of the man and the woman even above the blood of his recent kill. He paused, long claws poised over the mountain lion's open belly, from which curls of steam rose. He watched the truck's red taillights move up the highway through the snow. All around him, the ravens cawed, waiting for their turn.

When the truck disappeared, he returned his attention to the mountain lion. Against its will, the animal had answered his call earlier in the night, did his bidding, and fulfilled its purpose in frightening the woman. How terrified the creature had been to find itself in the realm of men.

Terrified more to find itself stalked by him through the trees. The predator had become the prey. The pathetic mewl it let out when he'd killed it was no better than the housecat it had injured in the alley.

Fear, he fed on fear, because he could not satisfy his other appetites. Yet, he could not stop trying. He reached inside the still-warm carcass and lifted out the liver. Row upon row of razor-sharp teeth sank into the organ until bile dribbled between them. But the warmth of this animal and its meat gave him no sustenance. Within minutes of eating, the gnawing hunger would return until he was consumed with it, consumed from the inside out.

Mountain lion, horse, elk—these were not what it—what he craved. No, that particular hunger built inside him with every passing moment. He must feed. Soon, he knew. Very soon.

But not here, not yet. He could go elsewhere, elsewhen to feed.

Here and now, the fun was just beginning. He would control his appetite a little longer for the sake of the game.

12

By the time Dylan was parking the truck outside the horse barn, Piper wasn't sure which was more harrowing—the drive through the snow as tires slipped at every turn, the truck shuddered at every gust, and the road disappeared in bursts of white—or the similarities in hers and Dylan's stories. Scratching noises under his deck. Scratching noises in the dumpster. Glowing eyes in the night they'd both decided were raccoons. The smell of something rotten and dead.

And as silly as it sounded, both of them couldn't brush off their feelings that something wasn't right. That something bad was coming.

She shared what her research had turned up on her phone this afternoon.

Instead of dismissing her as crazy, Dylan reached into his coat and pulled out her *Spine-Tingling Myths from Around the World* book. He tossed it across the bench seat.

"I was reading some of that earlier this evening." He sounded rattled. "Remember the Stagecoach Cannibal?"

Mention of that rattled *her*. How could she forget that little gem of a scary story? Dylan's brother had taken great glee in telling her that one when she'd first moved onto the ranch.

She flipped through the book, feeling colder by the second, before tucking it into one of her bags.

"You don't think . . ." she said.

Silence swelled inside the cab.

Then Dylan forced a laugh. "Listen to us. Getting carried away like a couple of scared kids. Something's happening all right. A bear got Lightning. Some nut job out there hurt one of my elk. And the animals are going crazy with these blizzards coming in. We need to calm ourselves down and be rational. Let's focus on Thunder, okay?"

He could say what he liked, but Piper couldn't help but feel all these events were connected. Though she put her faith in science and logic, *what if* there were more things in this world than could be explained by rational science? What if some guy was tromping around in the snow killing elk and wearing antlers on his head? That sure as hell wasn't rational in her book.

Dylan was right about Thunder, though. She took a deep breath and opened the truck door. Snow clawed at her face. Lights poured out the high barn windows, and she couldn't wait to get inside.

Dylan carried her medical bags while she carried the cat crate and clothes. Poor Osiris. He let out pitiful meows as the cold wind whistled through the holes of his cage. Dylan rolled back the barn door, and they hurried inside together. He turned to push the door closed again.

The rumbling sound prompted several horses to let out disturbed snorts and whinnies. Their large bodies rustled in the hay and their distinctive scent filled the air. One horse stuck his head out the stall midway down the long aisle.

It had been over a year since she'd stood in this barn and she had to admit, she'd missed it. It still smelled a tiny bit like freshly cut wood, having been finished right before she and

Dylan were Splitsville. He'd bought more horses for hunters to use as the final step in expanding the hunting operation after his dad died.

Though the reason for more horses and a bigger barn had infuriated Piper at the time, she'd liked the barn itself.

Halfway down the aisle, a stall door opened and Willis stepped out, his large belly appearing first. With a jolt, she realized she'd missed him, too.

He wore his signature red-and-black buffalo plaid coat and a worn pair of jeans more gray than black. His beard looked whiter than last time she'd seen him as he turned to face her, arms out like a gunslinger.

As she approached, he looked so grumpy she couldn't help but smile.

"Piper," he grunted.

She made herself sober her face. "Willis."

"You pissed me off plenty leaving my boy here." He lifted his chin at Dylan, who'd come up behind her to set down her black medical bags. "But I'm not gonna lie and say it ain't good to see you."

To both their surprises, Piper hugged the man. His arms stuck out for a moment and then slowly, came around her shoulders to return the hug. Two years ago, he'd lost his wife to lung cancer. It hadn't stopped him smoking, and the smell of cigarettes clung to his long hair. He yielded to the hug. Piper figured he didn't get many of those these days.

At last, he pulled away and said, "Enough of that, now."

"You're warm," she said. "You feel okay?"

"Don't worry about me. I'm fine. Worry about Thunder." He gestured at the stall door. "You better get in there."

Piper picked up a bag and opened the door to slip inside the stall. The little palomino colt lay on the straw, his legs tucked under him like a dog. His eyes were shut, and his head hung down. Thunder was the picture of misery.

Dylan hung an arm over the stall door. He looked damn

good like that, his broad shoulders filling out the brown oilskin rancher's coat and his cowboy hat pulled low over those hazel eyes. She could feel him watching her as she eased the foal onto his side to examine his abdomen. Thunder didn't react overly when she ran his hands over his belly, and there was no distension. She pulled her otoscope from the bag and looked at his eyes. Then she pulled up his lip to get a look at the gums, which were a little pale. Yellow discharge, hardly noticeable on his light muzzle, crusted his nostrils.

Piper listened to his chest with a stethoscope, and her heart sank.

"What do you think's making him colic?" Dylan asked. He sounded as anxious as a new father.

Piper looked up at him from where she squatted on her heels in the stall. "It's not colic."

"That's good, right?"

"This isn't any better. He's got pneumonia."

Willis sucked his bottom lip against his teeth. "Well, shit."

She stood up. "Pretty much. We'll get him on fluids and antibiotics right away. I don't have equine drugs, but I've got some broad-spectrum antibiotics that should do the trick. At least until this storm clears out and Dr. Rodriguez can get here." Piper came out of the stall and dug through the bag of medications until she came up with a couple of bottles.

"These might work." She put a hand to her forehead, thinking. "God, I wish I had a horse nebulizer. Then we could get those antibiotics right down into his lungs where it can do the most good."

Willis stirred beside Dylan. "We got one of them a few years back when Sage was having all those problems. Remember, Dylan?"

"How come I didn't know about that?" Piper said. "I don't remember Sage having issues."

"It was a year or two before you moved in," Willis said. "Believe it or not, there was an existence here before you, Piper, and we've gone on without you, too."

"Easy, Willis," Dylan said.

The older man dropped his head. "Sorry."

Piper stared at the two men, stung by Willis's reaction. "Okay. So great, there's a nebulizer. Where is it?"

"At the old stable," Willis said, in a more polite tone.

"That's disappointing." The old stable was on the other side of the ranch, nearer the cabins.

"Why doesn't Dylan here take you?" Willis clapped Dylan on the back. "The nebulizer was in the tack room last time I saw it. In a boxed kit with solutions and stuff. Should have everything you need."

She looked at Dylan and his expression told her he didn't relish the thought of going back out into the storm either. "Think it'll make a big difference?" he asked.

Piper watched Thunder, the way the little colt's sides heaved with every breath. His lungs had sounded so crackly.

"I think he's going to need every trick we can throw at him," she said. "I only hope it'll be enough."

—

With strict instructions to keep an eye on both Thunder and Osiris, Piper left Willis in the barn and followed Dylan back to his truck.

"Looks like a slight lull." Dylan held out his hand where snowflakes collected.

"Wind's not as bad as before, too."

They got in the truck, still a little warmer than the outside air.

Dylan started the engine. "This first storm's supposed to finish by tomorrow night."

"But the second one's coming early Saturday morning with even more snow."

He sighed. "This is what we're reduced to, Piper. Talking about the stupid weather."

For some reason, her heart jittered. "Well, it's some weather."

"You know what I mean." He sighed again.

Piper didn't know how to respond. Dylan turned onto the dirt road, invisible under the snow, but demarcated by the fence posts on either side.

The orange plow on the front of the Chevy pushed snow, with a whooshing noise, into satisfying walls on the side of the road, like frosting on a cake.

A little farther on, the first hunter's cabin came up on their right. Piper pointed. "I didn't see any cars outside the cabins the other day. Did you have to clear anybody out for the storm?"

Dylan shifted in his seat, focused on the road ahead. "Nobody was here."

"Business bad?"

He shifted again on the bench seat. "I stopped the hunts."

"What?" Piper stared at him, but he kept his eyes on the road. "Oh, no. You didn't have issues with CWD, did you?" Piper had heard a ranch in Gunnison had a mule deer with chronic wasting disease.

"Can you think of any other reason why I might have stopped them?"

Piper continued to stare. "You—you listened to me?"

"I still think you're wrong about it. But it upset you."

"We're divorced, Dylan. It's not your job to care what upsets me anymore." He'd never given an inch on the issue when they'd been married. If he had, things might have been different. It angered her he couldn't have done this two years ago. She'd had a million ideas for things they could have done on the ranch instead. "Why now?" She didn't bother hiding the sharpness in her voice.

For several beats, the only sound was the shushing of the windshield wipers and the bump and whoosh of the plow. She barely heard Dylan's whisper. "I miss you, Pie."

Something caught in her throat and she couldn't speak. *Pie.* It had been his nickname for her from the first day they'd ever met. It had been January, eight years ago. He was twenty-four, she twenty-three. She'd been in her second year of vet school at CSU. He'd started college a little later than most and was in his third year doing an Agricultural Business degree. It was funny, but they hadn't met on campus. It had been at the National Western Stock Show in Denver.

Triumphant, Piper turned around with a cup of steaming urine in her hand. The steer behind her bellowed at the indignity of his ordeal.

"Don't know what you're complaining about," she told the animal. "I'm the one covered in pee."

"That looks like fun," said a cowboy, arms draped over the pen fence. He wore a black cowboy hat, suede jacket, and just about the cockiest smile Piper had ever seen, which annoyed her even as she noticed how good-looking he was.

He said, "What's going on? You got a drug test coming up or something and needed some clean piss?"

Without meaning to, she grinned. "This fella is the one getting drug-tested. We make sure he's not on steroids or any other drugs that can be harmful to people."

"Who's 'we'?"

"The other vet students and me volunteering here. I feel kind of bad, though, knowing this guy's destined for the dinner table."

"Yum." He licked his lips and met her eyes. "That's a good-looking steak on the hoof there."

"'Steak on the hoof?'" She laughed. "He's a good-looking bovine though, as far as they go."

"Yep. He's a fine piece of flesh. And I've got an eye for these things." He looked her up and down and waggled his eyebrows at her.

Piper rolled her eyes and made a vomiting sound. But then somehow, when he asked her if she wanted to grab something to eat, she found herself saying yes.

They ended up buying big slabs of warm apple pie from a

booth and cups of hot chocolate. It was freezing and she could feel the heat coming off his body beside her on the bench of the picnic table.

"This is my favorite," she said, scooping a bite into her mouth.

"Makes sense, you being called Pie and all."

"It's Piper, you know."

"Sure, that's what everybody else calls you. But you're such a cutie, I think I'll always call you Pie." He smiled, lopsided, and boyish.

She set her spoon down and gave him a look. "Always? We met half an hour ago."

"I know, but you'll see. I gotta good feeling about us, Pie."

It should've scared her, that cocky certainty of his, but he'd smiled at her again, and when her heart flip-flopped in her chest, she'd had the funniest feeling he was right.

In the last few months of their marriage, he'd used her given name a lot in strained sentences. *Piper, you know that's not what I meant. What would you have me do, Piper? Piper, I'm not an idiot.* Every time he'd said her name, it made her bristle. But Pie? He hadn't called her that in a long while. Until now.

I miss you, Pie. He'd stopped the elk hunts on the ranch. She swallowed the lump in her throat and opened her mouth, shut it again. "Dylan?"

He looked at her, waiting, a fearful, hopeful expression on his face.

She couldn't keep looking into those intense eyes. She turned her gaze to the road and said, "Dylan, I miss—Oh my God, look out! There's somebody there!"

13

Dylan whipped the steering wheel to the right and by mere inches avoided the form lying in the snow in the headlight beams. The truck fishtailed and they swerved off the road into the fence. Two posts dragged behind them on the wire until they came to a stop. The plow bounced up and down on top of a mound of snow it had pushed beside them.

Piper wasted no time jumping out of the truck into about a foot of snow.

Dylan slammed his door when he got out. "Was that a woman?"

"I think so." Piper ignored the cold wetness going down into her boots as they picked their way back to the road.

Piper yanked out her phone and used its flashlight. "It's so dark out here." The snow reflected light, but the moon, already a miserly crescent, was hidden behind storm clouds.

Splashes of crimson appeared in the phone's beam.

"Do you think she's—is she dead?"

Dylan's voice startled her and she took a step closer to him.

They approached the woman slowly as if she might rise up like a horror movie zombie. Piper's stomach tightened. She'd seen plenty of dead animals, but a dead human was a far different matter.

Piper gazed down at a small blonde woman lying on her back in the road. Her face was so pale and her eyes closed. She looked to be in her fifties. Blood seeped under her right shoulder.

"What's she doing out here on my ranch?" Dylan looked at Piper, his face almost as pale as the woman's. "She looks pretty dead."

"Yeah." Piper should check, but the thought of touching the woman filled her with fear.

A raven screeched from his perch on a nearby fence post.

"Get out of here," Piper said, outraged on the woman's behalf. No way was she letting this human being be picked at by scavengers. She waved her arms at the raven until it flew away.

"Poor thing," Dylan murmured. "Where did she come from?" He turned around as if looking for answers.

The woman wore nothing but a dress and a shawl. A shawl? Piper shone the light over her body. The dress was a dark blue calico, covered in a thick layer of snow. She must have been out here for a while. A white bonnet lay askew under her head. It was covered in blood. Old-fashioned button-up shoes stuck out the hem of her dress.

"What's she wearing?" she said. "She looks like some kind of pioneer lady."

Dylan didn't answer. He was busy brushing snow off an object lying about a foot from the woman's right hand and lifted a rifle. Shiny brass winked in the light of her phone.

"What the—look at this, Piper. See this brass receiver? It's a Henry rifle."

He lifted it in Piper's direction and she shrugged. "So?"

"Yeah, okay, look who I'm talking to. So this is an antique. They used these rifles in the Civil War. This thing's worth tens of thousands. It's weird though. It looks like new."

"Everything about this is weird."

Dylan turned back around to consider the woman again. "What do you think killed her?"

"I'm not sure she's dead. I would've sworn her chest just moved."

"We should check." Dylan made no move to do so, though.

Piper's breath came in rapid clouds of vapor as she crouched beside the woman. She put her fingers to the woman's neck. Her skin was so cold. Piper couldn't find a pulse. She fought down her revulsion to put an ear over the woman's mouth.

Was that her imagination, or did she feel a whisper of breath? She waited. No, that one was definitely not her imagination. She straightened up. "I think she's alive!"

"Really?" Dylan looked much more alarmed at the possibility of a living woman being found on his ranch than a dead one.

As if in answer, the woman moaned.

"We need to get her out of the cold."

"You think?" Dylan sighed and bent to effortlessly scoop her into his arms.

"Wait, what if her neck—" But it was too late. Dylan was already carrying her toward his truck. Even with a woman in his arms, he managed the snow just fine. Her ex-husband was a strong man, she had to admit. And he still managed to keep the woman's rifle in one hand.

The woman's bonnet fell off her head into the snow.

"Pardon me if I don't wanna hang around here. Looks like the lull's about over," he said over his shoulder.

He was right. The snow was thickening and the wind had picked up again. She could barely make out his form as he moved away. She checked around on the road for anything else belonging to the woman, but there was nothing besides the small puddles of blood. She swept a booted foot back and forth in the snow but didn't find anything.

She hurried after Dylan through the deepening snow. He'd covered the back seat with a blanket, laid the woman down, and tucked it around her. Dylan had already turned on the engine and was buckling himself in.

"Get in," he said.

Instead, Piper opened the back door so she could examine her. Blood was seeping through the blanket already. She pulled it back to get a closer look when—

"Hey!" Dylan circled his arm at her. "Get in here."

"She's bleeding from somewhere. We should try to stop it first."

"Or, you might consider for a minute that whoever hurt her could still be hanging around. Get in the damn truck, Piper."

She'd been so focused on the woman's strange attire and confirming the fact of her survival, she hadn't thought of that frightening possibility. Someone—or something had tried to kill this woman.

Piper made a huffing noise, but got in the passenger seat and locked her door.

Dylan didn't speak as he concentrated on reversing the truck out of the snowbank and getting back on to what passed for a road. Piper got out her phone and dialed 9-1-1. A harried-sounded dispatcher answered.

"Good luck," Dylan said under his breath.

A minute later, Piper slammed her phone on the seat. "Emergency crews are tied up with other emergencies. They don't think anyone can get to us anytime soon anyway. I guess I'm going to have to try and help her the best I can."

"Piper, you're a good vet, but no offense, this woman needs a doctor. I'm going to try to get her to the hospital."

Piper didn't like the idea of him driving in this snow, but she had to agree it was the better option. "You think we can make it into town?"

"*We* aren't going. I'm gonna drop you back with Willis. There's no need for both of us to be out on the roads in these conditions. I need you to stay and help Thunder."

"Shoot. Thunder." She'd forgotten the colt for a few minutes.

"We didn't get the nebulizer. We were so close to the old stable, too."

"You'll just have to do your best for him with what you have. We got bigger problems now."

"What do you think happened to her?" Piper glanced back at the woman who lay so unmoving, she might have died. If so, it would certainly make things easier. Guilt stabbed Piper at the pragmatic thought.

Dylan pounded a fist on the steering wheel, "What the hell is happening on my ranch? Lightning, that elk, now a person. Willis was right. He said it was only a matter of time until somebody got hurt."

"So, you *do* think it's all connected."

"Is it an animal, Piper? Some kind of rogue, rabid bear?"

"I don't know. What about that guy in the snow I saw with the antlers?"

He gave her that look he always did when he thought she was being an idiot. "Come on. You know the snow was just playing tricks on you."

"We found the antler velvet in my clinic right after that."

He didn't have an answer for that. Piper was relieved to see the horse barn's lights shining through the snow up ahead.

"Where did this woman come from, Dylan? If it was an animal that hurt her, why was she walking around out there alone on your ranch? In nothing but a dress and shawl?"

"Mental health problems? I don't know. Or somebody could've hurt her somewhere else and dumped her body out there."

"In what vehicle? How did they get on your ranch? We didn't see any tracks. And there's the small matter of the fact she's not dead." Piper turned around to check the woman again. Her arm hung down and Piper felt a faint, thready pulse at her wrist.

"Maybe they didn't know she wasn't dead. Or they thought the cold would finish the job."

"She didn't have a purse or wallet, but maybe there's some

I.D. on her somewhere? I know this sounds crazy, but she looks like she came straight out of—"

"The 1800s? Yeah, I know. But unless we got ourselves a time-traveling woman, there's some other explanation, and I don't think I'm going to like it."

Time travel was exactly the crazy idea Piper was thinking.

Dylan didn't turn off to park by the barn and instead idled the truck in the road. "All right, you get inside and help Thunder."

"Let me look at the woman once more. I want to check the bleeding."

"Piper."

"Let me look, okay?"

She climbed out, and the cabin light in the truck came on. Piper pulled back the blanket to reveal the woman's calico dress. Most of the blood came from her right shoulder. The woman didn't stir as Piper unbuttoned the dress to the woman's navel.

"She's wearing a chemise," Piper muttered.

Dylan hoisted himself up and turned in his seat. "A what now?"

"An undershirt. An old-fashioned one." Piper grabbed the garment at the top and tried to tear it, but the fabric was so wet with blood, it wouldn't rip.

"Here." Dylan handed her a knife from a sheath at his hip.

Piper didn't say anything about her ex-husband being armed to the teeth. She had to concede—she was glad tonight.

Piper sliced away the chemise.

"Oh, wow," Dylan said.

Four diagonal slashes cut from her right shoulder, between her small breasts, and down to her left hip. Each slash was about two inches from the next, narrow at the ends and wider in the middle. It reminded her of the wounds on Osiris earlier in the night. God, was that really this same night?

Piper had seen a lot of damage inflicted by one animal on another. They were messy. These slashes were so perfect and evenly spaced as to look like some sort of Halloween makeup kit.

But the cuts were real. Muscle and yellow fat peeked through the wounds. She was relieved to see, however, that the wounds only seeped blood. Perhaps the cold had been a blessing by stopping the bleeding. While the injuries were gory, they didn't appear life-threatening. Piper guessed the woman's state of unconsciousness was caused by hypothermia rather than blood loss. She buttoned her dress back up, embarrassed for the woman's nakedness in front of Dylan, though he'd shown nothing but concern in his eyes when he'd looked at her.

Or maybe it was just the woman was middle-aged. But she was in good shape. Strong and fit for a woman of fifty or more. Piper hoped that strength would help her.

Piper checked under the woman's legs, then under her back and shoulders. She couldn't find any other bleeding other than a small scalp wound near her ear.

"Keep the heat blasting," Piper said. "I think she's safe to transport to the hospital."

Dylan nodded. "Take good care of Thunder. And yourself."

"You too. Don't get stuck out there, okay?" Piper considered telling Dylan to stay, that she would do her best to stitch up this woman's wounds and care for her. But that was insanity. He was right. She needed human doctors and medicine. Dylan had a four-wheel-drive truck with a snowplow and just as good a chance of getting her to a hospital as an emergency vehicle.

She started to close the door when she stopped. "Hey, Dylan?"

"Yeah?"

"I just wanted you to know. I—I miss you, too."

Before he could respond, she shut the door with a slam and walked toward the horse barn.

14

Piper rolled back the barn doors and stepped inside. A few horses nickered a welcome.

"I'm back," she said.

No answer came except for the soft stamping of a hoof on straw somewhere.

"Willis? You here?"

Her footsteps thudded on the wood floor as she walked over to Osiris's crate to peek in. He lay on his stomach, legs stretched out in front, and opened an eye at her in greeting, an encouraging sign.

Where was Willis? Piper didn't like being alone in the barn. She didn't want to be alone anywhere tonight and definitely not on this ranch.

She drew a deep breath as she walked down the aisle. Willis could be in the bathroom or grabbing some coffee.

She reached Thunder's stall and smiled at the sight.

Willis was sleeping next to the colt. He sat in the straw, his eyes shut and his back resting against the wall. His mouth hung open, and he snored. One hand rested on Thunder's flank.

She opened the stall door and was alarmed to see neither the colt nor the man stirred.

"Hey, Willis." She touched his shoulder and even through his coat, she could feel the heat radiating off him. She put the back of her hand to his forehead. His skin was so hot. Her hand was freezing, though, and that finally woke him.

"No! No, don't come near me!" His eyes flew open, and confusion swam there for a second before recognition took over. "Oh, Piper. You scared me." He rubbed a hand down his face and beard. "I was having a nightmare."

"And no wonder. You're burning up with a fever, Willis." Piper looked from him to Thunder, who'd gone downhill in the short time she and Dylan had been gone. "I'm not sure which one of you looks worse."

"I'm not gonna lie. I've felt better." He shivered. "I'm so cold."

She went out of the stall and dug around in her medical bag to come up with an aspirin bottle. "Here, take these." She shook out two pills into her hand.

He swallowed them down without water.

She said, "We need to get you into bed."

"Where's Dylan?"

Piper considered lying to save him worry, but he repeated the question. "We found a woman who was hurt. He's taking her to the hospital."

"Hurt?" Willis pushed himself up straighter. "W-what's g-g-going on?" His teeth chattered.

Piper put an arm under his elbow and helped him to his feet. "Let's worry about you right now, all right? I think we need to get you tucked into bed."

"I c-c-can't walk back to my trailer in the storm. Feel like crap. There's a s-s-snowmobile back of the b-b-barn. Keys are in-n-n the office."

"Well, that's good to know, but you're not going anywhere

in this weather. You can stay right here where I can keep an eye on you and Thunder. I'm putting you in the stable master's quarters upstairs."

When Piper and Dylan had still been married, she'd fitted out the barn's living quarters herself intending to bring her horse-loving identical twin sister out from California to live on the ranch. That idea went up in smoke when her marriage went kaput. She doubted Dylan had done anything with the quarters.

"No one's using them still, right?"

"No. But I d-d-don't need a n-n-nursemaid."

"I kind of think you do."

He sighed, but put up no more fight, leaning on her as she led him down the aisle and up the stairs that lay across from the barn doors.

It was a nice apartment, she thought, flipping on all the lights. If you didn't mind the horse smell. She certainly didn't. The kitchen lay to her left, open to the living room directly ahead. The living area and bedroom were much bigger than those of her small apartment. She'd decorated it with her sister's feminine tastes in mind. She guided Willis down the hall and into the bedroom.

He sank onto the bed with a groan. Piper knelt to take off his boots and helped him under the covers. It amused her when the gruff Willis snuggled under the rose-covered quilt on a satisfied sigh.

Once he was settled, she asked, "So, this snowmobile? It's working okay?"

"Yeah, why?" Now he was under the covers, his teeth had stopped chattering, and he wasn't shivering as hard.

"Dylan and I didn't get to the old stable to pick up the nebulizer. From the looks of Thunder, he needs it now more than ever."

"You're going back out there alone?"

"It's not far. Not even a quarter of a mile."

"You could get lost in this blizzard."

"Willis, I'm afraid if I don't do this, that little guy down there is going to die."

"You're more important than a horse," he said, closing his eyes. "Even if you did run off like an idiot and leave Dylan and me."

She patted his chest. "I *am* an idiot. That's why I told you yesterday I realized leaving you was the biggest mistake of my life. And leaving Dylan." She smiled. "But mostly, you, of course."

He didn't respond to her bad joke. His breaths grew longer, and she figured he'd fallen asleep. She got up and turned off the light.

As she was about to walk out, Willis spoke. "Dylan never stopped loving you, Piper. Not for one second." His voice sounded sleepy and weak, and he mumbled the last part. "Don't you forget it 'cause I know you love him, too."

She was halfway down the hall when Willis spoke again, clearer now as if he'd summoned all his strength to say it.

"A rifle's hanging in Dylan's office. Take it with you, Piper."

—

Piper found the keys to the snowmobiles hanging on hooks in the barn office. The room smelled of Dylan. She sent up a silent prayer for his safety out on the roads. And then added one for the woman.

She glanced around the office. Was it this tidy when they were married? Papers sat in an orderly fashion in an inbox. On top of a filing cabinet rested a trophy from his high school rodeo win. She smiled. To her surprise, a worn copy of Thomas Wolfe's *You Can't Go Home Again* sat on his desk. Next to it was a picture frame.

She picked up the black and white picture of her standing next to Lightning. In the photo, Piper was laughing, looking at something off-camera. Probably some joke one of the wranglers had made. They were always cutting up.

Piper had taken every photograph of her and Dylan and boxed them up and shoved them into the back of her closet. Like she'd done with the memories of her marriage and the deep ache of missing him. They might be hidden, but that didn't mean they weren't sitting there, present in her life every single day.

Dylan had elected to keep her picture on his desk.

What did that mean? That it didn't hurt him anymore to see her face? Maybe he'd gotten over her. When he'd said he missed her, had he meant it in a bittersweet way? Longing for something that could never be? Maybe he'd gotten over her so well, he missed their friendship. That thought made her feel like she was the one whose chest had been clawed open.

Or was there more to him saying he missed her? Did he miss her like she did him? Was there any undoing their mistakes?

She kissed her fingers and touched them to Lightning in the photograph. Over a year had gone by, and she hadn't visited her horse once. Now he was gone, and there was no undoing that mistake. This picture of him, healthy and whole, was how she wanted to remember him, not the bloody pieces of him strewn across the ground.

She couldn't save Lightning, but if she braved the blizzard, she might be able to save his colt.

With a heavy sigh, Piper took down the Ruger Magnum rifle hanging behind Dylan's desk. She opened the top drawer and found a box of .300 ammunition. With even greater reluctance, she sat down, pulled out the magazine as Dylan had taught her, and loaded it, double-checking the safety was on. She grabbed a flashlight and left the office with all its comforting traces of Dylan. She pulled on her gloves and hat. Then she steeled herself for the cold wind when she opened the door.

Once again, the crazy weather surprised her. The air hung still and the snow fell in thick, undisturbed curtains falling silently on the ground. Did blizzards have an eye like a hurricane?

It was so quiet.

And cold. Her breath hung in clouds as she stepped out. The snow muffled noises and obscured her vision in the already dark night. It was not the time to think of Lightning, of the elk, of the antlered figure in the snow, of the woman bearing the claw marks of a large animal. She might hate it, but the rifle in her hand gave her, all alone out here, a measure of confidence to face the night.

She walked, boots squeaking in the snow, to the back of the barn, where three red and black Polaris snowmobiles stood in a line. Even with Thunder so sick, Dylan driving an injured woman to the hospital, and Willis burning with fever upstairs, even with the fear licking up her spine, she couldn't contain a quick, sharp moment of joy at the sight of them.

"You've never ridden a snowmobile?" Dylan asked her.

"You ever gone surfing?" she shot back.

"Okay, fair enough. Maybe since I'm taking you snowmobiling, you'll take me surfing?"

"Sounds like a fair trade."

After brief instructions on operating the machine, he handed her the keys and she hopped on.

Minutes later, he caught up to her across the meadow where she'd stopped, having left him in the proverbial dust—or snow, in this case.

He flipped the visor of his helmet up and gave her that crooked grin. "Piper Mitchell is a speed demon."

"You sound shocked."

He shrugged.

"Guess you don't know me that well, then."

His nose crinkled up. "Nah. I think I know you better than you think."

"Oh, yeah. Why's that?"

"Because you're sitting on the fast snowmobile."

The fast snowmobile. She climbed on it now, wondering if Dylan had known her better than she thought all along.

15

Dylan gripped the steering wheel and leaned forward to peer through the windshield. The wind had died down, but the snow fell as heavy as ever. The windshield wipers swished back and forth. Music would've been nice, but he needed to concentrate on driving. Heat blasted out the vents and made him sweat under his jacket, but for the woman's sake, he didn't dare turn it down.

The odometer ticked over on his dash, marking off each hard-won tenth of a mile. One and three tenths more to go until he reached the end of the ranch road and the beginning of the highway. Five more minutes at his current speed. He could do five more minutes. And with any luck, he'd find a freshly plowed highway to take him into town and get this woman to the hospital.

Two-tenths of a mile later, a groan came from the backseat.

"Ma'am," he said. "Can you hear me?"

Another moan, louder this time.

"Ma'am, I'm getting you some help, okay?"

To his surprise, she'd pushed herself up to sitting with an anguished cry and held the Henry rifle in her lap. With visible effort and a grunt of pain, she clicked the lever down and up— plenty familiar with the action.

He heard the next bullet in the tube slide down.

Dylan slowed the truck to a stop and looked over his shoulder. He could grab the rifle barrel and wrestle it off her, but he'd rather not. "Whoa, whoa, easy. I'm turning on the light, okay?"

She blinked in the sudden brightness. She had blue eyes, even bluer than Piper's, and the whites showed all around. There were crow's feet around those eyes, but she was still an attractive woman. Her chest heaved up and down as she panted. Dylan winced, thinking breathing like that had to hurt her injuries something fierce.

"W-who?" She stopped to lick her lips. "Who are you?" Her voice came out hoarse and strained with some kind of accent.

"Dylan Kincaid, ma'am. What's your name?"

She didn't answer. Instead, she pressed herself further into the corner and gripped the rifle harder. "Where am I? Where's Anna?"

Irish. That's what her accent was. "We found you on my ranch. The Crazy K. I didn't see anyone else. Who's Anna?"

"She's the widow staying with us." Her voice caught on that word. *Widow*. "I hope she stayed in the cabin. I told her to stay inside when I saw it."

"Saw what?" he said.

"Where am I now?"

What had happened to this woman? Whatever it was, it couldn't be good. She looked so scared, he used a low voice like he did when speaking to a spooked horse or elk. "My ranch is outside Crested Butte. In Colorado. Where are you from?"

"Crested Butte," she whispered. "Crested Butte. I don't know that name." She clutched the blanket to her chin. "W-what are we traveling in?"

The question made Dylan's mouth go dry. "This is my truck, ma'am. I'm driving you to the hospital to see a doctor."

"How were we moving? Where are the horses?" She fingered the top of the door and looked around the cab, her eyes wild. "Where do those lights come from?"

Maybe she had a head injury. Or something much worse was going on. Dylan's imagination couldn't help but get the better of him. What if she'd been held captive for years by some crazy serial killer? Or some kind of cult leader? Someone into re-enacting the nineteenth century? Maybe she'd never been outside in the real world. That would explain how she didn't understand something as ordinary as a truck.

He ignored her questions for now. "How did you get hurt?"

Her eyes darted back and forth. They held a glassy sheen and he figured she was in shock. "Is it gone? I need to check on Anna. She's got children." Her voice sounded weaker, lost. The rifle barrel dipped toward the floor well.

"Is what gone?"

"The creature."

"Creature? What kind of creature?" Dylan swallowed and looked out the windows of his truck at the swirling snow. "A bear? A mountain lion?"

She shook her head and closed her eyes as if the ordeal of talking had exhausted her. "Something terrible. Like a man, but not. So terrible. My husband," she mumbled. "He's dead. He left three days ago to stake his mine and never came back. I found him."

Stake his mine? The conversation kept getting weirder. "You found him?"

"So much blood. He's dead. My husband's dead."

"I—I'm sorry," Dylan said, trying to hide his rising alarm.

"He was a mean son of a bitch, but no one deserved that."

"What's your name, ma'am?" he tried again.

"Hattie. Anna is all alone with her children. I hope she won't come looking for me. She needs to stay inside." She slid down the door of the truck, and the rifle clattered to the floor. "She won't know . . . what's out . . . there if . . ." Her voice trailed away to nothing as she lost consciousness once more.

"Shit." Dylan put his foot on the gas harder than he intended and fishtailed the truck a little. He needed to get her to the hospital fast.

His mind raced, and it never did well at high speed. He was a slow thinker. *List the facts, Dylan.* A woman, dressed in clothes from the 1800s, shows up on his ranch with claw marks raving about some creature like a man that attacked her. She has a friend in a cabin somewhere, but she's never heard of Crested Butte. She doesn't understand what a truck is. The woman has a husband who was staking a mine. Who's now dead. She knows her way around a Henry rifle.

"What the hell?" he said out loud. Those were some stupid-ass facts and none of them made any sense. Time travel was the only thing that did, but that particular option of explanation wasn't open to him seeing as it was impossible. What, did he think he and Piper drove through the ranch and somehow stumbled back into the 1800s? He wasn't Marty McFly and his truck sure as hell wasn't any DeLorean.

He turned on the radio and felt an embarrassing rush of relief that it worked. A static-filled Carrie Underwood song filled the cabin. Some idiot DJ had a sense of humor and decided "Jesus, Take the Wheel" was a good choice for this weather. He immediately switched it off.

"Come on, come on, come on," he said. At himself, the truck, the situation. He just wanted to get this woman to the hospital and off his hands and get back to Piper.

He wanted this storm to be over and everything to make sense again.

The odometer slowly rolled over. The snow fell fast on his windshield. The truck juddered over the snow, and the heat continued to roast him. He turned it off. Just for a minute or two before he got heatstroke in a blizzard. He was caught in some kind of monotonous white hell where he'd be stuck driving this road for the rest of eternity.

Hattie moaned on the back seat again. To be safe, he reached back and grabbed the rifle. He moved it out of her reach and rested it against the passenger seat. Dylan returned his gaze to the road and gasped, slamming on the brakes.

A big pyramid of logs blocked the road.

At first, the brakes did nothing. A steep drop waited on either side of the road, but Dylan made himself stay calm. The brakes bit in at last and the truck rolled to a stop, slowed by the thick snow and the uphill climb as much as anything.

Entire trees, their trunks a foot in diameter or more, lay piled on top of each other to form a barricade at least ten feet high. Higher, he could tell, than the elk fences. They stretched across the road, sticking out past the drop-offs on either side to block the only access in and out of the Crazy K.

Who put it here? And why? Dylan gripped the steering wheel and ignored the pounding pulse in his ears.

The truck's headlights lit up the trunks. The snow stopped completely like someone had thrown a switch. He leaned forward and squinted at the sight. The tree trunks had been stripped of their bark by way of long, deep, vertical scratches. Sitting atop the pile were four or five ravens, hopping about on nimble feet.

"What in the world?" His breath fogged up the windshield and he used his jacket sleeve to rub a clear circle.

Then he screamed. It was a manly scream, but still. He had to acknowledge he'd just screamed.

Hattie—likely disturbed at his shouting—that's what it was, shouting, not screaming—stirred on the back seat.

Antlers appeared at the top of the pyramid, rising up as if an elk were climbing up the other side of the pile. Bloody strips of velvet hung from the antlers, like the tattered flags on the battlements of a fort. The sight chilled him. Piper had told him the antlers scraping at her window were shedding their velvet, too.

His mind flashed to what he'd read in that book over dinner.

Dylan should throw the truck in reverse and get the hell out of there, but he couldn't get himself to move. He had to see what kind of elk was attached to those huge antlers. See what kind of elk could clamber up a pile of logs like some kind of damn bighorn sheep.

The antler rack rose higher until the dagger tines were visible. Long, rotting ropes of velvet hung from them. He watched, with trepidation, as the brow tines became visible, which meant the elk itself was about to appear.

Suddenly, it was imperative Dylan *not* see what came after the antlers. He didn't want to know what was climbing up the pile toward him.

But it was too late. A nightmare vision crested the pile of tree trunks.

This time, he didn't care the screaming coming out of him wasn't particularly manly. Hattie joined in from the backseat.

16

Piper sat on the snowmobile and wondered what she was going to do with the rifle. There was a storage box on the back of the snowmobile, which would come in useful for the nebulizer, but it wasn't long enough for the gun. She glanced around and caught the gleam of metal from the long pole of the powder jack, used for raising the snowmobile if it sank. It was strapped to the side of the machine next to—what else?—a handy-dandy rifle scabbard. Bless that gun-toting Dylan. She slid in the Ruger, put the key in the ignition, and enjoyed the growl of the engine coming to life to block out the eerie silence.

She guided the sled around the front of the barn and back onto the road she and Dylan had taken earlier. Heavy snow fell, and Piper took her hand off the handlebars to wipe her visor every few seconds. The snowmobile's headlight illuminated a narrow path in front.

Soon, splashes of blood appeared in the headlight's beam as she passed the place where she and Dylan had found the injured woman. What had taken an eternity in the truck took no time at all on the fast snowmobile, gliding across the snow. How far had Dylan and the woman gotten? Had he reached the highway yet? Maybe he was even now making his way toward town and the hospital. He couldn't get back fast enough as far as she was concerned.

Out here, she felt so alone. The new horse barn, ranch house, and staff trailers lay behind her. Ahead, no lighted structures were in view. Off to her left, trees blurred by in a dark smudge. To her right, a meadow stretched away to where the national forest ran up the mountain, a deep purple against the snowy night.

The old barn lay in that meadow and a short while later, Piper spotted it as a darker shape in the darkness. She held her breath, hoping the snowmobile wouldn't sink into the deep, fresh powder, and turned off the road toward the barn. The Polaris had no trouble trailblazing a new path.

Piper pulled alongside the barn door and cut the engine, plunging her back into an eerie quiet. Her ears rang in the sudden silence. Without the light of the snowmobile, it was very dark. The helmet visor made it even darker, leaving her blind, trapped. Though she could see better when she slipped the helmet off, she felt vulnerable without it.

She climbed off the snowmobile and clicked on the powerful flashlight. The barn doors weren't locked and slid back with a loud rumble. She fumbled around for the light switch and flipped it.

Nothing happened. Dylan must not bother powering the place anymore. It smelled of hay, but underneath that something rotten and unpleasant, like a kitchen with dirty dishes and old trash. She swung her flashlight around. Dylan looked to be using the old barn for hay storage and as some kind of tractor hospital. A dismantled John Deere rested in the aisle like a sleeping dinosaur. The sight of so many of its parts scattered around reminded Piper of Lightning with his guts spread about.

Stop it. She needed to focus on Thunder and getting that

nebulizer. Piper closed the doors behind her. It wasn't much warmer inside the barn, but closing the doors at least kept out the wind.

Something rustled in the hay and she whirled to her right, pointing her flashlight at the bales stacked in the disused stalls. Another little rustle came. It was such a small sound—like mice.

Hundreds of mice must live here.

Willis said the nebulizer was in the tack room. It lay at the end of the barn down the aisle, on the right side. This barn was much smaller than the new one, but at night, in the dark, the tack room seemed miles away.

She walked down the dusty boards, never before realizing how creepy a barn could be. A rustling came from the hayloft above as well.

At least with all these mice around, she wasn't alone. She swung her light from one stall to the next as she moved through the barn. Hay bales in that stall, an antique steam engine with flaking green paint in the other and so on, until she found herself at the doorway to the tack room.

She slid back the door and shrieked, dropping her flashlight onto the floor. It went out, plunging her into darkness even as it registered that all she'd seen was an old helmet hanging on the wall and the empty racks for the saddles. Somehow, her brain had created the image of a person standing there.

Piper knelt and retrieved her flashlight. She switched it back on, but the beam shone weaker. To Dylan's credit, he hadn't left much in this room, save the cracked helmet. It didn't take her long to find the dusty nebulizer kit sitting in the corner. By the dim light of the flashlight, she saw the kit contained the nebulizer itself, bottles of saline for mixing medicines, and a solution of chelated silver. Some people believed the silver interfered with microbes like bacteria and could help fight off infection.

She wasn't certain the silver would be safe for a young foal. She could call Dr. Rodriguez and see what the equine vet thought about it.

Something reverberated above her head, and she let out a strangled yelp, but it was only snow sliding off the barn roof. She didn't feel like hanging around any longer now she had the nebulizer. Any questions she had for the other vet could wait until she was back at the new horse barn—in the warmth and light with Willis sleeping upstairs and Dylan on his way back.

She'd nearly reached the barn door when her phone rang in her pocket. For the third time in as many minutes, Piper jumped about a foot. She tucked the nebulizer box under her arm and whipped out the phone. Expecting it to be Dylan, she said, "You at the hospital already?"

"Piper!" A man's voice came crackling over the connection.

"Yes, who is this?"

"It's Gilbert."

"Gilbert?" Why was Veronica's boyfriend calling her at four in the morning? "What's going on? Is Ronnie okay?"

"Oh, no." He groaned. "—you—seen her?" In his distress and with the static, Piper had trouble understanding him.

"What?"

"Have—seen her?"

"Have I seen her? Is that what you said? Gilbert, where is she?"

"That's just it." The static disappeared. "I don't know where she is. I woke up to go to the bathroom, and she wasn't in bed. I looked around the trailer"—Piper experienced an inappropriate rush of victory at his use of the word—"and she isn't here."

"Are you sure?"

"Of course, I'm sure."

"But where could she be? Is her car there?"

"Yes, yes. Both our cars. But Foxy is missing too."

Foxy was Veronica's Shiba Inu, a medium-sized orange dog with a curling tail that did, indeed, look like a fox.

"Maybe Foxy got outside, and Ronnie's out looking for her?" Piper tried to tamp down the contagious, rising panic in Gilbert's voice.

"Piper, I looked everywhere for her. I don't see any footprints or nothing. Her snow boots are by the back door still."

"Did you try calling her phone?"

"It's on the nightstand where she always keeps it. But I called the police. They thought I was crazy for worrying already. Nobody can get out in this weather. I've been looking for her for almost an hour, you know? Something's wrong."

"If Foxy is missing, she must have gone out looking for her."

"But why wouldn't she wake me to help? Why are her boots by the door?" He sounded like he was trying not to cry. "I'm really worried, Piper."

Piper's feeble reassurances made no sense. Why would Veronica have gone out on her own in the middle of a blizzard? "Well, now I'm really worried, too. If I hear anything, I'll let you know right away. You do the same for me, okay?"

"All right, thanks." He hung up.

Piper stood in front of the barn doors with a shaky, sick feeling. Where on earth was her best friend?

She shoved her phone in her pocket, jostling the flashlight in her hand. Its beam swept wildly across the barn, and in its light, she caught sight of a shiny, wet patch of crimson.

Blood. The shaky feeling doubled. She used her flashlight to follow the trail, which led in the opposite direction she'd taken down the aisle to the tack room. A foot-wide smear, as if something had been dragged across the floor, ran right up to the door of the feed room.

Piper froze for a moment, debating what to do. Part of her—most of her—voted to turn around, jump on the snowmobile, and get the hell out of there. Another part, though, the annoying, responsible part that had evolved beyond primal fear, thought she should check it out. After finding the woman on the road, there could be someone else left on the ranch who needed her help. Someone injured.

Or more likely dead, judging by the wide swath of blood.

Piper drew a deep breath and made herself take a step toward the feed room. That unpleasant stench from before grew. What had first smelled like dirty dishes and garbage sharpened into a coppery, tangy scent.

She was reassured it didn't smell like something decomposing though. Blood didn't always equal death.

She took another step and did her best to ignore the rustling in the hay behind her. Her hand trembled as she reached out and opened the door—and staggered back at the sight and smell. With a cry, she tripped over some twine and landed on her backside. Her phone rang in her pocket, but Piper didn't move to answer it. The flashlight had clattered to the ground beside her, and its light pointed straight at the open feed room to reveal the horror inside.

It was a nightmare. She must be having a nightmare. Piper couldn't believe what she was seeing.

She scrambled to her feet while the phone continued to ring in her pocket, and the rustling in the hay behind her grew louder.

17

Dylan watched in fascinated horror as the antlers cleared the top of the log pile. Ravens took to the air with hoarse cries. All of a sudden, the truck's headlights dimmed and still, the scant light revealed more from a nightmare than Dylan ever cared to see.

"He's back," Hattie said. "Do you smell it?"

He did. A disgusting, putrid smell. She reached around for her rifle, and when she couldn't find it, dissolved into whimpers.

Dylan picked up the rifle from the passenger seat and stared in horror as glowing green eyes appeared. They were set not in the face of an elk, but a man. Or as Hattie had said, *Like a man. But not.*

His face was terrible, rotting, and skeletal. His luminous eyes were too large. The monster cocked his head, like a bird of prey. With the creature's head at a different angle, Dylan saw its eyes didn't glow. They only reflected light, like a raccoon's. God, there hadn't been a raccoon scratching under his deck. Those glowing eyes he'd seen in the bushes had been this thing.

When the monster's eyes didn't glow green, they were much, much worse. They had no pupils, no whites. Just deep pools of blackness in his face. Smears of blood ran down his forehead, leaking from the base of the antlers that rose bizarrely from his skull. He turned to look at something off to his left, again with jerky, bird-like movements. The flesh of his right cheek was missing, revealing his jawbone.

The creature rose, revealing more and more of his body until he stood atop the barricade. He was tall and thin and wore no clothing, but his nakedness was hidden by the strips of decomposing flesh hanging, bloody like the velvet on his antlers, off his torso. The left side of his rib cage was visible. White bones gleamed in the dimmed headlights, and beneath them, the dark red of exposed viscera.

The creature held his arms at his sides, the fingers of his hands curled slightly. At their ends curved long, wicked claws.

It couldn't be real. It just couldn't. And yet everything he was staring at proved what his great-grandmother told him was true. A scary story turned horrifying reality.

"The witherling," Dylan whispered.

At the word, the thing's head snapped toward the truck like he'd heard Dylan speak. Those black eyes bore down at him, seeming to burn through the windshield.

Then, the creature shrieked. Hattie clapped her hands to her ears, and Dylan followed suit, but he couldn't block it out. Dylan recognized traces of noises he knew but put together, it was quite unlike anything he'd ever heard. The rusted-gate screech of a bugling elk, the scream of a mountain lion, a train stopping on rails. The sound grew, and as it did, the witherling—because what the hell else was he gonna call it?—the witherling's jaw came unhinged to open far too wide.

Something loosened deep in Dylan's gut at the sight of the creature's open mouth. It looked like every tooth he possessed was a canine. Dylan had been to the zoo once and seen a baboon yawn. That's what these teeth reminded him of. The long, sharp canines of a baboon, but with a mouthful of them, all curving to points as wicked and thin as those on the creature's claws.

Abruptly, the sound ended, and the witherling's mouth snapped shut.

What followed was worse.

Run. RUN. RUN!

The word came without the creature moving its mouth at all. It was inside Dylan's head, and outside his head, and all around. It was a whisper, but it was as loud as the shrieking had been. A voice, but not a voice. From something that was a man, but not a man. The hairs on Dylan's neck rose. The sound was filled with such evil, Dylan said an instinctive prayer.

Then he took the witherling's advice.

He threw the truck into reverse and went as fast as he dared in the snow, on a road with a steep bank on either side.

"Go, go!" Hattie shouted.

The headlights dimmed further as they shot backward down the road. All Dylan could see was the silhouette of the form with antlers atop his head striding down the piled tree trunks. The creature did not rush. He did not hurry. Sure-footed and calm, he made his way toward them.

It was the most chilling thing Dylan had ever witnessed in his life.

In the back seat, Hattie was doing her own praying.

The witherling walked toward them even as the gap between him—it?—and the truck widened. Dylan checked his rearview mirror and focused on the road behind him rather than the horror in front of him.

At last, he reached a place where the banks on either side rose up and evened out with the road. Dylan glanced over. The creature was some distance away now. He turned the wheel in a tight arc to turn the truck around to drive forward.

The tires sank into the deep snow on the side of the road. When he put the truck in drive, it lurched and stopped.

"Oh no, no, no."

"No, no, no," Hattie echoed in the back.

"Hang on."

He tried again and then once more, but the tires spun, sinking them deeper.

"I'm going to have to dig us out." He put a shaking hand on the door. "You keep watch for me." Down the road, the small antlered form grew bigger as it continued its relentless stride forward.

Hattie's pale face stared back at him. "Don't leave me."

"I'm not. I promise I won't leave you. You stay here in the truck and keep watch for me. Pound on the window if he's getting too close."

"He's so fast," she whispered. "You won't have a chance."

Dylan swallowed hard. If she told the truth, that was very bad news. "I don't have any other choice."

What's your plan, Kincaid? He needed to get the truck moving, but then what? He needed to warn Piper, get back, and protect her. Warn the others.

He handed Hattie the rifle and climbed out into the dark night.

In the truck bed lay a snow shovel. He pulled it out, the plastic handle cold even through his gloves. As fast as he could, he dug around the tires. The shovel crunched in the snow in a furious rhythm. His breath puffed out in a fog. For every shovel of snow he moved, he glanced over his left shoulder.

The figure was still advancing. A football field away. Then half.

He pulled the .357 from his holster and fired a shot at the creature.

It hit the witherling's leg, which buckled under him. A lucky shot. The thing crumpled to the ground, unmoving. With a little more luck, perhaps it wouldn't be able to get up again.

He jumped in the truck and restrained himself from slamming on the gas. He goosed the accelerator just enough to bump the truck up over the snow. They were on their way!

Dylan glanced in the rearview mirror and saw the witherling unfold itself and rise from the ground. He walked forward and then broke into a run.

"He's coming," Hattie said. "Go faster!"

Dylan pressed down the gas a little more. Something slammed into the truck bed. Hattie screamed. Dylan checked the mirror again and saw the witherling crouched in the truck bed.

The sight pissed him off. That thing better get the hell off his Chevy!

Dylan pushed the truck even faster, praying it wouldn't slide in the snow.

The sound of shattering glass filled the cab as the creature slammed its antlers into the back window. Hattie screamed and pressed herself down into the footwell of the back seat. The window broke with such force, the shards hit Dylan in the head and rained down around him in the driver's seat. The putrid smell was overwhelming, making him gag. Dylan swerved and the creature stumbled to the side. Somehow, though, the thing managed to stay in the truck bed.

A clawed hand reached inside. Hattie pointed the Henry and blasted the monster in the chest. Pieces of it flew everywhere. Dylan's ears rang from the deafening shot.

"Shoot it again!" he shouted.

Hattie cocked the lever and shot it again. Dylan pulled the wheel as hard as he dared to the left. The witherling, now off balance from being shot twice, flew through the air and landed on the ground to the right of the road.

Dylan straightened the truck and continued down the road, toward his ranch and the people he cared about.

"Is he moving?" he asked Hattie.

He could hear her brushing aside pieces of glass before climbing back onto the seat to peer out the broken back window.

"I—I don't see him," she said.

"Are you all right?" he asked her. The poor woman had

serious injuries and had experienced more of an ordeal than Dylan, and he felt like passing out himself.

"Poor Anna," she whispered. "We have to warn her. She has children. Just babies."

"We will. We're going to figure this out, okay?"

Dylan pushed the truck as fast as he dared. The plow bounced and slammed over the ground. He hated taking a hand off the wheel, but he had to call Piper. He had to warn her to stay inside with Willis no matter what.

And get the rifle down in his office.

He called her, but it rang and rang. As he waited for her to pick up, he kept checking his rearview mirror.

For now, at least, the monster stayed where it was.

18

Piper scuttled back from the tack room like a crab on her hands and feet until she managed to scramble to standing. She snatched up her flashlight, and though she didn't want to, pointed it at the room. The phone stopped ringing, but she barely registered the fact in the face of such an abomination spread before her.

Body parts were piled from floor to ceiling in bloody stacks. One was just a pile of severed arms, another legs—the limbs were all different skin tones. Some looked old, some young. One leg still wore pants. Suede with delicate red beading down the side. The cut ends of femurs and humerus bones gleamed blue-white through the muscle.

Worst of all was the mountain of heads. Men and women and even some smaller heads she hoped to God weren't from children. Black hair, brown hair, gray hair, and blonde hair. Redheads and bald heads. Some still had their eyes open, mouths agape. The eyes of others were shut tight as if blocking out the horror around them even in death. Half torsos hung from hooks in the ceiling to reveal racks of ribs like slaughtered cattle.

There must have been at least a dozen people's remains in there. All of them looked fresh. While the smell was bad, it wasn't like something rotting. It smelled like what it was. Fresh meat.

Piper vomited. Tears streamed down her face as she braced her elbows on her knees, her body shaking.

Someone, no, some*thing,* had made the feed room a meat locker. Full of human meat.

Who were all these people? How could the police not be hunting for a dozen or more missing people? What had done this?

Her mind sprang to the Algonquin legend in her book of the wendigo, a person transformed by cannibalism into a monster with a voracious craving for flesh.

Piper might not believe in the supernatural, but some psychopath could think he was a wendigo and be imitating one. Horror stories stole the legend and twisted it, making the wendigo a nightmarish, rotting elk. Maybe this psycho was wearing antlers on his head and going around eating people.

Piper forced herself to overcome her shock and get moving. After all, a monster was a monster. What mattered most was getting away from here. She picked up the nebulizer box and in her giddy terror, congratulated herself on remembering it. Then she hurried out the barn and even had the presence of mind to close the doors to better preserve the crime scene. The Polaris waited right where she left it. She strapped the nebulizer into the wire basket.

As she climbed onto the snowmobile, her phone rang again in her pocket. This time, she snatched it out and answered it.

"Piper!" came Dylan's frantic voice. "Oh, God. You were right. There's some kind of honest to God monster on the ranch."

Despite everything that happened, despite everything Piper had just seen in the feed room, hearing Dylan say that to her—

pragmatic, skeptical Dylan—iced the blood in her veins.

"Stay in the barn with Willis," he said. "Do *not* go anywhere. Go get my rifle down from the office. I want you to—"

"Dylan, I'm at the old horse barn."

A pause. Then, "What? Oh, God. No, Piper! No. How'd you get there?"

"On the snowmobile."

"Well, get the hell out of there!"

"I've got the rifle with—" But Piper had glanced down at the scabbard, which was unsnapped and empty. "It's gone! Dylan, somebody took the rifle off the snowmobile."

"Get out of there," he repeated. "You push that snowmobile as fast as you can and get back to Willis. Don't even try to get to the house. Just get inside the new barn and stay there. I'll be there in a couple of minutes. Keep—"

The phone cut off, and loud static blasted into her ear. She ended the call and shoved the phone in her pocket. Beside her, the barn door rumbled open.

19

Dylan swore and slammed his fist on the steering wheel. He didn't want to consider why Piper's call had been cut off like that. All he could do was hope when he returned to the barn, she'd be waiting there. If not, he'd go out looking for her.

His inability to protect Piper frustrated the hell out of him. It was the same helpless feeling plaguing him since she left. Every day, he went to bed not knowing how she was doing, if she needed anything, if she were lonely. He could have called her, he supposed. In the face of tonight's events, his stubbornness and pride were dumb reasons not to call the woman he loved.

He didn't want to die without telling her. As he sped down the snow-packed road, he was overwhelmed by the need to tell Piper he loved her. The need to get to Piper, waiting ahead, drove him as much as the need to escape the thing behind.

The wind shrieked again, whipping white clouds into the air. It obscured his view of the road ahead—and also his view in the mirror to see if the creature still pursued him.

"Hattie? You all right?"

She'd gone so quiet, he figured she must have lost consciousness once more.

"I don't know where I am," she answered in a soft, forlorn voice. "I don't know what that—that thing is. Everything is unfamiliar. And I hurt so bad."

Dylan cleared his throat and shifted in his seat. "Hattie, can I ask you something strange?"

"Yes," she whispered.

"Wh—what's the date?"

"It's March."

March? Uh, nope.

I think it's the eighteenth. It hurts," she said again.

"I know. We'll get you some medicine soon. But Hattie, what year is it?"

"The year? It's 1868."

Dylan's heart hammered in his throat. "When were you born?"

"1817. Why are you asking me?"

"Before I saw that monster back there, I wouldn't have believed in people traveling through time. But Hattie, it's a crazy old night."

"You're frightening me."

"I know and I sure am sorry for that. I don't know how to tell you this, but 1868 is about a hundred and fifty years ago." He told her the date.

"That's impossible." She sucked in a breath as she moved on the seat.

"You didn't understand how we were moving earlier. This is a truck with a combustion engine. There's going to be a lot of things you won't understand if you're telling the truth and you came from 1868."

"*Came* from 1868? You're mad." She started to cry. "Where's my cabin? Where's Anna?"

"Tell me what happened when you were attacked."

With a tear-choked voice, she said, "My husband didn't

return. He's been gone a few days and a big storm came up. Our supplies are running low. Anna's oldest heard something outside. We looked out the window and I glimpsed antlers. We needed meat. I grabbed the rifle and went after it. I followed the antlers a little ways off. I smelled something horrible." She took a deep, shaky breath. "Then I saw my husband in the snow, gutted like a fish. He never even left for the claim office. I had no love for the man, but to think of him lying there, so close to the cabin, for days?" She rubbed her face. "Then I turned around and—and that thing slashed my chest open. I screamed. I'm certain Anna must have heard. She must be so scared. I shot the thing, but it didn't hurt it. He grabbed me by the wrist and pulled me so hard, I fell over and hit my head. And that's all I know until I woke up in this—this truck."

"How many children are with Anna?"

"Three."

"And the oldest?"

"She's seven." Hattie stared out the window at nothing. "The youngest isn't even weaned. Around the same age as the baby I lost. My only baby," she murmured.

"I'm sorry," Dylan said, hating himself for having nothing better to say. "Anna will take care of her children. They'll be safe."

Hattie didn't say anything else. Her breathing evened out as she drifted back into sleep.

Dylan checked the rearview mirror over and over. Nothing but blowing snow. It fell heavier and the wind shrieked louder until he lost his bearings of where he was on the ranch. He had to go by his odometer.

"Two-tenths left," he said aloud, squinting at the dashboard. He glanced up to where a huge brown shape blocked the road.

It was a bear, its shaggy brown hair coated in snow. It looked at him, and its face was unlike any bear he'd seen before. It had cream-colored stripes of fur over its eyes and his muzzle was short and stubby. Something about the shape of its skull struck him as primitive. In his headlights, the bear pushed up onto its rear legs and stood.

And stood. It rose higher and higher until it was looming above the truck, and he couldn't see its head anymore. It was at least as tall as a polar bear. The animal didn't appear to know what to make of Dylan's truck. It flopped back down onto all fours—its legs were strangely long—and stared at him.

Not knowing what else to do, Dylan honked the horn. The bear turned his head sideways and opened his mouth to let out an ear-shattering roar. Then it lumbered off the road and away into the storm.

What had Piper's stupid little biologist friend said about the claw? That it came from some kind of prehistoric bear? *Prehistoric.* That was the word he'd use to describe that thing.

"What the *hell?*" he shouted, pounding his fists on the steering wheel. "What the hell is going on around here?"

Had some kind of portal to the impossible opened up on his ranch?

"Hang on, Piper, hang on," he said under his breath. To his great relief, the turn-off to the new horse barn appeared on his left.

He took the turn carefully and pulled in front of the barn.

There was no sign of the snowmobile. Maybe she'd parked in the back?

Dylan jogged around behind the barn. Only two Polaris machines squatted in the snow.

She should have been back by now. He ran back to his truck, slipping and almost falling over twice before he reached it. Piper was out there alone on a snowmobile.

No, not alone. There was some kind of monster witherling running around and a prehistoric, giant bear.

"Guess you better find her first, Kincaid," he told himself.

20

Long, sharp claws wrapped around the barn door. Piper didn't need to see any more. She rammed the key in the snowmobile ignition, and the engine roared to life. She pushed the thumb throttle down hard and shot off across the deep snow back toward the road.

Once on the harder-packed snow, she risked a look behind. In the darkness, an antlered form loped after her. It had the shape of a man, like what she'd seen outside her apartment window. It ran on all fours like an animal, though, and as it did, it let out a creepy, hyena laugh that froze her insides. She had the unpleasant impression the thing was enjoying itself.

She turned back around and watched the road ahead. In the distance, the high windows of the new barn lit up, beckoning her like a lighthouse beacon. The snowmobile roared faster as she pushed the throttle harder.

All of a sudden, beside her left hand, antlers appeared. She jerked the handlebars to the right and overcorrected back to the left. The creature galloped alongside her.

Looking up at her was the rotting, skeletal corpse of a man, with a huge rack of antlers protruding from his skull in a bloody mess.

Her brain couldn't make sense of it. A real-life monster like the stories in the mythology book. No serial killer was believing himself to be something supernatural. It was *actually* a supernatural monster. If she had any doubt, it vanished when the thing turned its head to look at her.

Bulbous black eyes. Row upon row of sharp needle teeth. Exposed jawbone.

It opened its mouth and let out a terrible scream, like a mountain lion's, but a hundred times worse. Piper swerved to the right again.

This time, the snowmobile jetted up a snowbank and jumped the crest. She landed hard in the deep snow of the woods. The creature behind her continued to give chase. Piper shot through the dark green blur of trees rushing by on each side.

A small aspen, its light trunk hard to see in the snow, rose up ahead. She slowed to go around it, and then pushed the throttle to go faster. She ground forward a short way before the snowmobile sank into the snow.

She was stuck. Without a shovel to dig the sled out, and no one to tow her.

Piper scrambled off the snowmobile and flipped up her visor.

Fear, like she'd never known, gripped her. She turned in a slow circle. The monster crouched on its haunches twenty feet away, at the very edge of the headlight's beam. How had it gotten in front of her? It stared at her with those large, inky-black eyes. It'd had no trouble keeping up with her through the snowy woods.

Piper backed away. She no longer had any idea where the road lay. All she knew was she must get away from that inhuman thing hunched before her with its gleaming, sharp teeth. With every step she took her feet sunk down a foot into the snow.

How could she get away from something that moved so fast? Panic overtook her thoughts, and she let out a sob.

Hush! came a sibilant whispered voice in her head. *It's time to play.*

The creature shot off into the woods leaving that horrible reek in its wake.

Piper's entire body shook. She swiveled back and forth, trying to peer into the dark woods. The wind whipped snow into her face. Already her feet felt frozen. She couldn't walk out of here. She had to figure out how to get the snowmobile out.

Of course! In her panic, she'd forgotten about the powder jack. Piper rushed to the sled. Her fingers, already clumsy in gloves, were numb as she dug through the snow to find the jack strapped above the skis of the snowmobile. She struggled to unbolt it.

Behind her, in the distance, something rattled in the trees. Was it the wind? She looked wildly around. Outside the beam of the snowmobile, all was pitch black.

It didn't matter. She had to concentrate on getting the snowmobile out. At last, she managed to free the jack. The plate would be located in the storage box behind the seat. Like a nightmare where her feet were stuck in place, she waded through the deep snow. It took her several tries to open the box. Now she knew how astronauts felt.

There came a faint growl, but she made herself focus on screwing the powder jack into the plate. The jack wasn't more than a long, slim, telescoping pole with a lever handle attached. A minute later, she'd managed to rope the powder jack onto the back of her sled.

Adrenaline fueled each pump of the lever that ratcheted the snowmobile a little higher out of the hole where it had sunk. Her shaky arms turned to noodles, but she kept pumping.

Another growl came, closer this time. Piper ignored it.

Click, click, click, click. The snowmobile rose higher and higher on the jack until at last, she could swing the machine away from her onto fresh powder. She cried out as her muscles screamed in exertion. It took all her strength to push the sled off its previous path and onto a new one. Once the snowmobile was on a new course, Piper flung herself onto the Polaris. Though she wanted to shove the throttle down, she eased the snowmobile forward and around the tree. As she swung in an arc, glowing green eyes caught in the headlight where a large shape appeared.

Piper gaped at the sight. It wasn't the monster, but it was every bit as terrifying and out of place.

A giant cat, like a lion, but larger, stood in the light. It was buff-colored with white spots down its sides. Its shoulders stood far taller than the snowmobile's handlebars. It must have weighed at least eight or nine hundred pounds. What interested her the most, however, were the long canines, which jutted down even with its chin. It opened its mouth in an uncertain snarl, which showed them off all the better.

Despite her fear, Piper was fascinated. It wasn't a smilodon, better known as a saber-toothed tiger. Its teeth weren't long enough. But it was most certainly a prehistoric lion of some kind. No modern lion had canines like that—never mind the fact it was the largest big cat she'd ever laid eyes on. And the markings on it were so unusual.

What would Nate say to this? she thought absurdly. Chilled, she remembered the *Arctodus* claw found in Lightning's spine. *Had* it been a short-faced bear that had left it? Anything was possible in her new reality where a monster and a prehistoric lion were running around on the same ranch. Who knew what else awaited her in the night?

For now, she and the lion were in a standoff. The animal was as uncertain about her as she was it. Or at least, it was uncertain about the snowmobile.

From above, close enough to make Piper yelp, came that hyena-like laugh.

The sound spurred the lion into action. Something shifted in its stance, and the animal made its decision.

When in doubt, it had decided to attack.

Piper gunned the throttle and roared over the snow, praying her instincts were right about which way the road lay. The lion behind her roared in answer. It was too dark to see anything in her side mirrors, but she sensed the animal moving behind her. She sensed, as well, something moving above her through the branches. The creature.

The trees were too dense for her to go this fast. The primal part of her brain wrestled with her intellect, which won. She made herself slow. No way could she risk getting stuck in the snow again.

How fast could this lion go? Her speedometer read fifteen miles an hour. Surely the animal could move that fast, but perhaps not in the heavy snow.

All of a sudden, a giant paw shot out and grazed her hip to leave a searing line of pain. The big cat's claws sunk into the seat of the Polaris. Piper veered sharply around a tree and the lion fell off. With so many trees, she didn't dare look behind her.

Thick snow obscured her vision. Her heart thundered in her chest. A minute later, with no sign of the lion, the trees ahead thinned. Hope surged inside her. The road stretched out fifty yards away. She allowed herself to put on some speed. Twenty miles an hour. Twenty-five.

The road was a bright white path in the night compared to the dark woods. Not far now. At the edge of the forest, the monster dropped from a tree to block her path.

Piper swerved and caught the edge of a tree with the front of the snowmobile. She flew through the air and landed on her back in the beam of the headlight. Stunned, she picked up her head, but the snowmobile's headlight blinded her. She made out nothing but the silhouette of a man and antlers. The thing advanced on her slowly, unhurried.

Off to her right, from deeper in the woods, the lion growled.

Which one would kill her first?

21

Dylan returned from behind the barn to his truck and wondered what to do with Hattie. Drag her along on his search for Piper? Bring her into the barn?

He should bring her inside and warn Willis of what waited out there. Willis could call the hands and warn them, too. No one should go outside. He hefted the slight woman out the backseat and carried her to the door. He slid it back and slipped them both inside.

The barn was silent. Even the horses made no noise. He couldn't shake the feeling that everyone was waiting in fearful quiet.

"Willis? Where are you?"

What to do with Hattie?

She moaned in his arms. "It hurts." The woman wasn't aware of much more than her own pain. She struck him as the tough, mountain-woman breed, and her fear and pain left him uneasy.

The apartment. She needed to be in bed. He carried her up the stairs, winded by the effort, and flipped on the lights in the apartment.

Someone screamed in the bedroom to his right. He jumped, and the action jerked Hattie enough that her eyes popped open.

Not as gently as he wanted, he dumped Hattie on the couch and dashed into the bedroom. He found Willis sitting bolt upright in the bed.

"No! Get away from her!" Willis screamed. Livid spots blotched his pale face, crisscrossed with blue-black veins. The whites of his eyes had gone red with blood.

"Willis!" Dylan was shaken to the core at the sight of the changed man who looked like some kind of medieval plague victim. "It's me."

Dylan crossed to the bed and grabbed Willis by the shoulder. "It's me, Willis. It's Dylan."

"Run, Piper!" Willis cried, voice rough as splintered wood.

Dylan shook Willis by the shoulder, hard, until recognition lit his eyes. He turned and grabbed Dylan by the arm with both hands.

"Help her, Dylan. Help Piper! The monster has her."

Dylan's breath caught and his chest squeezed in an icy vise.

"The monster's got her, Dylan. It's holding her. Help her!" Then Willis collapsed back onto the bed, spent at this effort. He stared, glassy-eyed, at the ceiling for several seconds before his eyes shut.

Dylan didn't need any more prompting. He tore through the apartment, with a hurried, "Stay here. I'll be back," at Hattie on the couch, and thundered down the stairs and out the barn.

He jumped in his truck and took off in the direction of the old barn. The snow and wind blew harder than ever.

A minute later, through the thick, falling flakes, light appeared to his left in the woods.

He pulled the truck even with the light and jumped out, leaving the engine running. The wind clawed at his jacket, and he pulled his .357 out of the holster. He carried the gun in his right hand and used his left to stop himself from falling over.

His legs sunk knee-deep in the snow as he climbed the shallow bank toward the light.

"Piper!" The wind carried his shout away.

He cleared the top of the bank and reached the edge of the woods. There, in the headlight beam of the snowmobile, stood the creature, holding Piper in its arms, her yellow puffer jacket the only splash of color in a scene from a black-and-white horror film. Dylan ducked behind a tree. Willis, somehow, had seen this. Had known this was happening. Dylan hoped he could sneak up on the creature and take him unawares, maybe shoot a leg out again without hurting Piper.

Piper was frozen in its arms, unstruggling, and she stared at something off to her right. Dylan followed her gaze and in his shock, clutched the tree to keep from staggering over.

A monstrous lion-shape crouched in the snow, the details hidden in shadow. A lion? Short-faced bears and lions and witherlings?

Dylan didn't know what to do. If he shot the lion, the witherling could take off into the woods with Piper. If he shot the witherling, it would drop Piper, and the lion could get her.

Before he could make a decision, a terrible noise filled his head.

She's mine! it hissed, coming from all directions at once.

The lion flew through the air, and the witherling tossed Piper to the side, launching itself to meet the big cat in a terrifying clash of growls and screams.

"Piper!" Dylan shouted.

She spotted him and started toward him, and then, to his astonishment, turned back to the snowmobile and pulled something from the storage box. Behind her, the witherling and lion rolled on the ground in a blur. Piper clambered through the snow and reached his position behind the tree.

"Come on." He grabbed her hand and half-dragged her down the bank as they slipped and slid through the snow to the road. Once they reached the truck, he shoved her in the open driver's door, and she scooted over so he could jump in beside her.

"Hold this." He handed her the gun and she took it without argument.

He turned the truck around and headed back to the new barn. Any second now, he expected one or both nightmares to follow them onto the road.

Piper kept looking over her shoulder.

"You see anything?"

"No."

"Are you okay?" he asked.

"Not exactly, but I'll live. You?"

"Been better." He gripped the wheel and fought the slipping tires. The four-wheel drive made it feel like the truck was trying to go in four different directions as they slid all over the road.

It wasn't far to the barn though, and he turned off the road to park in front, stopping the truck as close as possible to the door to block its entrance.

Dylan dove out the truck and almost ripped the barn door off its tracks to slide it open. The wind howled, and the snow fell so fast, it covered his arms in the time it took to open the barn. He hurried Piper out of the vehicle, and she almost fell out the passenger door and into the barn, gripping a box in her arms. He followed her and shut the door. It could be padlocked from the outside. From the inside, there was nothing more than a heavy latch hooked into an eyebolt. He hooked it closed and prayed it held.

Piper backed away from the door, clutching the box to her chest.

Dylan turned his head to read the print on it. "The nebulizer? You went back for the damn nebulizer?" He stared at the woman in astonishment.

"I wasn't leaving it there. I went through hell to get it."

To his surprise, Dylan let out a laugh. He grabbed her by the wrist so the box fell from her hands, and pulled her into his arms. "God, you're a dedicated vet, I'll hand you that, Piper."

She shook against his chest. He ripped off his gloves and threw them on the floor so he could stroke a hand down her hair. Her left ear was bleeding.

"What happened?"

Piper's hand drifted up to her ear lobe and she looked at the blood on her fingers. "The—the creature touched my earring and hissed like it hurt it. It ripped my earring out." She took out her other earring and held it up for him to see. "It's silver, Dylan. Maybe it's a weakness like so many monsters have." Her voice caught. "This can't be real. There's no such thing as—as whatever the hell that thing is."

"A witherling," he said. "That's what my great-grandmother called the monsters she said lived in the forest around here. Guess she was right." He gave a half-smile.

"A witherling. This is so crazy. What are we gonna do?"

He held her tighter and rubbed his hand over her back. "Shh. Shh, Piper. We're going to figure this out." He meant the monsters out there. Of course, he meant that. But he meant something else, too, and she seemed to sense it.

She stilled in his arms and tipped her head to look back at him. "We will." She reached up and ran a hand down his cheek. "I know we will." Then she blew out a shaky breath.

"We need to check all the doors and windows in this place," he said. "Secure them the best we can."

He jogged down the aisle on the left side, she on the right. Each stall had a window that could be shuttered. They went in each stall, brushing by startled horses, to ensure the shutters were latched closed. Thunder barely stirred when he went in his stall. He led the colt's mother into the stall with him.

They might not have much time together.

The entire time they worked, he knew they both waited for a sign of the witherling, or a growl from the lion, but they heard nothing. The expectation frazzled his nerves.

The side door had a regular deadbolt lock. As he expected, it was already locked.

For good measure, Dylan rolled a hopper of alfalfa pellets in front of the barn door and another in front of the side door. Then he turned around and saw Piper pull her hand away from her upper thigh, her fingers covered in blood.

In two steps, he was at her side. "You're hurt."

"It can wait. First, you need to warn everybody on the ranch, and I need to call the cops."

"And tell them a—a—"

"Monster is after us? No. We'd sound crazy. We'll tell them it's a psychotic person trying to kill us. That ought to get their attention. And there's something else you need to know, Dylan."

He didn't like the tone of her voice. Liked less the story she relayed of what she'd discovered in the feed room of the old barn.

"A dozen people?" Dylan scratched the back of his head. "I was in that barn two days ago. You'd think I'd have noticed a bunch of corpses in there."

"We can think it all through after we make some calls."

Dylan nodded and walked away to give Piper space to call 9-1-1 for the second time that night. He dialed Raymond's number. It rang and rang. He was about to give up when the man's sleepy voice answered.

Dylan explained as matter-of-factly as he could.

For a few moments, there was stunned silence on the other end. At last, Raymond said, "Hey, man, you getting into Michael's peyote supply?"

"I'm as serious as I've ever been about anything. I need you to call the others and tell them to stay in their trailers. Willis is already with me." Michael was in one trailer with his girlfriend, Tanya, and Kyle was in another with his wife, Michelle, and their teenage son, Quinton. Randy, like Willis, lived alone in the last trailer.

"You think anyone's going out in this weather?"

"Tell them," he insisted. "Keep their animals inside. Nobody sets foot outside until we figure out what the hell to do."

When Dylan got off the phone, Piper was just ending her call. "How'd it go?" he asked.

"Same story as before. Everyone's busy with other problems and no one can get to us. And how unlucky is this? I got the same dispatcher. I got the impression she thinks I'm making this stuff up."

"Can you blame her?"

Piper shut her eyes and shook her head. Then her eyes snapped open. "Willis. I need to check on him. You got to the hospital and back faster than I'd expected."

Dylan's stomach sank. "I never got to the hospital. Hattie— that's the woman—she's upstairs on the couch. And Willis is in bad shape."

"Okay. So we fix up Hattie, do what we can for Willis, give Thunder a nebulizer treatment—"

"Check your injury."

"Eventually. And then what?"

Dylan stared back at her. "No, we check your injury now. And then we take care of everybody else. Then we come up with a plan. This is my ranch, damn it, and I will defend it."

22

Piper's heart sped up as Dylan strode toward her. Without warning, he pulled down the edge of her waistband and tugged one leg of her snow pants down past her hip.

He sucked in a breath. "Does it hurt?"

She shook her head. "I think I'm too cold and numb to feel anything." She craned around to look at the scratch. A glistening red line curved from her hipbone to the outside of her thigh. It was deep but not as bad as she'd feared. The lion must have only grazed her with one of its claws.

"You think it needs stitches?" he asked.

"Don't think so. I'm more concerned about infection from a cat scratch."

"A cat?" He quirked his eyebrows at her. "That was a little more than a cat."

Dylan bent and slid her pants down farther to where the scratch ended mid-thigh. His hand, by some miracle, was warm as he ran it down her leg and up to her hip. Now it was her turn to suck in a breath. Her heart pounded harder.

The ol' ticker's certainly getting a workout tonight, she thought, and then wondered if she was suffering shock.

She could still see the creature's inky eyes staring down at her, feel the curl of talons against her arms and legs as it had cradled her against its stinking body. No, she didn't want to think of that now. She didn't want to think of it ever again.

Fortunately, Dylan's touch proved to be all the distraction she needed at the moment.

Her ex-husband peered at her wound, his breath warm on her thigh. It was strange that it was strange to have him touch her. This man knew every last inch of her body intimately, had taken it many times, owned it as only a husband could. His hands all over her had once been natural. Now it was thrilling in its strangeness—familiar and forbidden all at once.

He looked up at her with those hazel eyes, and her breath caught. For several heartbeats, they stared at one another until she cleared her throat. "See? It's going to sting like a mother later, but I'm okay." She started to ease her pants back up.

"Shouldn't you at least clean it?"

"Um, yeah, that's a good idea. I've got some antiseptic wipes in my bag."

She took a step, but Dylan put a hand on her arm. "I'll get them."

"I got this."

He balled his hands into fists and blocked her way. "God, Piper, you never let me take care of you. For once, would you just let me?"

"Fine." She stood awkwardly with her pants down and watched him rummage around in one of her black bags. It would have been faster to do it herself, but this time, she let him take care of her.

"Do you think they killed each other?" she asked, as he turned around with a triumphant look and several foil squares of wipes in his large hand.

She'd always loved his hands, big and strong. And skillful.

"We can hope." He ripped open a square with his teeth.

Piper resisted telling him that wasn't particularly hygienic. "I don't like waiting here like sitting ducks."

"I know. But this barn is new and well built. Everything is locked up tight. I've got my gun." He bent once more to inspect the scratch. "We're going to need more guns and way more ammo, too."

"Guess th-the thing, the witherling or whatever took your Ruger."

"It was my dad's."

"I know. I'm sorry."

A second later, he ran the wipe over the wound, and Piper hissed.

"You sound like a goose," he said. "Did I ever tell you about the time that goose—"

"Chased your brother around the pond?" She smiled. "Only a couple dozen times."

"Sorry."

"No. It's a good story."

He used three wipes, and Piper's leg burned in earnest.

"There." Dylan pulled her pants up, and as his hand grazed her hip, it curled possessively around it and squeezed. "That's all the doctoring I know how to do."

Piper swallowed hard. "Thanks. I appreciate it." She wanted to step into his arms again. See what would happen. But people needed her right now. "I'm afraid you and I have a lot more doctoring to do tonight."

Thinking of people who needed her made her remember Gilbert's call. But there wasn't anything she could do for Veronica right now, and with a little luck, she might be able to help the people waiting for her upstairs.

All she could do for her best friend was offer up another prayer.

—

Dylan insisted Piper go up the stairs first so he could guard her back, and he carried her medical bags. She decided she didn't mind one bit. When she reached the apartment, all the lamps blazed. The woman, Hattie, he'd said her name was, lay on the flowered couch asleep. Even across the room, Piper could see the woman's breathing was rapid.

Dylan followed and set the bags next to the sofa.

"You didn't even cover her?" she asked and, annoyed with herself, heard the criticism in her voice.

"Willis was ranting about you being grabbed by the monster. I ran out of here as fast as I could."

"Willis? How could he know what's out there?"

"I don't know. He told me the monster had you in its arms. It was like he was dreaming. Or—or having a vision or something. He was seeing it happen in his head. I know that sounds crazy."

"Crazy is the theme for tonight."

"You need to brace yourself before you go see him."

Dylan disappeared down the short hallway. Piper covered the woman with a blanket and followed him into the bedroom.

Willis twitched on the bed, eyes wide open in horror. From time to time, he let out a low moan. His face was splotchy, and the whites of his eyes had gone red with broken blood vessels.

"Some kind of virus?" Dylan asked.

Piper went over and laid a hand on the man's forehead. "He's burning up. Even more than before."

Willis thrashed under her touch, insensible. He was muttering something under his breath that sounded like, "Don't. Don't. Don't."

She said, "I'll give him a sedative, and then we're going to get to work on Hattie."

Piper retrieved the pills from her bag and brought a glass of water. She and Dylan stared down at Willis, who was muttering something else now. "Stop. Stop."

"It probably is a virus or bacteria," she said to Dylan. "And a nasty case of conjunctivitis."

She acted confident, but the truth was, the sight of Willis terrified her. It would be bad enough to see Willis sick enough to be delirious with fever, but having visions of the monster? Accurate visions?

There was no explanation for that other than something sinister.

Dylan coaxed Willis into a sitting position, and for the few moments it took to get the pills down him, he knew Dylan and Piper were there with him.

"Hopefully he can get some sleep," Dylan said.

"What he needs is a hospital."

"Yeah." Dylan stared at the man, and Piper could see he worried as much as she did about the explanation for the man's illness. Then he caught her looking at him and gave her a bracing smile. "But since we can't get him to a hospital, he's lucky to have you. Ready for Hattie?"

She nodded. Dylan turned off the light, and they left the room to return to the woman on the couch.

A wave of overwhelming uncertainty threatened to crush her as they took a few moments to stare down at their next patient.

"It's like stitching up a dog, right?" she said to Dylan.

Never mind human doctors used different medications, different dosages—even different suture material.

"Sure." Dylan gave her a crooked smile.

A strong gust of wind whistled around the living room window, and Piper shivered. Hattie slept soundly on the couch. Piper crouched down and gave her an injection of Valium to sedate her for the coming procedure. Hattie winced at the shot but didn't open her eyes. Her breathing indicated she was in pain, but she didn't stir when they spoke to her.

As Piper set out all her materials and tools, she and Dylan caught up on what had transpired while they'd been apart.

"I'm sure Veronica is out looking for her dog," Dylan said. "She lives forty minutes from here. It can't be related to what's happening on the ranch."

Piper didn't bother reminding Dylan she'd seen the witherling in town. He knew already and was only trying to reassure her.

He told her about the animal that ran in front of his truck. That Dylan had seen a prehistoric short-faced bear running around in the blizzard didn't surprise her at all after everything else that had happened. Nor that Hattie claimed to believe the year was 1868.

"You got any theories?" he said.

"I'm a nerd. When I need info, I look in a book." She pulled the myth book out of her bag. "Why don't you see what else you can find in there while I work on Hattie? That Valium's taken effect. I'll use a local anesthetic, but I'm worried it's still going to hurt like hell." Piper sighed. "I don't even know if I'm doing the right thing stitching her up. I don't know what the infection risk is. But I can't leave her like this."

Together, they carried the sleeping woman to the kitchen counter, which Piper had wiped down with bleach. She leaned down and spoke in the woman's ear, offering up reassurances and explanations in equal measure. Hattie nodded, but Piper didn't know how much she comprehended.

Which was good. It was going to be a long and painful ordeal for everyone involved. Once she'd got Hattie numb and cleaned the wounds, Piper settled into the familiar rhythm of suturing. The woman trembled but made no complaint. With Hattie's eyes shut, she wasn't sure if she was asleep or not.

"The witherling reminds me most of the wendigo." Piper pushed the curved needle through Hattie's flesh with a wince. "But Native American wendigos don't have antlers. Herne the Hunter does, this ghost guy in England. What has antlers or horns?" Piper was babbling and forced herself to steady her hands.

"Leshy," Dylan said.

"What?"

"My great-grandmother was Russian. She told me about

Leshy, this horned god of the forest there. He usually had wolves and bears running around with him." Dylan shuddered. "Anyway, she said this old god came to America and cursed anyone evil and greedy to become these hungry witherlings that hunted and ate humans, who called wild animals to help them."

"Like a wendigo."

"Yeah. She moved to Colorado as a young woman. She said people used to disappear all the time from the forest, and she saw a witherling eat her friend. My parents told me later it was a mountain lion."

Piper thought of the mountain lion in the alley. "Maybe, maybe not. What else did she say?"

"She claimed she saw a witherling right here on our ranch. It touched her forehead and then vanished. She was in bed for days with a fever and had nightmares of a giant boar eating a man. Then one day, she was fine, and the fever lifted. My dad assured me it was only Great-Granny had the flu."

"Some flu." Piper glanced toward the bedroom where Willis rested and noticed Dylan do the same. "Why didn't you ever tell me any of this before?"

"I haven't thought about it since I was a teenager camping in the woods. She died when I was six or seven. She had dementia so nobody took her seriously, and my mom made her stop telling me that stuff."

"Can't imagine why." Piper tied off a suture as another gust of wind shrieked at the window. This crazy weather. She jerked at the thought. "Draugrs."

Dylan held up the book. "Saw them in here. Zombie type dudes from Nordic mythology with horns on their heads."

"Draugrs can control the weather, Dylan. What if the witherling is causing this blizzard?"

He glanced at the window. "It does feel unnatural."

Could this really be happening? She and Dylan were getting their information from a book of *myths* and his great-granny with dementia. And yet, she'd seen the witherling herself.

"Maybe these witherlings might have inspired stories around the world. Werewolves, vampires, ghouls. The stories might be rooted in some truth. This thing could have all kinds of powers."

"Great. So expect anything?"

"We should be prepared for anything, yeah."

For a few minutes, the only sound was the wind, the click of her needle holder, and Dylan flipping through pages.

"Listen to this." His voice grew excited. "There's a story in here about a werewolf that could time-travel to find new human victims and sometimes brought them through time with him. What if the witherling did that? Pulled through prehistoric animals from the past? Grabbed Hattie back in 1868 and pulled her through to here?"

Piper's fingers tightened on the needle holder as she sutured. Time travel, as crazy as it sounded, made the most sense. "If that's true, how are we going to get Hattie back?"

Dylan shook his head on a shrug. "You're asking me?"

"Yeah. You solve problems, Dylan."

He gave a crooked smile, but it faded. "Don't have any answers for this problem."

"All right, let's find and summarize as many monster facts as we can."

By the time Piper finished with Hattie, they'd compiled a list of witherling possibilities.

Dylan's piece of paper was scrawled with questions.

Draugrs cause madness in people and show up in their dreams. Can witherlings?

Some legends say wendigos can touch people to give them a fever and visions. Only killing the wendigo can save a fever victim. Great-Granny? Willis?

Vampires bite and turn people.

Werewolves come out at full moon. (Only crescent moon now)

Immortal?

A lot of monsters killed by silver, fire, beheading, stake in the heart. Witherling didn't like silver earrings. What else? Ghouls killed by consuming human food.

Slender Man tricks people with voice.

Shape-shifters can turn into different people. Do witherlings change form?

Piper read the growing list over Dylan's shoulder. Despite all the mythology information, no clear facts presented themselves. Piper knew there was only one way they'd learn about the witherling, and it was the one thing she never wanted to do again.

See it in action.

—

Piper had never been so exhausted. She hadn't been this tired when she pulled that all-nighter for a pharmacology final or worked a few twenty-four-hour shifts at the emergency clinic when she was in vet school. The closest feeling to it was in the days after she'd left Dylan and moved into her apartment in town. She'd hardly slept for a week.

This tiredness, however, topped even that.

She sat in the hay of Thunder's stall, her back leaning against the next stall where his mother whinnied from time to time in concern. Dylan, eyes closed, sat beside her, the folktales book in his lap. The high barn windows had changed from black to gray to white as the sun came up. White was all that could be seen as the blizzard continued to howl and scream.

Piper had done her best to stitch Hattie up. Now she and Willis slept upstairs.

Thunder's ribs heaved with perhaps the slightest bit less exertion after his nebulizer antibiotic treatment. Osiris rested comfortably in his crate.

Whatever monsters waited out on the ranch had left them alone through the wee hours of the night.

Now all the immediate, pressing needs of the living things around them had been addressed, they needed to come up with some sort of plan, but she couldn't think straight without some sleep.

She let herself slide down into the hay, using her coat as a pillow, and curled onto her side. The straw was scratchy, but she was too exhausted to care. Dylan set the book aside and slid down as well until he lay behind her. She sensed his hesitation. A moment later, he rolled onto his side too, and his arm came around her. They lay side-by-side, a small distance between them, and waited for something.

Her. He was waiting for her. Had been all along. Waiting for her to finish vet school, waiting for her to move to the ranch, waiting for her to be his wife, waiting for her to accept him.

Waiting for her to come back.

She'd been waiting, too. Waiting to figure it out, waiting to see how they fit together, waiting for some elusive fulfillment.

Piper scooted herself back against him until he threaded his other arm under her head. Now they lay tucked together, his knees behind hers, her back pressed to his chest, his arms wrapped around to shelter her.

His breathing was slow and deep, the comforting sound of a big man on the edge of sleep. For the first time in a long while, Piper felt safe. She sighed and shut her eyes.

She had one last thought before drifting away.

They fit together just fine.

23

Dylan shifted against Piper, in that hazy place between sleep and waking. His hand curled around her hip and pulled her tighter. She felt so warm and good. She groaned and pushed back against him harder.

She had his attention now. He opened his eyes to figure out what else, besides the aching throb in his jeans, had awoken him.

At first, he thought it was the wind.

Then he knew. Waylon. He could hear the dog howling outside in the distance. Long, high-pitched, frightened howls.

Piper stirred in his arms. Dylan eased her away and sat up.

Thunder rested across from him, looking brighter than the night before. He might have smiled if he weren't so concerned for his dog. A glance at the high barn windows revealed an astonishingly blue sky.

The calm between the two blizzards.

Another long howl, closer now, sounded from outside the barn. Dylan jumped to his feet.

Piper mumbled something.

Dylan snatched his jacket off the stall door and shrugged into it. He hadn't thought of Waylon all night. Or the dog door in the house. He reached outside the stall and grabbed his hat off the hook and shoved it on his head.

"What's going on?" Piper sat up in the straw and watched him pull on his boots.

For one brief moment, he let himself admire his ex-wife. Even with the dark smudges under her eyes and the straw in her red-gold hair, she was beautiful. She hated her freckles, but he found them charming. They made her look young and innocent. While those sexy, big blue eyes of hers staring up at him said otherwise. Color spotted her cheeks. Was she embarrassed to wake in his arms?

He wished he could grab her right now and go for an actual roll in the hay. He suspected she might let him, too.

Piper stood and brushed herself off. "Dylan?"

He shook his head. "Sorry." There wasn't time to think through the implications of sleeping together—well, not *sleeping* together. Literally sleeping together. But it was a start. He felt it in his bones. If he played it just right, showed her what he already knew she wanted, he'd have her back in his life, back in his house, and back in his bed soon enough.

There was, however, the small matter of a monster running around on his ranch, but compared to winning back an ex-wife, that was a much simpler problem.

Kill the thing before it killed you.

Waylon howled, closer still.

Piper stared at him. "Is that—"

"Waylon. Yeah. I'm going to find him." He took the handgun off the stall door and put it back in his holster before opening it. "You go check on Willis and Hattie."

Piper put a hand on his arm. "Be careful. Maybe witherlings can trick people."

He looked at her hand. On impulse, he bent down and kissed

her. "I love you."

Then he strode down the barn aisle, wishing he could have seen her reaction, but knowing it was better not to look back.

—

He shoved aside the hopper of pellets. When he rolled back the barn door, a pile of snow fell in, along with the bloody, severed head of an elk, wedged between his truck tire and the door.

He swore and bent to pick it up with his gloved hand.

Behind him, Piper paused on the staircase to the apartment. "What is that?"

He held it up so she could see. Blood dripped onto the wood floor.

The eyes had been gouged out and the antlers ripped out of the skull like the other elk hanging over the pen fence. Where were the antlers? Judging by the ragged bits of neck muscle and skin hanging down, the elk's head had been ripped off its body.

He didn't like to think of the strength it would take to perform such feats. Anything that could rip the antlers out of an elk's skull and tear its head off could have ripped open the barn door while they slept.

"Maybe it was the bear? Or the lion?" Piper asked. She didn't sound like she believed it though.

He shook his head. Dylan knew a message when he saw one. The witherling wanted them to know it had survived whatever battle it had with the lion, which was terrifying enough. If a huge prehistoric lion couldn't kill that monster, what chance did a human have? But the elk head suggested it wanted them to know it had been thinking of them last night. It wanted to make sure they didn't forget it was nearby. It was *toying* with them, and that made him angry as hell.

He heaved the elk head as far as he could from the barn door. It landed with a bloody plop to sink into the snow.

"Maybe you shouldn't go out there alone," Piper said.

"You come lock the door behind me and go check on Willis

and Hattie." There was no way he wanted Piper out there.

"I'm not locking you—"

"Just do it, Piper."

She stood on the stairs in obvious turmoil. He could see her wondering. Lock him out or leave her and the others vulnerable inside? At last, she came down the stairs to stand beside him.

Cautiously, he stuck his head out the door and looked around. He had to squint against the blinding white snow, sparkling in the sun. It was so cold, his breath came in vapors. Nothing moved—like the cold had crystallized everything.

Waylon howled from the direction of the house. Dylan grabbed the shovel by the door and dug a path out around his Chevy, almost completely buried in snow. It was awkward in his snowshoes, but he was sure glad he'd kept the pair in his barn office.

Piper watched in silence until he cleared enough snow to close the door again. Her grim face disappeared as he shut it. He heard her latch it closed.

Dylan rested the shovel against the barn. The outside walls were coated in snow, stuck there by the wind. He set off toward the house on his snowshoes.

The gun in his holster was precious little comfort. The witherling could be slowed, it was true, but it recovered with shocking speed. Even assuming the prehistoric bear and lion didn't operate by some supernatural rules and could be killed by a gun, a .357 wouldn't stop them—or at least not fast enough to save him—unless he got the perfect headshot.

He wished he'd grabbed his sunglasses out of the truck. He squinted as he kept scanning the blinding white snow for any sign of danger. Sweat broke out under his shirt and coat as he tromped over the snow. Every few steps, his snowshoe sank deep enough he had to pull it back out. As he came around the corner of the barn, he spotted Waylon, his floppy ears down. The dog sat in crimson-stained snow next to a dark form lying beside him. He was about halfway between the house and the barn. Waylon threw back his speckled head and howled again.

Dylan picked up his pace. His heart beat fast from the exertion, but more from the way the dark form on the ground lay so still. It had to be a person. He could see that as he drew nearer.

Waylon spotted him, and the dumb dog bounded toward him with fresh baying. The snow was so deep, most of his dog disappeared with each bound. By the time Dylan reached Waylon, sweat coated his back. Waylon had made it no more than thirty feet away from what waited in the snow. From *who* waited in the snow.

Someone lay on their back, arms and legs spread wide like they were about to do a snow angel.

Dylan stepped closer, his snowshoes swooshing and looked down at the person. A furred parka hood was pulled low over their face, almost obscuring it. The bloody elk antlers had been stuck through holes in the hood, to make the person look like they wore them.

He bent over and flipped up the top edge of the hood so he could see the person's face.

Dylan staggered back and covered his mouth. "Oh, no."

Waylon trotted over a rise in the snow and down the other side. He plopped down, threw back his head, and howled.

He followed his dog over the rise. That's when Dylan saw the other body.

What was left of it.

24

Piper's legs trembled as she climbed the stairs to the apartment. Whether it was from Dylan's profession of love or the shivering overtaking her body, she didn't know. Both things had her rattled in equal measure.

She should have told Dylan she loved him too before she shut the door on him. What if he'd taken it as a metaphorical shutting of the door? What if something happened to him out there?

But maybe it was good she hadn't said it. Piper thought she wanted him back, but what if it were only the loneliness of this past year? What if the events of the past few days had made her desperate to share her fear with Dylan, and she'd mistaken this feeling for wanting to get back together? Telling him she loved him would give him false hope and break his heart again.

He was still Dylan Kincaid and she was still Piper Mitchell, two very different people.

Which was why they worked so well, she thought. Except some of those differences were non-negotiable.

And yet people could change. Dylan had stopped the hunting on the ranch, hadn't he?

He still wanted children though, and she didn't. Did she? Piper shook her head. She wasn't sure anymore. Truth be told, this past year, she'd experienced the first inklings of an ache in her chest when someone brought a baby into her clinic. She'd assumed it was her own perverted sense of wanting what she couldn't have. Trust her to start thinking about kids after she'd divorced her husband—in part—for wanting them.

She reached the top of the stairs and stood there in indecision.

If Dylan still loved her, if he wanted her back so badly, why hadn't he come for her? He should have ridden into town like the cowboy he was, marched into her clinic, and demanded she come back home.

Which would have driven her further away, and he must have known it, too. If she'd run away with some childish hope he'd chase after her and validate his love, she was more immature than she cared to admit.

"Grow up, Piper," she said out loud.

She'd hurt her husband—ex-husband—and his pride. She'd been the one that left him. And if she wanted her marriage again, she was the one that had to come back.

Was that what she wanted?

She was scared. She'd seen what her father's affairs had done to her mother over the years. How her father had changed and warped her mother from a strong and vibrant woman into a brittle, colorless mouse of a person.

But Dylan hadn't ever cheated on her. Had she been using their differences as an excuse to leave him before he could hurt her? To somehow punish Dylan for her father's transgressions?

The idea horrified her. Another shiver ran through her, and she found herself thinking another unpleasant thought. Maybe she'd been in denial about a lot of things.

In the past few minutes, for example, she'd been trying to avoid facing another truth, but as her teeth chattered, she couldn't ignore it any longer.

Piper had a fever, and the witherling had touched her.

—

To her surprise, when she opened the apartment door, Hattie was standing in the kitchen. The woman was bent over the stove, twisting the knob to turn the gas burner on and off again.

"Hey," Piper said. "How are you?"

Hattie straightened up and winced at the movement. She was pale, but not deathly so. "I'm kind of hungry. Do you have anything to eat?"

Piper shook her head. "No. We'll need to get up to the house to grab some food. You should be resting. I can get you some water at least."

Hattie let herself be led to the couch.

"I'd like to check your wounds if that's all right?"

The woman nodded and turned her head to the side in embarrassment as she unbuttoned her dress.

Piper sat next to her on the couch and examined the stitching. It was red and puckered around the edges, but she saw and smelled no sign of infection, and her skin was cool to the touch.

Unlike Piper's.

"I'll give you some more medicine for the pain." Piper buttoned up the dress for the woman who was now crying. "I know you must be scared, Hattie. We're going to do everything we can to help you and try to get you back where you belong."

"I don't know where I belong," she whispered. "My husband brought me out to Colorado from Boston for a new life. He's dead now. Everyone I loved in Boston is dead, too, save a few friends."

Piper explained to the woman about their witherling time travel theory. She took it with pioneer practicality, which was to say a quiet, brave sort of acceptance. Piper squeezed her hand and fetched Hattie a glass of water and some tramadol. The woman swallowed down the pills and lay back on the couch, looking miserable.

"Hey." Piper grabbed the remote off the coffee table. "You want to watch some TV?"

Hattie gave her a blank look. "TV?"

"You might as well enjoy being in the future, right?"

Piper turned on the television and a college football game came on.

Hattie's eyes widened, and her mouth fell open.

"You can watch different things if you want." Piper showed her how the channel buttons worked, but the woman looked too amazed to do anything but stare at the screen in awe, jaw agape.

Piper took her hand and squeezed it, before saying she needed to check on Willis in the bedroom. She found him tangled in the sheets, thrashing back and forth. His eyes, if possible, looked redder.

"Willis?" She approached the bed with trepidation, worried he'd turned into a monster himself. "It's me, Piper."

To her relief, his thrashing subsided. "Piper? Is that you?"

"It's me, Willis. It's Piper."

She sat on the bed and took his hand in hers. It was warmer than her own fever-hot hands. "You look like hell. How do you feel?"

"Like I'm in hell." He grunted. "You're okay." His voice cracked. "I've been seeing the most terrible things, Piper. They seem so real."

In his agitation, he moved his legs back and forth on the bed.

"Shh, Willis. It's okay. You're just sick, that's all. It's the fever."

A lie, of course, but a necessary one.

"I saw a monster. He had you and I—I thought he was gonna kill you." To her horror, the gruff man began to cry.

"No, Willis. Shh, it's okay. I'm right here."

"Where's Dylan?"

"He's gone to check on Waylon. Feed him," she improvised.

"Get us some food. You hungry, Willis?"

He shook his head. "Dylan's okay?"

"Yes."

"I—I saw the monster with Dylan too. It was—" his words cut off on a half-sob. "It was eating his leg. And—and he was still alive."

A cold chill slithered down Piper's spine, like the time outside her clinic when she got hit by icicle run-off down her coat.

"No," she said with a shiver. "That's just the fever talking."

Never mind Willis had seen exactly what happened to Piper. Saw the monster holding her in its arms. And yet she was okay, wasn't she? But Willis had said he thought the monster was *going* to kill her, not that he'd seen it happen.

Did Willis have some sort of psychic connection to the witherling?

The answer to that made her shiver again. Perhaps the witherling could send visions to its victims, but were they of real things?

"No," she said louder and squeezed his hand hard. "I'm not going to let anything happen to Dylan."

Willis smiled at her as another tear slid into his beard. "You two made up yet?"

She smiled back. "It could happen."

"I told him, Piper. I told him he had to forgive you for leaving him. Just like you'll forgive him for Allison."

Piper's hand went limp in Willis's, and her stomach tightened. Allison? The older sister of that trampy wrangler, Holly?

"Allison was foolish payback, that's all." Willis's eyes shut.

Piper swallowed, thinking as fast as she could. "That's right, Willis. And it didn't last long, right?"

"Couple weeks is all," he said. "I told him he was stupid when I saw her coming out of the house one morning. Slinking off, more like."

Piper's heart seemed to relocate to her throat where it pounded out a tattoo. Allison, the twenty-five-year-old woman who worked as a bartender at the Black Diamond bar where Veronica had seen Dylan and Holly together. Piper knew she was twenty-five because she'd once joked with the woman she wasn't old enough to be in a bar, let alone bartend, and she'd revealed her age.

She was attractive enough if a man liked everything Piper wasn't. Allison was short and busty with bleached-blonde hair and a lusty laugh.

"When was that again?" Piper asked, not feeling bad for an instant taking advantage of Willis's feverish state.

"'Bout a month after you left," he murmured. "You hurt him, Piper. He just used Allison to hurt you back."

"What about the other women?" Her other hand, the one not holding Willis's, bunched up in the blankets as she waited.

His face scrunched up. "No other women. It's always been you he wanted."

No other women. She'd figured he must have been with women over the past year. So why did it hurt so damn much to find out about one?

A month, though! A month after she'd left. That bastard. He'd done it to hurt her back, Willis said, but she was sure he must have enjoyed himself immensely all the same. Holly was too young? Well, then, just try the slightly older sister.

She couldn't help but see her husband—for he was still her husband at the time—in bed with Allison. His warm, strong hands on those big breasts of hers, grabbing her hips, driving himself—

A pounding came from downstairs and she jumped off the bed as if she'd been caught doing something wrong. She couldn't shake the image swimming before her eyes of Dylan and Allison naked together.

No wonder Holly hated him. All of a sudden, Piper felt a bizarre sympathy for Holly, a woman she'd wanted to punch in the face all this time. Poor Holly. Not only had Dylan rejected her kiss and fired her, but he'd also gone and slept with her big sister. Piper would never, in a million years, sleep with her own sister's crush.

What a skank.

"Piper!" came Dylan's voice from below. "Open up!"

Waylon added his barking to the pounding.

For the briefest moment, she considered leaving him out there. Let the witherling or bear or lion have their way with him since he'd clearly had *his* way with *Allison*. The moment only took long enough for her to lick her lips, but her hesitation shamed her.

"Stay here," she said as if Willis were about to charge down the stairs himself.

Seconds later, she was unlatching the hook, and shoving open the barn door.

Dylan stood in the snow carrying Veronica in his arms.

25

"Oh my God." Piper clapped a hand over her mouth. "Is she—"

"No. You wanna let me in?"

Waylon shoved his way past Piper and ran up and down the aisle, his claws clicking on the wood floors.

Piper stepped back and let Dylan carry her friend into the barn, slamming the door shut behind them. Dylan moved toward the stairs, but she stopped him.

"Let me see her."

Waylon danced between them, barking and barking.

"Shut up, Way!" Dylan shouted. "Where do you want me to put her?"

"Here." Piper moved to an empty stall and opened the door. She dashed into the tack room and brought out a horse blanket, laying it over the straw. Dylan set Veronica on it.

"Where did you find her?"

"Halfway between here and the house."

"What's wrong with her?" Piper crouched beside her friend.

"Veronica? Can you hear me?"

"Hypothermia, I'd guess." Dylan disappeared into his office, Waylon on his heels.

"Ronnie? It's Piper. Can you hear me?"

Veronica groaned, and her eyelids fluttered.

Dylan, pale and shaken, returned from his office carrying a space heater. He plugged it in a nearby socket and set it outside the stall.

Piper ran a hand down her friend's forehead. "How did she end up here?"

Dylan raised an eyebrow at her. "How do you think?" His face darkened. "I found Raymond out there too." His Adam's apple bobbed up and down. "Most of his lower half was gone like he'd been—like he'd been—"

"Oh my God. Eaten?"

Dylan nodded.

Piper put a hand to her chest in shock. Raymond was such a devoted family man to his wife and two children. How could he be dead—a husband and father snuffed out in such a gruesome manner?

Dylan put his head in his hands with a heavy sigh. "God, his wife, and kids. I'm gonna need to check on them. And tell them."

"I'm sorry. I'm so sorry." Piper's anger with Dylan receded in the face of people dying,

Still, she found herself wanting to survive this ordeal if only to rip into Dylan. A month after she left him? Really?

Her brain swirled with all of it—Raymond dead, Dylan and Allison, and now her friend showing up on the ranch. She returned her attention to Veronica.

Waylon stood in the aisle, legs braced wide, and howled at them.

"What's wrong with him?" Piper asked.

"He's just overexcited."

"Well, make him stop." It was unfair because she'd always loved that stupid hound, but her irritation with Dylan extended to his dog just then. "Get him out of here."

Dylan grabbed Waylon by the collar and dragged him up the stairs where he must have put him in the apartment. Piper hoped Hattie liked dogs.

She pulled off Veronica's gloves and checked her fingers for signs of frostbite. Dylan returned and knelt beside her to help take off the woman's socks. They checked her feet too.

"Everything looks good," she said. "She's not even wearing any shoes, and her feet are fine. I don't think she was out there long." She pushed up Ronnie's jacket sleeve to feel the skin on her arms. "She feels pretty warm."

Piper looked up to find Dylan staring at her.

"You *look* warm. Your cheeks are red." Dylan leaned over Veronica to peer at Piper's face. Then he put a hand to her cheek. "Piper, you're burning up."

She jerked back from his touch. "I'm fine."

"No. You're not." He stood up to loom over her. "Let me see your scratch."

"No."

He crossed his arms over his chest. "Do it."

"Would you stop bossing me around?"

"Piper."

A muscle twitched in his jaw and she could tell he was clenching his teeth.

"Let me see it," he repeated. "You've got a lot of people—and animals here—who are counting on you. So you have to take care of yourself."

She rolled her eyes, knowing he had her. "Fine." She stood and yanked down her pants to her knees. "There. Are you happy?"

"Am I interrupting something?" Veronica murmured from where she lay in the straw.

Before they could respond, her eyes closed again, and she was quiet.

Dylan's mouth twitched as he twirled his finger in the air to indicate Piper should turn around.

She turned in a slow circle so he could see the scratch running over her hip and thigh wasn't raging with infection. Then, with her backside to him, she bent over and pulled up her pants. When she turned back, he smiled.

But the smile didn't reach his eyes, which were grim. "I was hoping it was the scratch causing the fever."

"I know what you're thinking and don't say it, okay? I can't handle it right now."

"All right." His lips thinned with an expression of concern she'd never seen on his face before. "I say we call the authorities again. Try to get all of you to the hospital."

"Agreed. You call this time. I'm going to let Gilbert know Ronnie's here."

They pulled out their cell phones and at the same time, said, "My phone's dead."

"I'll use the one in the office." Dylan walked off and returned in a minute, his forehead furrowed. "Line's dead. Shit!" He swiveled on his heel and shoved open the barn door.

Piper left Veronica lying in the stall and followed Dylan to the door. She watched him stride through the snow, bloodstained from the elk's head, and open the driver's side of his Chevy. He scooped out snow that had blown in through the broken back window and climbed in. A few seconds later, the engine cranked and clicked, but failed to turn over. Through the window of the truck, she saw Dylan slap his hand onto the steering wheel. He got out, slammed the door, returned inside the barn, and marched into his office. He returned carrying some keys in his hands.

"The snowmobiles?" she asked.

He nodded, looking angrier than she'd ever remembered seeing him. Which was saying something.

A couple of minutes later, he returned inside, swearing a blue streak.

Fear knotted her guts. "Both of them?"

"What do you think?" He threw his hands in the air. "Of course, both of them!"

"Hey, it's not my fault, okay."

"Sorry." He took a deep breath. "Sorry, I know. That *thing* disabled all the vehicles so we can't get off the ranch. And with the road blocked with that log pile, no one can get to us either. We've got no phones, no way in or out. We're screwed, Piper."

She ignored the throbbing in her head and the ache in her joints and made herself stay calm. This was just like an emergency in her clinic when people were stressed out and worried. The more agitated they got, the calmer she became.

"You're right," she said. "So, we need to come up with a plan. A different plan than calling for help or driving somewhere."

"My plan is to kill that fucker."

"I like that plan," she said. "Let's figure out how to do it. We know it doesn't like silver. You got any silver bullets?"

"Yeah, Piper. I've got loads of silver bullets. You know. For dealing with that little werewolf problem we got here on the Crazy K."

She ignored his sarcasm. He always got testy when he was scared. "I'll take that as a no. Anyway, even if it doesn't like silver, we don't know for sure it can destroy the thing. But I think any weapon is a start, right? We need guns—"

"The guns you always hated?"

She ignored him. "And we need food. That means going to the house. Should we move everyone there?"

He narrowed his eyes at her. "Sure. I'll just throw three people on my back and hike up to the house on my little snowshoes. It'll be no problem."

"Okay, fine. We'll stay here. You don't have to get so pissy."

"Well, you're not helping, Piper. And besides, the barn is way more secure. Almost all the windows on the first floor are shuttered and the barn door is strong. You seriously think we should hunker down in the *house* with all those windows and the sliding glass doors and—"

"Okay, okay. I get it. God, Dylan. My point is, you need to get up to the house to get—"

He snapped his fingers. "That silver dagger! My dad has a silver dagger that was his great-grandfather's from Scotland. Some kind of ceremonial thing or something."

"Great," she said, taking her turn at sarcasm. "Then you can hunt down the witherling, wrestle it to the ground, and stab it with your little antique silver dagger."

He glared at her. "You got any better ideas?"

She sighed. "I'm just going to suggest you stop and think this through. That thing out there is smart. You can't go after it half-cocked."

"Are you saying I'm not smart? That I'm stupid?"

"Why are you always so defensive about being stupid?"

"Because you treat me like I am!"

"Maybe you are sometimes!"

He tucked his chin back in shock. "What the hell, Piper?"

"You slept with *Allison?*" Her voice ratcheted up an octave. She took a step forward and socked him in the arm, but his heavy coat provided too much cushion to make any impact. "You seriously slept with that skanky hoe bag a *month* after we split up?"

"Shit." Dylan went very still. He looked like she'd punched him in the face instead of the arm. "How did—"

"How did I know? Willis told me and don't you dare get mad at him. He's crazy with fever."

"Piper, you'd just left me."

"Exactly. I had *just* left you. And you immediately ran out and slept with Holly's sister? How could you?"

"I was trying to get back at you."

"Yeah, that's what Willis told me. But how come I never even knew until now?"

"Why would I have told you? We're divorced now, remember? Are you telling me you haven't slept with any other men since we split up?"

Piper stared at him. She wanted to lie, to lash out and tell him she'd been with many other men. But as much as she hated Dylan in this moment, she couldn't make him hurt as badly as she was just then. "Yes," she whispered. "There's been no one since we split up."

Several emotions crossed his face. Relief, shame, anger.

She cleared her throat. "I think you misunderstood my question about why I'm only finding out now. You said you did it to get back at me. So why didn't you tell me? Rub it in my face?"

"Because I was ashamed of myself, okay? I only used her to make you mad. When I realized what I was doing, I didn't have the heart to hurt you back."

"Oh, yeah. Used her. I'm sure you didn't enjoy it or anything. How many times was it, Dylan? How many times did it take you to feel ashamed? How many times did you screw that girl? What did you do with her?"

"That's none of your business, Piper."

"None of my business? It's nothing *but* my business." She was shouting now but didn't care. "You were still my husband."

"And you made it pretty clear you didn't want me to be anymore."

"Oh, give me a break. You couldn't wait for me to leave so you could nail the first thing that sidled up to you."

Dylan put his hands on his hips. His lips thinned to a white line and his chest heaved. He seemed unable to speak.

She was pushing too hard, but she couldn't get herself to reign it in.

He closed his eyes for a minute and curled his hands into fists before blowing out a long breath. "I'm sorry your dad cheated on your mom. But I'm not him. You always expected the worst of me and—"

"You thought you'd deliver?"

He snorted. "Yeah, Piper. You totally got me. Except for one thing. Answer me this. If I was always wanting to cheat on you, why didn't I do anything until you left me? Why wasn't I cheating on you our whole marriage?"

"How do I know you weren't?"

His eyes narrowed further. Now she knew she'd gone too far. Not for one second did she believe Dylan had ever cheated before.

He turned his back on her and stepped out into the snow. He turned around to close the door and looked at her with such venom, it burned like acid. "If you really think it's your business, I'll tell you. But just remember, you asked for it." He held up three fingers. "I nailed Allison three times. What did we do? She said I could do whatever I wanted with her. You know what I like. Use your imagination." His mouth twisted in a sneer. "And for the record, I *did* enjoy it! Now I'm going up to the house!"

He slammed the barn door so hard, Piper was scared it would come off its roller.

Then she ran over and retched in the utility sink, but nothing came up from her empty stomach. She stood gripping the sides of the sink and trembled with pain, impotent rage, and fever.

How could she have ever thought she wanted that man back?

A rustling of straw came from the stall where Ronnie lay.

"Where the hell am I?"

26

She deserved that, Dylan thought, as he trudged through the snow.

How dare she bring up Allison when Raymond was dead? A man was dead. Had been *eaten*. Every time he thought of it, of the man's wife Irene, a block of ice lodged under his sternum.

It wasn't the time to worry about an argument with his ex-wife. And yet . . .

He replayed Piper's stricken face from moments before and shoved it from his mind. She deserved it.

She thought the worst of him, she got the worst of him. If she wanted details, who was he to hold back?

Except that he had. He hadn't told her details. Nothing real. He told her he'd done whatever he'd wanted with that woman. And he had. Which was to say, not much at all. Certainly nothing requiring imagination.

After word got out about his and Piper's split, Allison had been making eyes at him for weeks down at the Black Diamond. Dylan knew her reputation, knew it would be easy. So he'd invited Allison back to his house one night and gone through the motions as quickly as possible. As if checking off a box with the most minimum effort necessary for hitting the requirement. *Get revenge on wife who left you by sleeping with another woman. Check.*

Sure, he'd enjoyed himself. For about five seconds. The lead-up had been awkward and felt plain wrong. Guilty, mental intrusions of Piper plagued their short foreplay. And the aftermath of those five pleasant seconds? He'd been crippled by overwhelming remorse that left him lying in paralyzed horror all night beside the sleeping Allison. At last, the sun had come up and after another horrifying hour, he'd asked Allison to leave. He'd shut the door on her with a sense of relief that was destroyed when he'd spotted Willis walking toward his porch, shaking his head in disappointment at the retreating Allison.

So, yeah. A real good time.

When Piper showed no sign of coming back or even returning his calls, he'd seen Allison twice more out of spiteful rage. But both those times had gone just like the first, and he'd ended up hating himself more each time he'd done it. Even after signing the divorce papers, he hadn't been able to escape the self-hatred and regret dogging his every step for a year now. And the irony was, after officially being divorced, he felt too guilty—and worn out—to sleep with any other women.

What he'd done as a form of revenge against Piper had backfired. At first, he'd fantasized about Piper discovering his indiscretion, imagined the hurt it would inflict upon her if someone let it slip down at the Black Diamond. But it hadn't taken long until the weight of it hung like a millstone around his neck, and he'd ended up praying she never, ever found out.

Because the truth was, he *had* still been married to Piper when he slept with Allison. He'd let his temper get the better of him when Piper left. Let himself believe she deserved what she got. And he'd cheated on the woman he loved. She'd never found out about it until now, and she'd never come back regardless, so it hadn't made any difference in the end.

But he had to live with cheating on his wife and that made a difference to him.

He was a man of integrity. Or he'd thought he was.

Dylan continually scanned the area around him as he snowshoed across the stretch of land toward the house.

Man of integrity? He snorted. Any thoughts of that had disappeared when he'd made those three stupid, anger-filled mistakes with that young woman. And now he'd let his temper get the better of him again at a time when it really *might* have made a difference with Piper. Sleeping with her in his arms last night, he'd hoped, really hoped, that they had a shot at putting the pieces back together.

Deep down, he always knew he'd have to tell her about Allison to do that. But he would never have chosen to do it like he had.

Why had he told her those things?

You idiot, Kincaid!

It pierced him to his core to recall what she just told him. That she hadn't been with any other man. He'd tried his hardest not to imagine her with anyone else, but the sensible part of his mind knew she must have been. And he'd been wrong.

It broke his heart as surely as it gave him hope that she must love him still.

Not that it mattered now. He'd seen the look of utter destruction on her face as he'd slammed the literal door on her. Piper would take that as symbolic or something.

"Stupid. Stupid. Stupid," he said with each arduous step.

Stupid Willis and his stupid fever.

Which reminded him Piper had a fever too.

And Raymond was dead.

Everything came crashing down on him at once. He wished he could sink into the snow and go to sleep and wake up to find everything had been a bad dream.

Raymond would be alive and well. No monsters would be

loose on his ranch. He never would have slept with Allison.

And Piper would still be his wife.

Tears stung his eyes. Probably from the biting cold.

He neared the place he'd found Raymond and considered what he should do with the body. The logistics of dealing with half a corpse was enough to make his knees buckle. But he would have to tell Raymond's wife about it. She'd want to bury him. He supposed he could drag the man's torso up to the house and put him in the garage under a tarp.

The land dipped down into the spread of bloodstained snow, and Dylan saw the problem had been solved for him.

Raymond's body was being completely devoured by something he couldn't quite wrap his head around.

He reached for his gun, looked toward the house, and wondered if he could make it there. Then he glanced back at the creature eating what was left of his friend and decided he didn't like his odds.

27

Piper rushed to her friend's side. "Veronica? Are you all right?"

Ronnie sat up and spit a piece of straw from her mouth. "I—I think so. Where am I?" She glanced around. "Is this the barn on the Crazy K?"

Piper nodded. "You don't remember anything? How you got here?"

She shook her head and looked around with the wide eyes of someone seriously freaked out. "No. All I remember was Foxy whining to be let out. I opened the back door, and he raced out into the blizzard. He was going nuts. Barking his head off. He tore off into the storm, and I followed. It was dark. Pitch black."

Piper raised her eyebrows. "So, you followed him? Without boots?"

"I just stepped out on the deck to call him back." Veronica frowned and looked down at her chest. "I was wearing my robe. This is Gilbert's jacket." She pulled the coat away from her and peered down at it. "How did I end up in Gilbert's jacket?"

Piper had no idea. "You went out on the deck to call for Foxy and then what?"

"I hope Foxy is okay. Maybe he made it back to Gilbert?"

"Probably." Piper didn't hold out much hope, but what good would it do to say so? "What happened after you went outside?"

Veronica's frown deepened. "I sort of remember a dark blur coming at me out of the corner of my eye and then—that's it. I woke up in this stall." She lifted a finger toward Piper. "And your pants were down. But I must have been dreaming that." Veronica rustled her hand through the straw. "I have to say the guest accommodations kind of suck here."

Piper didn't have it in her to smile. Instead, she faced a terrible realization. The witherling stalked Piper in town. It came to Dylan's ranch. The creature had somehow brought her best friend here.

That wasn't the random workings of a mindless monster, which was all she'd assumed witherlings were. Nightmarish beasts that hunted humans and ate their flesh. Terrifying, but simple. Yet this one seemed to be orchestrating an elaborate plan of terror against her personally. Why?

"Piper, I'm scared." Her bottom lip trembled. "How did I get here?"

She explained how Dylan found her lying in the snow.

"I need to use the bathroom and call Gilbert."

Piper sighed. "Our phones aren't working."

"The blizzard?"

"If only. You go to the bathroom. Then I'll catch you up." She pointed next to the tack room. "There's a bathroom on the left there or a nicer one upstairs in the apartment. Willis is in the bedroom and another woman we found in the snow is on the couch."

"What?" Veronica put up her hands. "Never mind. Tell me when I get back." She disappeared into the barn bathroom and shut the door.

Piper headed back to Thunder's stall. He looked better than

last night, which cheered her. As long as Veronica was in the bathroom, she might as well start another nebulizer treatment on the little colt and get some more antibiotics in him.

She wondered if she should get antibiotics in *herself*. But part of her suspected antibiotics wouldn't cure whatever this was.

Thunder allowed Piper to strap the nebulizer mask to his muzzle, and the machine whirred away. She leaned against the stall and fought to keep her teeth from chattering.

A loud hissing woke her, making her realize she'd fallen asleep on her feet for a second. She turned around to see Veronica returning from the bathroom. Osiris had pressed himself back in his crate, which sat in the aisle, and was hissing and spitting.

Piper was glad to see he was up and moving, but disturbed by his behavior. Was it a coincidence that Waylon barked so much at Veronica, and now the cat was hissing at her? Maybe Osiris was traumatized by his own experiences last night.

Veronica didn't seem to notice the cat. She stopped in the aisle outside the stall and stared at Piper.

"You all right?" Piper asked.

For a moment, her friend didn't answer. Her dark eyes drilled into Piper with an angry expression. She stood very still in the barn aisle, hands fisted at her side. Piper shrank back and put a hand on Thunder.

"Ronnie? You okay?"

Her friend's face shifted as she wrinkled up her nose. "Yeah. I think so. These horses smell."

Veronica laughed, and Piper decided she was being paranoid. Waylon and Osiris were understandably jumpy and anyway, why would Veronica be angry with her? That was ridiculous.

But for a moment there, she would've sworn Veronica was looking at her with pure hatred.

More likely, her friend was suffering shock. At this point, Piper thought she was too. Between finding out monsters were real, discovering a human meat locker, Raymond getting eaten, and learning about Dylan's affair, she felt punch drunk.

The fever wasn't helping.

Veronica pulled something from Gilbert's jacket pocket. "I found this in here." She handed over a wallet.

Piper took it and flipped it open to see Raymond's driver's license. How had his wallet ended up in Gilbert's jacket, which was on Veronica? It couldn't mean anything good, given what happened to Raymond. She glanced at his I.D. He was thirty-seven.

Tears stung her eyes. "This man is dead," she told Veronica, unable to meet her friend's eyes when she said it. "He's—he was—an employee of Dylan's. A ranch hand."

Veronica stared, uncomprehending. "What do you mean he's dead? Why was his wallet on me? In Gilbert's jacket. Piper, I want to get back to Gilbert. Now."

"I'm afraid that's not possible at the moment." Piper stuck the wallet in her pocket. Raymond's family would want it back. For now, she had to focus on those she could help. "The road out is blocked. We're stuck here. And once I tell you what's outside, you won't want to go out there for a while. In the meantime, I need to feed the horses and muck out their stalls. I can tell you everything I know while I work."

"Okay." Veronica didn't look very happy about any of this, but she added, "I'll help."

Piper was grateful for her friend's offer. She was shivering and weak from the fever.

They started at one end of the barn at the last stall, where a chestnut mare stood stamping impatiently.

"We'll just have to muck out around her," Piper said.

Veronica picked up a shovel and stepped into the stall. The horse screamed and reared up to wave her front hooves in the air.

"Whoa, whoa." Piper squeezed in next to Veronica. "You get out of here, okay? Whoa, it's all right, girl."

Veronica slipped out the stall. Piper put a calming hand on

the mare's neck and talked her down with soothing words.

First Waylon, then Osiris, and now this horse. It was weird. Piper didn't like it, not one little bit.

She turned around and studied her friend, who stood outside the stall with a bewildered expression.

"I'll do this stall and you take the next one." Piper pointed to where Hank, an old dapple-gray pony, waited with a forlorn expression.

But as soon as Veronica stepped into that stall, the same thing happened. Hank was ancient and partially blind, but he whinnied and bucked and pawed at the woman.

"Get out of there!" Piper shouted.

Veronica slammed the stall door and looked at Piper in alarm.

Something about her friend was spooking the animals.

"I guess horses don't like me," she said.

"I think they don't like what touched you," Piper said slowly. *It touched you, too, and the animals aren't acting like this with you.* She ignored that thought. As she mucked out the stalls, she told Veronica what happened.

By the time she'd finished her recitation, one side of the barn was mucked out, and all the horses were fed. Veronica helped bring them food and water, but any time she got close to the horses, they shied away or reared up.

Piper shivered violently and knew she'd have to leave the other side for Dylan to clean.

"I need to rest," she said.

"Let me help you." Veronica led her to the same empty stall where she herself had been lying earlier. She acted calm, even in the face of Piper's theory that the witherling had carried her off into the night and left Veronica on the ranch as a message to Piper. Piper remembered how wendigos and some vampires loved to fill their victims with fear before killing them. Perhaps the witherling did, too.

Mission accomplished, witherling, Piper thought with a

hysterical giggle. She was terrified.

But for Veronica's part, she didn't seem too afraid.

In fact, she was strong as she shouldered some of Piper's weight and eased her onto the blanket in the straw. How was it her friend had suffered hypothermia, endured some sort of ordeal of her own all night, but seemed unaffected?

Piper, aching and weary, sank down onto the blanket. She couldn't fight it anymore, and her teeth chattered so hard, she worried she'd chip them. She just needed to rest a few minutes, and then she should check on Willis and Hattie again.

Her eyes shut, and she fell into a terrible dream.

28

So far, the animal either hadn't noticed Dylan, or it was too interested in polishing off Raymond and didn't care Dylan stood there frozen with indecision.

And just plain frozen, he thought, with a bizarre urge to laugh.

Whatever the hell that thing was, it didn't belong in this time. Dylan wasn't a freaking paleontologist so he had no idea what it was. All he knew was it was an ugly son of a bitch, and he sure as hell didn't want it eating him.

It looked like some kind of butt-ugly pig, he decided. A pig that stood a full head taller than his own six feet, with a long snout. Smelled kind of like a pig too, with an added layer of the scent of bloody meat. The animal had a sloping back, skinny legs with cloven-hoof feet, and a swishy little tail. Funny bumps stuck out on either side of its massive, jutting jaws. Its teeth made Dylan want to piss his pants. Long, angled canines kind of like pig tusks and a bunch of other big-ass teeth protruded from its slathering mouth. It had to weigh at least a ton.

He hated the thing on sight. It was some kind of, some kinda—hell pig!

He suddenly remembered his dad watching a documentary about prehistoric creatures. His dad had loved watching those nature shows. Some British guy had been droning on about these hell pigs.

That's what that thing was.

A disgusting crack filled the air as the animal bit into Raymond's skull. Suddenly he remembered his great-granny and her nightmare of a giant boar eating a man. Was the witherling even now traveling back in time to touch his great-grandmother's forehead? It was insane to consider, but had she actually seen this very moment and unknowingly caught a glimpse of her grown great-grandson in the future?

He wished his great-granny's vision had been a little more informative. For instance, did he get out of this situation alive, and if so, how exactly?

Nice and easy, Kincaid. Nice and easy. His snowshoes had sunk into the snow as he'd stood there staring like a moron, wasting precious seconds thinking of his great-grandmother.

He had to yank his feet free, and still, the hell pig paid him no attention. Raymond's last act might just be giving Dylan time to slip away. He sent his friend a silent thanks.

His snowshoes crunched with every step as he sidled in the direction of the house. He didn't dare turn his back on that thing. He'd moved about twenty feet away when the creature stopped eating and lifted its head to regard Dylan with its beady eyes.

Everything inside him shriveled in fear. He froze again.

There was no frame of reference for dealing with this animal. Should Dylan be big and scary or shoot at it to scare it away? Or would that enrage the thing? Should he avoid eye contact?

He settled on playing it cool even if he felt anything but. "You stay there, buddy." He used a soft voice as he stepped backward. "I'm going on up to my house and you just enjoy your snack, there." He winced, realizing what he was saying about poor Raymond.

Another step backward. And another.

The pig stared at him for a few heart-stopping seconds but must have decided Dylan was retreating and therefore not a threat. It returned to its awful, bone-crunching meal.

Dylan got a good fifty feet away, and his confidence surged. The house lay a hundred yards away or so. He could see his back yard surrounded by bushes, the cedar deck with the sliding door he'd left unlocked. A football field was all. He could do this. Time to pick up the pace.

He walked forward, sparing one more look over his shoulder at the beast. To his alarm, Raymond was all gone. The hell pig was rooting around in the bloody snow, maybe hoping to find any remaining morsels.

Every few steps, Dylan looked over his shoulder. Seventy yards to the house. The animal trotted around in a circle, tail held high, as it continued to nose around in the snow. Sixty yards to the house. A reassuring look to see it had buried its muzzle deep in the snow. Fifty yards to go. He glanced back. The animal had stopped rooting around and held its head high in the air.

Like it smelled something.

Forty yards to the house. It wasn't easy to run in snowshoes, but Dylan did anyway. This time, when he looked back, the animal was looking right back at him.

It was walking in his direction, still sniffing the air.

Thirty yards to the house. He heard a loud grunt and this time when he looked back, the hell pig was charging toward him. The snow slowed the beast, but it was still doing better than Dylan on his snowshoes.

Could he make it thirty yards in the time it took that thing to make seventy?

Dylan whipped the gun from his holster, took the time to aim, and fired off a round at the stampeding beast. His fingers were clumsy in his gloves.

He missed. Two more rounds, two more misses, and the distance was shrinking between them. Another shot clipped the animal in the shoulder. It let out a pig-like squeal of rage but didn't slow in the slightest.

Dylan shouted on a burst of frustration and adrenaline, tearing across the snow. His cowboy hat flew off his head. Maybe the pig would get distracted by it. He didn't bother looking. He could hear the hell pig snorting and grunting and crunching over the snow behind him. The hat must not have tempted it, because it didn't sound like it was slowing down.

Louder and closer. Dylan scrambled through the gate to his yard, taking a costly second to shut it. He was almost to the bottom of the half-flight of stairs to the deck when he heard the gate smash. Dylan scrambled up the steps but fell halfway up on his snowshoes. He could smell the animal and sensed its heat behind him. He could hear its wheezing breaths and caught sight of its whiskered chin just feet from his arm as he pulled himself up on the deck railing.

Somehow, he managed to stay upright and reach the top of the stairs. The hell pig struggled a bit itself on the snowy steps but crested the flight just as Dylan's hand closed around the sliding door handle.

He yanked it open, and the hell pig launched itself across the deck. Dylan pushed through the door just as the creature lost its footing on the snowy, icy deck. That didn't stop it from biting down on Dylan's foot, the last part of his body not through the slider.

The aluminum snowshoe crumpled under the strength of the animal's jaws.

Dylan screamed at the white-hot pain as his foot was crushed in his boot. The animal began to pull him back through the door. His gloved fingers curled around the edge of the sliding door, but he didn't know if he could hold on.

His hand started slipping out of the glove. A sudden

splintering noise was followed by a loud crack. Dylan, freed from the beast's jaws, flew forward into the house as the deck gave way beneath the hell pig's feet. The animal fell ten feet below.

It screamed as a leg snapped beneath it. Dylan hung onto the edge of the sliding door and peered through the hole of his ruined deck to the ground below, where the animal lay thrashing in pain.

A slender white bone stuck out its lower leg. It screeched and screeched.

Something stirred in Dylan's chest. With everything that had happened, it took him a second to recognize the feeling.

Pity. He couldn't help it. He felt sorry for the thing. He pulled the gun from his holster, took aim at the creature's beady eye, and squeezed off three shots. The animal's cries ceased in an instant. Dylan's ears rang in the sudden silence.

Stunned at the rapid turn of events, he staggered back onto his butt to sit on the family room floor. His foot throbbed. He ripped off his gloves and leaned forward to use his bare hand to push the glass door closed. The hell pig was dead, he knew, but he liked having the door shut.

And God knew what else was out there. He hadn't forgotten about the short-faced bear and saber-toothed cat, not to mention the witherling. He took the snowshoe off his uninjured foot. The other was too crumpled to remove. Instead, he gingerly eased his boot, still attached to the snowshoe, off his foot, dreading what he would see.

A mangled, pulpy mess? His bones sticking out? He peeled off his sock with a pained yelp and stared down at his normal, intact foot. A deep indentation from a large tooth marked the top, but it hadn't broken the skin. It would leave a hell of a bruise, to be sure. It was possible some bones in his foot were broken too, but he was relieved to see no obvious signs of damage.

He glanced at the bent snowshoe and sent up a quick prayer of thanks. It had saved his foot.

The snowshoe couldn't be salvaged, but he had more in the garage. Anyway, with the plan he was hatching, he wasn't going back to the barn on snowshoes. He was anxious to get on with that plan so he could return to Piper and the others.

Bringing weapons to the barn was first on his list. Also, he needed to check on Raymond's family and talk to them, no matter how much he dreaded that particular chore. He wanted to look in on Michael, Kyle, and Randy too. Then, with any luck, his Bobcat here might be able to haul those logs off the road.

"You got a lot to do, Kincaid, so get off your lazy butt."

Dylan got up off the floor and put some weight on his foot to test it.

It hurt. It hurt badly, but he could still walk on it. He hobbled across the family room and into the hall to open the door to his garage. He flipped on the light and saw nothing disturbed.

The old beat-up white Bobcat S300 tractor sat off to the right.

Dylan limped over, pulled open the cracked glass door on the front of the vehicle, and sat inside the cab. It was nothing more than a torn leather seat and some controls on either side. A coated metal grid of three-inch squares, which would leave him open to the cold and snow, enclosed the cab. It sure beat snowshoeing though, and the heater blasted air so hot, it could warm him even with the open cab.

Holding his breath, he reached up and turned the key. The engine rumbled to life. He pushed the green button on his left and everything looked in working order. Letting out a sigh of relief, he turned the engine off. Killing himself with carbon monoxide would be pretty dumb considering what he'd survived in the past twenty-four hours.

Now to gather his supplies. While ignoring his throbbing foot.

First, he took several rifles, handguns, the silver dagger, two stainless steel knives, and box upon box of ammo out of his gun cabinet. The silver dagger was arguably one of the most important items to bring if Piper's guess was correct about how to kill a witherling. He tucked it into the knife sheath on his left hip. It was too long to fit properly, but he still managed to snap the leather strap over it.

Then he rummaged in the kitchen for as much food as could be found in a bachelor's pantry. The clock on the microwave told him it was 8:48 a.m. The weatherman had said the next blizzard was due this afternoon. Outside his kitchen window, the blue sky had already disappeared as gray clouds scuttled over the mountains.

From his bedroom, he grabbed his cell phone charger and strapped on his watch. He hated not knowing the time. He swept out the contents of his medicine cabinet into a plastic bag and swallowed down a couple of anti-inflammatories for his foot.

As he loaded everything into the cramped cab of the Bobcat, he rammed as many sleeping bags as he could fit around the items. Two extra pairs of snowshoes went in.

The garage was a little messy, even by his standards, and it took another ten minutes to locate the tiki torches from a summer party Piper threw a few years ago. That happy, sunny event was from another life, another life where tiki torches were just festive lights and not something he hoped would deter monsters.

A quick check of his watch showed him twenty minutes had passed since he'd been in the kitchen. The urge to hurry up gnawed at him until he grew frantic with it. Another twenty minutes to get the chains on the tractor's tires.

Two minutes to find the cans of torch fuel behind a box of Christmas decorations. And at last, two more minutes to figure out a way to wedge the torches through the grid of the Bobcat cab. The pain in his foot was slowing him down, no matter how much he tried to ignore it.

It had been over an hour since he'd left Piper at the barn, with no weapon but the old Henry, and sick and injured people in her charge. She'd be worried. Or not, considering how he'd left her. Could be she was hoping some prehistoric beast ate him. If so, she'd almost got her wish with that hell pig.

Then he remembered she had a fever. He was ashamed he'd forgotten, but maybe a hell pig made a good excuse. More anxious than ever to get to her, he wondered what state he'd find her in. He couldn't bear finding her splotchy, red-eyed, and raving like Willis.

The last thing he grabbed was his shotgun. There was barely room for him to climb into the cab. He buckled his seat belt, pulled down the safety bar, and laid the 12-gauge over his lap. Once the engine turned over, he hit the garage door button.

As the metal door rose, he screwed up his face in confusion.

In the distance, the red anti-predator lights blinked on and off on the elk pen. Dylan checked his watch to see it was 9:35. In the morning.

And yet outside, it was now completely dark. Not the dark gloominess of a gathering storm. The sky was the thick black of night. The sight chilled him as much as the cold air blasting into his garage. Had he traveled through time? How could it be dark already?

Dylan eased the joysticks forward and the Bobcat inched out of his garage like a tentative mouse poking its nose out a hole. He flipped on the headlights on the top of the tractor, lighting up the snowy driveway. The Bobcat ground its laborious way down the curving driveway and onto the road back toward the horse barn. The snow chains clinked along.

The thought of driving this thing several miles up the road to try to clear the pile of logs struck him as a bad idea in the dark. In this unnatural dark.

Ignoring the excruciating pulse of his heartbeat in his foot as the Bobcat jostled him, he worked the sticks to turn onto the road. As soon as he cleared the house, the barn came into view. The red anti-predator lights blinked on and off around the barn, too.

For a split second, he caught the flash of glowing green

among the red lights. It winked out so quickly, he couldn't be sure he'd seen it. He slowed the tractor to a stop and stared at the horse barn below.

He waited a full minute, wasting the tractor's fuel until he decided his eyes were playing tricks on him.

And regardless, he wasn't leaving Piper alone down there. If the witherling was hanging around outside the barn, it would get inside to her over his dead body.

He pushed the joysticks forward again and the little Bobcat bumped along in the dark down the road toward the barn.

Toward Piper.

And most likely, toward danger as well.

29

Piper moaned, vaguely aware of the straw poking her in the back, but she couldn't open her eyes. She was trapped in that twilight place between waking and dreaming, caught in a dream where she saw the world through another's eyes.

It was not a place she wanted to be.

He called up the wind, conjured the snow to swirl about him, summoned a deeper dark around the trailer like a cloak. Inside, he sensed the dog. Its predatory instincts were dulled by domestication, by a pampered life, but deep down, it was still a hunter and therefore could not disobey his call.

Moments later, the door of the trailer opened, and the dog shot into the night. It barked in defiance, but it could not go against his will. He sent the dog away into the blizzard.

The woman followed the dog outside. Dressed in a robe, she was a small shape in the face of the raging storm. He could smell her warm flesh, a beacon in the cold. He wanted to rip and rend and devour.

But he had a higher purpose for her.

The woman turned as if to go inside. He didn't hesitate. His long limbs raced on all fours over the snow and slammed into her body. Under his dark touch, she became unconscious in a heartbeat.

She was as nothing to him as he lifted her over a shoulder and shot through the night. With his speed, time held no meaning for him. In an instant, he was in the old barn.

He laid the woman down on the dirty floor. If he wanted any chance to resist temptation, to complete his task, he must first feast before touching her.

From his storehouse, he selected the arms and legs of a man he had snatched from another time, a time when the buffalo still roamed the plains. He ate quickly, the cold meat bringing him little pleasure.

After he had taken his fill, he crouched over the small woman. There, at the shoulder, where the collarbone arced to her neck, he sank his sharp teeth into her tender skin. The poison dripped from his mouth, flowed into the wound he'd made.

She stirred until he laid his clawed hand on her forehead and sent her back into the darkness.

When he knew she slept again, he left her. Back over the snow, he raced into the night. The need for warm meat was too strong.

And somewhere, in the storm, a man sought this woman and her dog.

All alone.

Piper cried out as she saw the figure of Gilbert, hunched against the wind, tramping around the trailer in the snow. Before she could see any more, a noise mercifully woke her.

Barking.

She sat up. Waylon was barking in the apartment upstairs. Piper staggered as she got up. She was so weak, the stairs rose as formidable as Everest, but she gripped the railing and hauled herself up, one slow step at a time.

Halfway up, she stopped to catch her breath. Waylon was snarling now.

Piper opened the apartment door to a confusing scene. Veronica stood in the short hallway to the bedroom. Willis, unconscious, lay at her feet. Hattie held the old rifle pointed at Veronica. Waylon, hackles up, growled and snarled from his position at Hattie's side, staring Veronica down with his one blue eye and one gold.

She must have been asleep for a long time. The living room window revealed darkness outside, and the lights were on throughout the apartment.

Where in the world was Dylan? She had the presence of mind to think, for one brief moment, that he might have died out there, and their last moments together had been full of rage.

"What's going on?" Piper said, alarmed at how weak her voice sounded.

"Willis came bursting out of the bedroom like a loony," Veronica said, staring down at him. "Raving on and on."

"Yeah." Hattie lifted the rifle to gesture at Veronica. "He was raving about you. Said you got the monster in you."

Ice crystals formed in Piper's blood, cutting into her heart as her fever dream came thundering back into her head. She looked from Waylon, who she'd never seen so demented, back to Veronica. "Ronnie? Can you show me your shoulder?" She pointed toward her right shoulder.

"What? No. Why?"

Waylon's snarls subsided to low growls as if he expected the humans to work this out, but he'd be on standby all the same, thank you very much.

"Because I think the witherling bit you. Just pull down your pajama shirt."

"Bit me? That's ridiculous. Don't you think I would've told you?"

Hattie raised her rifle again. "Do it. I think that man's right about the monster in you. You touched him, and he went down like a sack of potatoes." She glanced at Piper. "She bent over him and I swear, it looked like she was goin' to eat him."

Veronica looked at Piper and held up her hands, imploring. "Piper, this is crazy. It's me. It's your friend, okay? I was just trying to help Willis."

"Fine. Then show me your shoulder." Nausea rolled in Piper's stomach as she remembered a German shepherd she'd put down. He was vicious. Piper saw the stitches his owner received in his forearm, fending off an attack from the dog. The shepherd would bark and snarl at his front window at every living creature that walked by the house. He'd turned on a dog, a nice yellow lab, at the boarding kennel and almost killed it.

Yes, the dog was vicious. Eighty percent of the time.

The other twenty, he would come up, tail wagging, and sit at your feet to be scratched behind his ear or bring a ball for fetch, playful as a puppy. It had dismayed Piper that when the owner brought him in for the euthanasia appointment, the friendly version had shown up that day.

That same sick feeling returned when Piper looked at Veronica, at her familiar face, at her sweet friend who had always been there for her over the years. Which was she? Friendly or vicious?

No, this was Ronnie. It was just a nightmare she'd been having downstairs. From the fever.

And yet . . . Willis had dreamed real things too. Piper knew what she would see even before she lunged forward and yanked down the front of her friend's pajama top.

Veronica shrieked as Piper revealed a deep bite—two horseshoes of seeping punctures in her friend's shoulder.

"It *did* bite you!" Hattie said.

"So what?" Veronica snarled. "I must have been unconscious when it happened. So it bit me. That creature's not a vampire."

"We don't know much about witherlings. Maybe it *is* like a vampire and can turn you into a monster, Ronnie."

"You're crazy. You think I'm going to start running around

eating people now?"

That was *precisely* what Piper thought, but it was too terrible to admit.

A loud scrabbling noise came from above her head. Something was crawling on the barn's roof. Waylon barked again, backing into the kitchen.

Veronica made an odd growling noise. And then, her eyes went black, the whites disappearing as if ink had spilled across them in an instant. She opened her mouth to reveal a full set of curving, sharp teeth and sprang at Piper.

Piper screamed and with a deafening shot, Hattie fired the rifle on Veronica.

On what had been Piper's best friend.

30

Cold wind hurled snow at Dylan through the open grid of the Bobcat cab. His pulse beat in his foot, like another heart resided there. Something had to be broken for it to hurt so badly. The little tractor crawled down the hill, struggling through the thick snow. Now he wished he had the plow on the thing instead of the bucket. He'd planned to use the bucket to remove the logs from the road, but there was no way he was driving that far in this weather, in the dark, with all manner of creatures waiting out there.

He kept looking around, aware of how the slow tractor made him a sitting duck.

The snow was light enough he could still make out the landmarks of his ranch. The lights came on in Randy's place, and Dylan's gaze flew to the cluster of trailers, where the lights already glowed in Kyle's and Michael's windows. What did his ranch hands make of the sudden darkness? He pictured them in their homes, staring out at a day turned inexplicably to night. If only he could call them. Or drive his truck out to bring them back to the barn.

Raymond's wife and children must be waiting all alone in their place, for a husband and father who'd never come back. Call him old-fashioned, and Lord knew Piper had enough times, but he felt better about the safety of women and children in dangerous situations when there was a man around to protect them.

Ominously, Raymond's trailer remained dark. He'd been so concerned about breaking the news of Raymond's death to the man's wife and children, and how he could get them to safety, it hadn't occurred to him none of that might be necessary. Maybe no one was waiting there. Maybe his whole family was already dead.

How had Dylan ended up in this nightmare? If these stupid blizzards would wrap up, he could make everything all right. He'd clear the road and get everyone off his ranch. Hunt down that monster and kill it. But Piper suggested the witherling might be controlling the weather.

So what then? The blizzard would never end. Not until Dylan killed the witherling.

"So you'll hunt the bastard in the snowstorm if you have to."

He wished he hadn't spoken out loud. Was it his imagination, or had the snow thickened in an instant? Disoriented, he was unsure where the road was that would lead him to Piper.

It wouldn't do to lose his bearings out here. He made himself focus on the red anti-predator lights on the horse barn. They guided him in like ground control waving in an airplane.

For a brief moment, the snow cleared like curtains parting. He caught movement near the barn.

Dylan squinted hard as if that would give him night vision. A vague, dark figure crouched on the ground. Huge antlers appeared, disappeared, appeared, disappeared in the blinking red lights. The dark shape scrambled up the side of the barn with the deftness of a monkey and pulled itself onto the roof. Black birds—crows or ravens?—perched along the entire ridgeline.

More snow swirled around him, and he couldn't see anything but the flying flakes in the light of his Bobcat and the blinking red lights on the barn in the distance.

He pushed the sticks forward as far as they would go. The tractor's engine responded with a whine, but the tires could only go so fast over the snow.

"Come on, come on." His heart lodged in his throat, hammering so hard, it threatened to suffocate him with dread.

Piper was down there with a creature that could rip the antlers from a skull. It could rip the top off the barn if it so chose. She and Willis and Hattie and Veronica—it would be like shooting fish in a barrel for the witherling.

He followed the red lights, praying with all his might.

"Not far now," he said.

Something slammed into the Bobcat with an ear-splitting roar.

31

"**R**onnie," Piper shouted, as her friend—or at least her friend's body—crumpled to the living room floor.

For now, she ignored the clomping noises coming from the roof, Waylon barking under the kitchen table, and Willis groaning in the hallway behind her. She rushed to Veronica's side. Her friend lay in the fetal position, clutching her right forearm to her chest. A small pool of blood spread onto the carpet.

That's gonna be a bitch to clean up. Piper almost laughed. The fever was adding to her slaphappy feeling. Her head felt like a balloon on a string floating high above the terrible scene.

Veronica whimpered, and Piper eased her friend over.

"You should stay away," Hattie said.

Veronica whipped up her head with a snarl.

"Oh, God!" Piper jumped back from the sight of all those teeth, at the unfamiliar face staring up at her from Veronica.

Hattie cocked the rifle again. Blood was seeping through her dress. Not an alarming amount, but enough to concern Piper. If she didn't have other things to worry about, that was.

"Don't shoot her!" Piper pleaded. "She's already hurt. If we can kill the witherling, she'll be cured."

Hattie had to shout to be heard over Waylon's barking. "You don't know that."

Piper didn't. But she had to at least hope there was a chance of saving Veronica.

Footsteps moved back and forth on the roof above, but the scene unfolding here took all of Piper's attention.

Hattie stood with the rifle pointed at Veronica. "And she isn't hurt that much. Looks like I just grazed her arm."

"She's my best friend," Piper said. "We can't kill her."

Even as she said it, Veronica uncurled on the floor and pushed herself up to a crouch, hissing. Hattie shot a questioning look at Piper. All the while, the rifle stayed trained on Veronica.

"Just—just hang on a second." Piper stood and raced out the room. Adrenaline helped her ignore the shivering that racked her body and the screaming ache in her joints.

She half-fell down the stairs to the barn floor below and snatched her black medical bag. By the time she returned, Hattie held the rifle on Veronica, who hunkered in the corner of the living room beside the TV stand, snarling and growling much like Waylon continued to do under the kitchen table.

With shaking hands, Piper filled a syringe with ketamine. She hoped her addled brain was calculating the correct dosage. And that humans were dosed in a similar way to dogs.

"Ronnie?" Piper held the syringe tucked at her side.

Her friend's head snapped in her direction. So there *was* something of her left inside after all.

"I've got something to make you feel better." Piper stepped toward her friend.

Veronica moved in a blur, launching herself at Piper with fingers curled like talons.

No. Make those actual talons.

Veronica knocked her to the ground, and the syringe flew

from Piper's hand. Veronica shoved Piper to her back and lunged over her, teeth bared. Piper grabbed her friend's shoulders and managed to hold Veronica at bay. Blood dripped from the wound on the woman's forearm onto Piper's chest.

"I'm goin' to shoot her," Hattie shouted, as Waylon howled under the table.

"No," Piper ground out. The effort of holding off Ronnie made breathing difficult. "Help. Me." Even if she wanted Hattie to shoot her friend, she was just as liable to hit Piper instead.

Hattie used the stock of the rifle to bat Veronica away, catching her in the shoulders with a crunch that made her howl. There was a clatter as Hattie spun her rifle back around to aim it at Veronica again. Piper groped around on the floor, plucked up the syringe, and didn't hesitate to plunge it into her friend's bicep.

Veronica howled again. Piper crab-crawled away, toward the hall where Willis lay moaning. She stood up and leaned against the wall. Dizzy. She was so dizzy.

Veronica scuttled back to her corner by the television.

Hattie stood in front of Piper, blocking the hallway in a protective stance that touched Piper. Hattie gasped and struggled to hold her rifle up.

"Wait," Piper said. "I gave her some medicine to make her sleep. It will take a few minutes."

Hattie nodded. The injured woman had paid a price for her exertions. Piper almost laughed again. What a fine group they made. Hattie clawed up by a witherling. Veronica, bitten and turned. And her and Willis in the grips of some kind of fever that gave them terrible visions and left them weak as kittens.

At least the noises from the roof had stopped for the time being. Piper didn't like to think about what was up there. With their luck, it was a hungry pteranodon.

Veronica continued to make deep-throated growls, like Osiris when he was angry. Gradually, they grew fainter and more sporadic. Then, with a thud that made Piper wince, Ronnie slumped to the floor and cracked her head on the TV stand on the way down.

"Quick." Piper darted forward. Her vision tilted, and she clutched at the wall for balance. "Help me move her into the laundry room."

Piper grabbed her friend's foot. Hattie held up her rifle, obviously debating the wisdom of setting it down.

"She's out. It's okay."

Hattie set the rifle on the couch and grabbed Veronica's other leg. Together, they dragged her through the kitchen and into the small laundry room. Waylon darted from under the table, barking his disapproval every step of the way.

Veronica's arms trailed behind her over the laminate flooring. Where her nails had once been, the fingers now ended in curving, dark claws. Her black hair swept over the floor like a mermaid's floating underwater. If Piper ignored the mouth full of vicious teeth, her sedated friend still looked as beautiful as ever.

Piper and Hattie managed to slide Veronica into the laundry room. It was tiny, not more than a closet, with the washer and dryer taking up almost all the room. Veronica lay on the floor in front of the machines. Piper didn't have the heart to leave her friend in total darkness. She flipped on the light so she wouldn't wake up disoriented. There was no lock on the double doors. Piper slammed them and pulled a chair over from the kitchen table to wedge under the two lever doorknobs.

She didn't expect the ketamine's effect to last too long. Piper turned around to survey the kitchen, wondering what else she could use to secure Ronnie inside the laundry room. She could tie the two doorknobs together. Or maybe she could find duct tape to secure her friend's hands and feet.

Before she could act on these ideas, a dreadful ripping noise came from overhead. Like something was tearing off the very roof. Hattie looked at her, mouth hanging open, and as her gaze moved upward, she readjusted her grip on the rifle.

Waylon's bark cut off with an odd little whine.

"Waylon?" Piper asked.

His hackles rose, and his lip curled back in a menacing snarl as he took a step toward Piper, appearing ready to attack *her*.

32

Dylan's entire world flipped as the Bobcat fell onto its left side. He knocked his head into the side of the cab. Canned goods, boxes of granola bars, and water bottles rained down. A bottle of pills rattled past. One of the snowshoes slid loose, along with a stainless steel knife, clattering to land on the cab's grid. His rifles and other weapons had thankfully stayed wedged on either side of his seat among the sleeping bags. The dagger hilt dug into his left side, and he readjusted it and made sure the snap on the knife sheath stayed secure.

He looked up, through the right side of the cab, which had become the top of the tractor. A huge, dark shape loomed over him in the swirling snow, fleshy lips pulled back to reveal a fearsome set of teeth.

The short-faced bear was back and man did it look angry. Or hungry. Or worse, Dylan thought.

Hangry.

A giant paw swiped down at him, and he shouted. Large, black claws scrabbled at the open squares of the cab. One claw was missing, and blood stained the brown fur on that paw. Dylan knew just where that particular claw had ended up. An electrifying fear zipped down his spine and along every nerve ending as he remembered what this bear did to Lightning.

Although Dylan suspected the bear hadn't peeled the poor horse's legs. Maybe it hadn't even attacked the horse, to begin with, and had only scavenged the body.

But the bear wasn't averse to killing its food if needed, judging by its obvious interest in making Dylan its dinner.

Its claws hooked over the grid, but the squares were too small to allow anything else to reach through.

Dylan shoved off the safety bar and unbuckled his seat belt so he could feel around in the cab to locate the shotgun. The bear leaned down and pressed his black nose against the squares to sniff. Dylan pushed himself as far back from the bear as he could. The snuffling noises were familiar, like Waylon smelling at a rabbit hole. But the stench of the bear was eye-wateringly worse than anything Waylon had ever given off. It smelled like a dog who'd rolled in wet grass and skunk and garbage.

The bear bit down on the metal grid with a noise that gave Dylan goosebumps. Its jaws were no doubt strong enough to open up the cab as if it were no more than a can of baked beans, but the bear couldn't get a good enough hold to bite down. It used its paws to hold the tractor like a dog with a chew toy and attempted to bite it again. Its teeth screeched on the metal, but the cab remained intact.

For now.

Dylan's hand closed on the shotgun barrel as the frustrated bear let out a roar that made him drop the gun and slap his hands to the sides of his head to cover his ears. Hot breath blasted him in the face, rank with the scent of blood.

When the bear stopped, Dylan waved a hand in front of his nose. "Oh wow, you have *got* to brush your teeth."

He chuckled, a sure sign he was panicking. The electrifying fear had left him numb rather than energized and angry.

Think, Kincaid!

His fingers groped in the dark again and once more managed to locate the shotgun. He swung it around, ready to aim it through the grid when the bear shoved the Bobcat so hard, Dylan slammed into the left side of the cab. The little tractor started to slide down the snowy hill toward the horse barn.

Then Dylan was flipping again, and the Bobcat was upside down. A crack like a muted gunshot filled the cab, and he hoped it didn't come from him. He regretted taking off his seatbelt as he found himself in a ball of tangled limbs on the ceiling, which was now the floor. The silver dagger, fortunately still in its sheath, jabbed his hip. Somehow, he'd managed not to hit his head when he flipped this time, but his foot throbbed after getting banged up. The cracking sound must have come from a tiki torch wedged through the squares. It was now snapped off, leaving a splintered bamboo stick protruding out of the cab like a spear.

The Bobcat's engine, insulted too many times, decided to stall. In this upside-down world, the tractor's joysticks were above him. He used one to haul himself upright into a cramped crouch. The headlights, now on the ground, illuminated the snowy slope stretching down before him—and a giant bear's feet.

For one ridiculous second, Dylan thought those feet looked like what a grizzly bear's would look like—if it were wearing its own pair of bear slippers.

Impossibly huge.

It stood in front of the Bobcat and seemed to be intrigued by the bucket, which was dangling from the flipped tractor above Dylan's head. The bear stood on its long hind legs and grabbed hold of the bucket and jerked it. The entire tractor rocked up and down, up and down. Dylan hung on to the joysticks above him.

Now he knew how those kids in *Jurassic Park* felt. *Where was Sam Neill when you needed him?*

The bear roared again, not unlike a T-Rex, he imagined. Dylan, afraid to let go of the levers, had to endure the barrage on his eardrums with nothing more than a pained wince.

Giving up on the bucket, the bear moved to the side of the Bobcat and once more shoved its nose against the squares to sniff. Dylan scrabbled around on the ceiling-now-floor of the Bobcat in a desperate search for the shotgun. He came up empty. The cab was tiny. Why was it taking so long to locate the gun?

The bear curled its claws around the squares again, and this time, a screaming, wrenching noise filled the cab as it managed to stretch the squares on the grid. Dylan figured no one would hear him screaming over the racket, so he went ahead and indulged himself. These were no manly shouts, either. He knew and did not care that he was screaming like a little girl.

Meanwhile, his fingers managed to close around the shotgun, which he'd finally found above his head, rammed behind the joystick.

He went to pull it out, and nothing happened. The shotgun was stuck fast.

One of the rifles then. But before he could unstuff a sleeping bag from beside the seat and grab one, the bear ripped apart the metal strips between several squares of the grid all at once with a loud *Sproing!* The bear could now plunge its massive paw inside the Bobcat like it was a grab bag, and Dylan was the prize.

In the face of that swiping paw, Dylan abandoned finding a rifle in favor of the weapon at hand. He grabbed the top of the tiki torch and rammed its splintered end at the bear's foreleg as hard as he could.

The bear let out a yelp of pain like the time Waylon's tail met a terrible fate under the runner of a front porch rocking chair. Enraged, the bear knocked his head into the tractor's side like a battering ram. Already top-heavy and on a hill, the Bobcat flipped onto its right side.

The tractor slid down the icy slope, scooping loads of snow into the cab with Dylan. In a stroke of good luck in a day that had not seen much, the tractor slowly righted itself as it reached the bottom of the hill. The contents of the cab shifted once more with a tremendous rattle.

Dylan reached up in his correctly-oriented world and started the tractor's engine with a hope and a prayer. It struggled, twice. He craned his neck around and saw the bear standing at the top of the hill as if deciding whether or not he was worth the trouble. The engine caught and rumbled to life.

The bear headed down the slope, but with perhaps less enthusiasm than before. More of a half-assed lope than a sprint. Dylan wrenched the shotgun out from beside the joystick. He whipped around and stuck it out the side of the cab where the bear had created a big hole. Aiming it as far back as he could with the angle, he fired off a shot. It had no chance of hitting the bear, he knew, but he hoped it would have the desired effect.

"Please, please, please," he breathed.

At the sound of the shotgun blast, the bear shied away. It spun off its path toward the tractor and instead veered to its right, galloping toward the national forest, a dark mass hurtling through the swirling snow.

"That's right, buddy. I ain't worth your time." Still, in the grip of panic, he chuckled. "Too tough and bitter."

Dylan turned back around to ease the joysticks forward.

That's when he saw the witherling was no longer on the roof. He sighed with relief.

Then he saw a section of the roof was torn back.

33

"Waylon?" Piper held her hands up in surrender. The dog growled, then whined, growled, then whined, like he fought some awful inner battle for control. "It's all right, boy."

Whatever was out there was affecting Waylon, making him act against his will.

Hattie hefted her rifle up and readjusted it to aim at the ceiling where the racket continued.

Waylon took another step toward Piper, and she backed her way out the kitchen into the living room.

"Come here," said a hoarse voice behind her. She whirled around. Willis leaned against the wall of the little hallway. He waved his arm in a beckoning circle at her and Hattie. "Both of you. Get in the bedroom."

He half-slid, half-staggered backward down the hall and into the bedroom behind him. Piper and Hattie followed. Waylon burst into a run and the two women sprinted for the bedroom door. They'd barely shut it when the dog slammed into it with such force, he let out a *Yipe* followed by the *thud* of his body hitting the floor. The dog stayed quiet, perhaps knocking himself unconscious for the time being.

The ripping noise continued to come from the living room as something tore its way into the apartment through the ceiling.

The bedroom door, at least, had a lock, and Piper used it. She stumbled back toward the bed, overcome by another wave of dizziness.

"You two all right?" Willis asked. He was positively ghoulish now. Piper had seen better-looking corpses. For real. She'd done a three-hour stint in a human anatomy lab once.

Hattie didn't bother replying. She backed into the far corner by the nightstand and slid to the floor with the rifle propped over her lap.

"Piper?" Willis peered at her. "You don't look so good."

Looking at his ghastly face, she laughed. "You don't either." The room spun, and she shut her eyes tight against it.

"I've been better, I'll admit," he said. "Where's Dylan?"

"I—I don't know." Piper shook not only with the fever, but the panic she felt every time she thought of her husband. Ex-husband. "I haven't seen—"

Willis let out a scalp-tingling shriek and scrambled onto the far side of the bed beside Hattie. He stared at the bedroom door and shouted in a voice she hardly recognized. "The Stagecoach Cannibal! The Stagecoach Cannibal!"

Piper staggered with a fresh wave of dizziness and tumbled onto the bed.

The winter of 1883 had been long and hard for Adam. His brother was holed up in their cabin with pneumonia, which was real unfortunate. Between the two of them, Amos was the real hunter. Adam hadn't found any game in days. He was afraid Amos was gonna die and leave him all alone in this God-forsaken world. And he might die then too.

Spring had teased and tantalized him with a glimpse of warmer weather at the end of March. He'd managed to shoot a rabbit. His mouth twisted in shame as he recalled the pride with which he'd presented the scrawny thing to Amos. His brother had choked down some of it and left what remained of the tough, gamey meat to him. Adam vowed next time he'd bring back a deer.

Then Spring betrayed herself to winter's charms once more with a blizzard that trapped them in the cabin for days. He'd listened to Amos wheezing and rattling like an old stovepipe through these past long, cold nights.

In the end, Adam burned the table and the logs they used for chairs, and it still wasn't enough to keep them warm.

The blizzard finally loosened its grip last night. Now Adam ventured farther afield than he ever had before in search of food. But it was useless. There was none to be found.

Then he heard it. A whinny. Surely not?

His stomach growled at the thought of fresh meat. Horse steaks sizzling in the frying pan over the fire.

He came over a rise and saw it. The mail coach. He slid behind a tree and leaned out to watch. The stagecoach was gliding along on runners, following its route from Aspen to Crested Butte. What mail delivery could be so important to venture out in this snow? The driver struggled to coax the four horses along in the deep drifts.

"Bit off more than you could chew, huh?" Adam chuckled.

The stagecoach neared his hiding spot, and Adam hoisted the rifle to his shoulder. Like he'd planned it all along. Like he was born to do this.

Two gunshots, in quick succession, knocked the driver and the guard clean off the seat. For a split second, Adam thought he'd triggered an avalanche, but it was only the report of the echoes.

The stagecoach door opened, and a man emerged, hands raised in the air in surrender. Adam hadn't considered the possibility of passengers. What in tarnation would possess a person to make this trip in March?

He didn't hesitate. The shot blasted the man back into the

coach.

Adam waited a good amount of time until venturing down to investigate. When he did, he got a surprise.

A woman cowered in the coach, cradling the man's head in her lap.

"P—please don't hurt me."

Adam looked at her in consideration. Pretty and young. If it weren't for this infernal hunger plaguing him, he might have entertained himself with her for a few days.

As it stood, he took her out with another shot. Four shots for four beasts. He chuckled at his efficiency in hunting humans, at least.

Then he shut the stagecoach doors, climbed up into the driver's seat, and spurred the horses on.

Piper shook her head back and forth. She could hear Hattie shouting, but couldn't open her eyes. Something was coming, she knew. Hattie needed her help, but all she could do was sink back down into the nightmare, the sensation like dark, cold water closing over her head.

The horses. That's what he'd intended. But horses were useful. As he'd pulled the young woman from the stagecoach, meaning to bury her and the man some distance from the cabin, her dress had ridden up and one tender, pale leg—still warm—had splayed to the side.

Adam swallowed hard at the sight of it.

How long had it been since that stringy, old rabbit? His mouth watered, and his stomach rumbled.

He went to the woodpile and fetched his ax, whistling a tune. Something about a washerwoman.

Tonight, he thought, his belly would not go hungry. He and Amos had survived this winter. They'd survived that blizzard. And they would survive this mountain.

This, too, felt natural. Easy. Like pulling the trigger on the driver and guard. He'd been born for this.

Adam hefted the ax onto his shoulder, gazed once more at

the woman's leg, and brought the ax—

"No!" Piper screamed in unison with Willis.

A gunshot rang out in the bedroom, the blast cutting through the nightmare's cobwebs in her brain.

Piper's eyes flew open to see a set of antlers, covered in rotting strips of velvet, ramming through the bedroom door. At the sight, every cell in her body crystallized into shards of icy fear. She shot up and joined the other two on the far side of the bed, where Willis knelt on the floor. His lips moved silently as if praying. Hattie stood in the corner clutching her rifle.

"I don't know how many bullets I have left!" Hattie shouted. In her distress, her Irish accent thickened to fresh-off-the-boat levels. "And anyway, I don't think guns kill the thing."

"Save your bullets until you can get a direct shot," she told Hattie.

There was a window behind them, but it was a two-story drop out into the storm. They were trapped.

The door splintered under the sharp antlers' onslaught, and Piper caught a glimpse of the witherling's terrible and inhuman face.

Piper. You will die.

Piper shook her head as if the action might dislodge the words. She glanced at the others to see if they too reacted to the witherling's disembodied voice in their heads, but all they looked was scared. She had a sneaking suspicion the thing was only talking to her.

The noise of the breaking door sounded louder than even the ringing in her ears from the gunshot. The witherling's entire head burst through the door, and it stumbled into the room through the splintered pieces of wood. It recovered from the stumble and unfolded to its full height at the foot of the bed.

Hattie fired a shot into the creature's face. It exploded into a bloody mess and shattered the dresser mirror behind it. The monster flew back with an inhuman scream and collapsed onto the floor.

"Is it dead? Hattie asked.

"It's not moving."

Willis rose up on his knees to peer over the bed. "Did you kill it?"

"We need to burn it to do that," Piper said. For a quick moment, hope surged inside as she imagined them escaping the barn, dousing it in gasoline, and burning it to the ground with the witherling inside. "Hurry, we have to burn it!"

At her words, the witherling crawled toward the side of the bed where all three of them huddled.

Hattie fired her rifle, but nothing happened save a clicking sound. Before Piper's eyes, the creature's bloody pulp of a face started to rearrange into its version of normal.

Piper sensed they had seconds before it healed. She stood. "Come on!" She grabbed Willis by the shoulder and tugged at his flannel shirt. "Come on!" She used every bit of strength left in her body to launch herself over the bed and out of the bedroom. Hattie and Willis followed behind as quickly as wounded, feverish people could go.

Piper headed down the short hallway and tripped over Waylon's unmoving body. She registered that fact as a brief, physiological sensation of shock that twisted her gut and made her heart pound hard.

No time. She moved into the freezing living room. The wind moaned through the ragged hole in the roof above them, sending in swirling snow. Piper fixed her eyes on the apartment door, intent on one thing. Getting out of there.

The lights went out to plunge them into complete darkness. She froze, and Willis and Hattie ran into the back of her. Instinctively, they reached for one another's hands. Piper held Hattie's hand in her left, and she didn't doubt Hattie held Willis's.

They stood stock-still for a moment, trying to get their bearings in the eerie, black silence, except for the cold air whipping down from the roof. No sound came from the bedroom behind them. Piper led the way toward the apartment door, inching along like a first grader on a field trip using the buddy system.

A thump came from the laundry room. Hattie let out a small gasp. Piper heard a scrape. It sounded like it came from near the television stand to their right. She yanked on Hattie's hand and pulled them in the direction of the door. Without warning, the apartment door flew open on a blast of icy air and slammed shut again. Thuds moved down the stairs into the barn below.

"The creature?" Hattie whispered. "Did it leave?"

Before Piper could answer, the chair under the laundry room doors crashed to the floor. Her threesome scattered in the dark.

"Bedroom closet," Willis hissed and Hattie's hand was snatched from Piper's.

The laundry room doors smashed open so hard, they banged into the kitchen counters on either side. Piper pelted down the little hallway, remembering, with a hollow pain, to avoid Waylon's body. In the dark, she sensed Willis and Hattie dart into the bedroom on the left, presumably to take safety in the closet. Piper dashed to her right to disappear into the bathroom.

Which had a lock on its door.

She stood in the dark, cool bathroom and listened to the sound of Veronica moving around in the living room. There was a smashing sound that might have been a lamp on an end table.

Piper's chest heaved with each breath. An anvil of dread pushed down on her lungs. As she backed away from the door, her legs brushed against the toilet, cold enough she could feel it through her jeans. The adrenaline, combined with the fever, left her sick and shaky and she worried she'd vomit. She almost laughed, thinking she was at least in the right room to do so.

She didn't know how much longer she and Willis and Hattie could push themselves in their present states.

Ronnie—or whatever creature she'd become—continued bumping around in the living room like a mindless zombie. Hot tears clogged Piper's throat, but there was no time to cry. *Think.*

What next? She couldn't hide in the bathroom forever. And Hattie and Willis couldn't stay in the closet indefinitely either.

Where was Dylan? The fear gnawed at her heart, nibbled around the edges of her mind until she'd lose the ability to think if she weren't careful.

Piper reviewed her options. Escape the apartment and Veronica—to the barn below where she assumed the witherling had gone. Escape the apartment *and* the barn, and she'd find herself stumbling around in a blizzard filled with prehistoric beasts and deadly cold.

Gradually, a light grew in the bathroom over the sink. Puzzled, Piper watched the little nightlight plugged into the socket under the mirror as it grew from a barely perceptible yellow to a faint glow. It was enough light to illuminate her face in the mirror.

Horrified, she saw the whites of her eyes were bloodshot and her cheeks blotched with mottled pink. She looked nearly as bad as Willis.

In the mirror, the shower curtain billowed outward as if on a sigh. Goosebumps rose on her arms. She continued to stare at the reflection, unwilling to turn around to face the shower.

The curtain rings made a soft clinking on the metal rod as the shower curtain inched open.

34

A scream worked its way up from Piper's stomach where it lodged in her throat. She turned toward the shower, and the smell hit all at once. How had she not noticed it before? How had she not noticed the antlers protruding above the curtain rod?

The shower curtain continued its slow, relentless slide, but Piper couldn't move. She'd heard of people being paralyzed with fear before, something that had always sounded like a ridiculous notion. Now that she was experiencing it herself, it was all too real and understandable.

Fight or flight? Her body chose to freeze. She watched in silent terror as the shower curtain opened to reveal the witherling standing in the tub.

It was well over six feet, and its antlers scraped the ceiling. In the low light, its black eyes gleamed with the purest evil Piper had ever seen. Its lipless mouth cracked open to expose a set of jaws consisting of sharp, curving canines of various lengths. The hands curled at its sides ended in razor-like black claws.

The skin on its torso had peeled away from flesh to hang down over the creature's groin. The witherling's rib cage was a mess of broken, jagged, and missing ribs. Beneath them, the dark, meaty liver and the paler stomach shifted with the monster's breaths.

This evidence of the witherling's reality fascinated Piper. It wasn't a figment of her imagination or plucked from a horror film. It was actual flesh and blood and anatomy and organic matter. All this she understood. This thing standing before her with an insatiable appetite and endless capacity for evil had once been a lonely man in the mountains with no one but a sick brother for company. It—he—had been a human being once, before he'd been transformed into this nightmare.

Despite knowing what heinous act had led to that transformation, for the briefest of moments, she experienced something that might have been pity. "Adam?"

At the name, the creature hissed. Some part of the monster recognized that name. She knew it.

"Please, Adam. Don't hurt me." She held up her hands, and the witherling cocked its head. Good. The witherling had tainted her mind with fever and visions of this man's life before, and she would use it against him. "Adam, you don't want to do this."

He ran his tongue over those sharp teeth with something almost like a smile.

In an instant, she realized her mistake.

That thing standing before her might have *been* human, but it was fully monster now. Its eyes, twin pools of evil, showed Piper she could expect no mercy from such a being.

It hissed again and stepped over the edge of the tub.

Piper's legs cooperated at last. She stepped toward the door, feeling behind her for the knob. The witherling's hand lifted as her own twisted the door open.

Waylon stood in the hallway. Her relief at finding him alive evaporated when his hackles rose, and he slunk forward with a snarl.

Piper would rather take her chances with the Catahoula. She stepped into the hall. Waylon launched himself, and she braced for impact, but he sailed past her to grab hold of the witherling's leg.

Tears sprang to her eyes. Waylon, bless him, was trying to protect her. A savage snarling erupted behind her, followed by the sound of ripping flesh. Waylon let out a high-pitched yelp.

She fought the strong desire to turn back to help the dog and instead staggered into the dark living room.

But Piper had forgotten about Veronica.

35

Dylan pulled the Bobcat beside his Chevy in front of the barn. A foot of snow piled up against the barn door. He tried to climb out of the cab, but the door was jammed. The poor little tractor's beating had warped the frame. He shoved his shoulder against the Plexiglas. It groaned open about an inch. He slammed it again so hard, for a moment his shoulder hurt worse than his foot. The door gave all at once, and he staggered out of the Bobcat.

His foot screamed in pain as he tripped into the snow.

And then a woman screamed from inside the barn.

Dylan reached into the tractor for the shotgun and tucked his left elbow against his hip to reassure himself the silver dagger still hung there. The barn door also proved tricky to open with the heavy snow blown against it. It shrieked back on its rollers. A pile of snow dumped inside on the wood floor.

Dylan glanced around the barn, in total darkness. The horses were restless, kicking and whinnying in their stalls. A high-pitched yelp came from upstairs followed by a burst of ferocious barking. Waylon.

He ignored the pounding pain in his foot and ran to the staircase leading to the apartment. He took one precious moment to unsnap the knife sheath housing the silver dagger and then pelted up the stairs, tripping painfully once in the dark. Heart in his throat, he shoved into the apartment.

There it was. The terrible stench. Sounds of a struggle and Waylon's growling and heavy breathing greeted him.

Before he could figure out what was happening, Waylon's front paws crashed into his chest, knocking him off balance and shoving him backward. The dog was berserk, snarling and snapping at him like a rabid animal. Dylan grabbed his four-footed friend by the scruff and sent him sailing through the open door. Waylon smacked down the stairs with a squeal as he slammed the door shut.

I'm so sorry, buddy.

He turned around where two dark shapes rolled around near his feet.

One of the dark shapes on the floor hissed. Two glowing green eyes looked up at him.

"Dylan!" said Piper from beneath the creature. Panic and hysteria laced her voice.

He withdrew the dagger from its sheath and rushed to Piper's aid, but she shouted, "No! Stop! Don't hurt her. It's Ronnie."

Ronnie? He didn't care who it was. He wasn't about to let Piper get killed. He lifted the dagger high.

"Behind—you," Piper ground out.

Dylan whirled around. He registered another set of glowing eyes before a rack of antlers smashed into his arm and sent the dagger flying.

White-hot pain lanced up his forearm. He tumbled back onto the floor to land beside the wrestling shapes of Piper and Veronica. He braced himself for the impact of the witherling, hulking over Dylan in a crouch, while his fingers groped in the dark for his dagger. He was sick of spending his time of late trying to find weapons just out of reach.

"Dylan!" Piper screamed again. "You have to kill it!"

What did she think he was doing here? Having a tea party?

There! His fingers closed around the ornamental hilt when—

He screamed as teeth sank into the top of his leg with a pain unlike any he'd ever known. It was like burning knives dipped in battery acid plunging into his flesh. If the witherling pulled away, it would rip a mouthful of that flesh away with it. With no hesitation, Dylan grabbed the antlers in his left hand. The creature released his leg to turn and hiss at him again, its green eyes glowing radioactive in the dark as that gaze latched onto the silver blade in his hand.

It *knew*. It recognized the silver. Hope rushed Dylan like a linebacker, weakening him almost as much as the pain. The silver could kill the thing.

The witherling snarled, slicing its claws across Dylan's stomach. His coat protected him from getting his guts spilled, but the searing pain of the slashes made him drop the dagger again. The witherling rose to its feet.

"Dylan!" Piper shouted. She bucked Veronica off her and into the witherling, knocking the monster to the floor. It batted Veronica away like a fly.

The scuffle bought Dylan a fraction of a second to roll over onto his hands and knees to search the floor. In the dim light, the witherling crept toward him, its obvious need to play with him becoming its weakness.

It wasn't the only one who could play games. Dylan curled himself into a ball, screaming with the pain he didn't have to fake. The dagger was back in his hand, where he gripped it with all his might.

Somewhere off to his left, Piper grunted with the effort of fending off Veronica, who must have attacked her again. Dylan forced himself to still, waiting for the witherling to get within striking distance.

The witherling drew in a deep, shuddering moist breath as

it neared him.

Its long arm swung out to slash him again. *You will suffer.*

"No!" Dylan shouted. He exploded upwards, blocking the pain in his foot, his leg, his stomach. He lunged with all his remaining strength and drove the blade between those glowing eyes right up to the hilt.

The witherling recoiled with an unearthly shriek of a thousand rusted gates. The pain in his leg evaporated, followed by the bizarre sensation of the wound knitting closed.

All the lamps came on, and weak daylight leaked through the hole in the ceiling. Dylan rolled to his side toward Piper. Veronica had tumbled off her to writhe in agony on the floor. The claws on her hands shrank back into fingernails and she clutched her jaw, where a mouthful of canines shrank to ordinary human teeth. At last, she lay still, blinking up at him in confusion.

Piper scrambled up off the floor and clung to Dylan's side. Together they stared down at the witherling lying by the couch. The silver dagger smoked and dissolved into the creature's head. The antlers receded into the skull, fast as a time-lapse video. As with Veronica, the claws and teeth shrank and evolved to a human's. The black sightless eyes staring up at them morphed into a human's blue eyes surrounded by white. The broken rib cage closed back up over the exposed organs, the torn skin wrapped back around flesh, and lying before them was the body of an average-sized man of thirty or so. A dead man, at that.

Piper's fingers dug into his arm. "What are we going to do about—"

Dylan guessed her sentence was going to end with "his body," but before their eyes, the body decomposed, increasing the stench in the apartment. In seconds, the rotting corpse reduced to a skeleton, and the skeleton disintegrated into a pile of dust, which flew up through the open hole of the roof and was carried away on the wind. The smell dissipated in an instant and the air felt clean again.

Piper's mouth hung open as she and Dylan stared at each other. "Did that—" she pointed at the spot where the witherling had lain—"did that seriously just happen? Like something out of *Indiana Jones?*"

Dylan blinked. "Unless the ranch hands are playing the most elaborate practical joke ever."

They continued staring at each other in stunned shock and as if on cue, started to laugh.

Veronica sat up, blinking some more. She had her palms pressed to her temples. "My head hurts," she moaned.

"Let us out!" came a muffled voice from the bedroom.

Dylan hurried down the hall and Piper followed.

"You're limping. What happened? And that?"

Dylan waved her off as she pointed at the big bruise blooming above his left eye. "Later."

In the bedroom, they found a kitchen chair propped against the closet door.

"Get me out of here!" Willis pounded on the inside of the door. "Hattie's not doing well."

"How'd they get in there?" Dylan asked.

"The witherling must've trapped them inside."

"Why didn't it just kill them?" Dylan asked.

Piper shrugged, but the casual gesture was overcome by a shudder. "Guess he was only focused on me."

"But why?"

Willis pounded on the door again. "Let me outta here, Dylan."

Dylan set the chair aside, and Willis and Hattie tumbled out. Willis, his eyes clear, looked restored to health.

Well, as restored to health as a man his age who smoked could look.

"What happened?" Willis glanced outside the bedroom window where heavy snow still fell, dashed about by the wind, but in daylight. "The dark is gone." He put an arm around a very pale Hattie, whose dress stuck to her chest with blood.

"It's midmorning," Dylan murmured. Louder, "We killed the monster. We killed the witherling." He pulled Piper fiercely against him, looking down at her face no longer burning with fever. Relieved, he tucked her head under his chin and sighed. "It's over."

36

Piper was exhausted, but the aching in her joints had disappeared and she now shivered not from fever, but because the snow and icy wind still blew through the open roof. The four of them returned to the living room to find a dazed Veronica sitting at the end of the couch.

Willis and Hattie sat on the loveseat, both looking as tired as Piper felt. Willis reached behind him to pull the throw blanket off the back of the sofa and pulled it around the both of them. If Hattie was offended at huddling under a blanket with a strange man, she was too worn out and in too much pain to protest.

Something scratched at the apartment door, making Piper jump. Then they all looked at each other as they heard a whining sound. Dylan rushed to the door and threw it open. Waylon cowered in the doorway.

The Catahoula slunk in and licked Dylan's hand over and over in contrition.

"It's all right, buddy." Dylan's voice was overly gruff as he bent down and stroked the dog's face. "I knew it wasn't you. You didn't mean it. You're sorry. And I'm sorry I had to knock you down the stairs."

"He fought it earlier," Piper said. "He tried to save me." She came over and rubbed the dog's floppy ears. He pressed his cheek into her hand in apology.

"Piper, Willis, you feel all right now?" Dylan asked. "I mean, no fever? No visions?"

They both assured him they were fine.

"I—I think when I killed the witherling, my great-granny's fever must have been cured in the past." Dylan grinned. "That's why she got better. I saved my great-granny too."

Willis opened his mouth, and then shut it, as if too exhausted to inquire about such a bizarre statement.

"Piper?" Veronica said from the couch.

Piper came and settled on the couch by her friend. Dylan sat beside Piper. Waylon jumped onto his lap, looking ridiculous.

Veronica turned tear-filled eyes at her. "Did—did I hurt you?" She pointed at Piper's face and let out a sob.

Piper put a hand to her cheek, recalling Ronnie had scratched her there. "It doesn't hurt."

"I think it's healed," Dylan said. "Look at Waylon."

The dog's side was crisscrossed in what appeared to be freshly healed scars. Dylan pulled apart his jeans on the top of his right thigh where the witherling's teeth had shredded the denim and revealed a mess of pink scars. "It bit me here and—"

"He. *He* bit you there." Piper knew it was weird to defend a monster, but she couldn't help but feel a need to recognize the human tragedy in all of this. "The witherling was a man once, named—"

"Amos," Willis said.

"That was his brother," Piper said. "He was Adam."

"No. He was Amos. His brother was Adam."

Piper didn't feel the need to argue. She held up a hand where the snow collected in her palm. "The witherling might be dead, but we still have to see out this blizzard. What do we do now?"

Dylan's hand went to his head out of habit, but his cowboy hat was gone. "Damn hell pig," he muttered.

"What?"

"Hell pig. There's more than a blizzard out there to worry about. We got all kinds of prehistoric monsters running around. That giant bear flipped me in the Bobcat. All the way over." He twirled his index fingers over each other.

Piper stared at Dylan, amazed and grateful he wasn't more injured. She tried and failed to imagine what she would have felt if he had died.

"A giant bear?" Willis said. "Flipped you over? In a tractor?" Then he added, "I need a smoke." His hand reached into the pocket of his flannel shirt but came up empty-handed.

Dylan told them about his encounters with the short-faced bear and described the hell pig.

"Sounds like an entelodont," Piper said, unable to hide a little spark of excitement. "I saw one at a museum in Denver. It was fascinating."

"Well, I saw one in the flesh today. And I never want to see another hell pig as long as I live."

"They're more closely related to hippos than pigs."

Dylan laughed and pulled her against him—and Waylon—in the process. "You know you're such a nerd," he said into her ear so only she could hear. "That's part of why I love you."

As if in agreement, Waylon licked her chin.

She smiled at Dylan, cuddling the Catahoula like he was a lapdog. She hadn't forgotten the argument about Allison they'd had before he'd left her in the barn. But right now, everybody was alive and the witherling was dead, and that was all that mattered. There'd be plenty of time for discussion later.

The thought both cheered and terrified her.

"So how many of these ancient beasts are roaming around out there?" Willis asked.

"Maybe when the witherling died, it pulled the prehistoric animals back to their time?" Piper said.

Hattie stirred on the loveseat. "Then why am I still here?"

Her voice sounded so sad, Piper winced. Of course, Hattie must have hoped the witherling's death would return her to her own time. What a blow to find herself still here. The woman had done too much while suffering serious wounds to fend off first Veronica and then the witherling. Now, she looked like all the energy had drained out of her.

"I want to go home." Tears slipped down Hattie's cheeks.

"Shh." Willis put an arm around her, and she leaned her head on his shoulder.

Piper clapped her hands. "All right. We need a plan. Hattie needs more painkillers. And I need to check on Thunder and Osiris."

"I'd like to check on everyone in the trailers," Dylan said. "I'm gonna try out the truck." He pointed at a lamp. "The lights are back on." He rubbed Waylon's side. "We all healed from our wounds. Maybe the truck will work again too."

Piper said, "And our phones!"

"I need to call Gilbert," Veronica said, in a near-catatonic voice.

Piper didn't know how to tell her friend about her vision. She had a terrible feeling Gilbert was dead. But she didn't know for sure. Maybe he was back in their trailer, frantic to speak with his girlfriend. She pulled her phone from her jeans pocket. "Needs charging."

"Mine, too," Dylan said. "You got your phone, Willis?"

The man scratched at his beard. Hattie, eyes closed, rested her head on his shoulder and readjusted herself when Willis spoke. "Do I ever have my phone?"

Dylan sighed. "No phone calls for a little while then."

"I've got a charger in my bag downstairs," Piper said.

"I say we move camp to the barn below," Dylan said. "Everyone will be warmer down there." He sent a woeful look at the hole in the ceiling.

Together, Dylan, Willis, and Piper moved the furniture out

from under the hole in the roof. Dylan retrieved some plastic sheeting from the laundry room, and he and Willis managed to tack it up. The wind whistled through it, so who knew how long it would hold.

Like her and Dylan's relationship. The huge hole of divorce had ripped through their hearts, and nothing more than a flimsy plastic sheet of tentative hope protected them from hurting each other even more.

She rubbed her hands up and down her arms and made herself take one step at a time.

First step, get somewhere warmer.

37

Moving downstairs was not as simple as it sounded. Piper gave Veronica what was meant to be an encouraging smile, but her friend didn't respond. Veronica still sat in shock on the couch. Hattie had collapsed on the loveseat.

Willis helped Hattie to her feet. Dylan limped to the door, while Piper propped up Veronica. Their group carried all the blankets and pillows to be found in the bedroom closet and stopped at the top of the stairs to lock the apartment door behind them.

With the power back on, a welcoming yellow light glowed from below, but everyone hesitated to move toward it. They descended the stairs slowly, and not just because of Hattie's and Veronica's conditions. It was caution and a healthy dose of fear of what might await them in the barn. Welcoming yellow glow or not, they'd all been spooked by the unbelievable events that would forever change the way they saw the world. As for herself, Piper couldn't stop imagining a Utah raptor—not a velociraptor, because that would be small and ridiculous, she thought with a smile—tearing its way through one of the shuttered barn windows.

Waylon whimpered, but they found nothing out of the ordinary in the warm, horse-scented barn below. The first thing Piper did was plug in her phone to charge, eager for a connection to the outside world.

Willis and Dylan explored the tack and feed rooms and tromped up and down the aisle checking each stall.

The witherling might be dead, but it would be a long time before Piper could relax.

Dylan came out of his office wearing an old hat. It was crumpled and brown instead of his usual black, but it was still a Stetson, and so a reassuring sense of normalcy returned with him wearing it. Besides which, he always looked damn fine in a cowboy hat.

"Going to see if my truck will start." Dylan, armed with his shotgun, and once more safe under the protection of a hat, slid open the barn door. Cold wind and snow howled outside. The blizzard was going as bad as ever. Piper ignored the urge to stop him, to make sure he never left her sight again.

She craved rest and time to process all the horrors of the last couple of days, but before that could happen, her patients needed her.

Willis helped her make nests in two stalls for Veronica and Hattie. Ronnie was so spent, she fell back onto her blanket in the straw and closed her eyes. Would there be any lingering effects of Veronica's transformation to half-witherling and back again? Piper's stomach clenched. So much was unknown. Other than letting Veronica sleep, Piper didn't have the faintest idea of how to help her friend.

Piper turned her attention to Hattie in the next stall. She got down on her knees beside the woman lying on her blanket. Hattie sucked in a breath when Piper peeled away the dress from her chest to inspect her wounds. They seeped blood, due to all her activity no doubt, but there was no sign of infection.

Piper hoped a shot of tramadol would take the edge off.

"You done in there?" Willis asked.

"Yep."

Willis squeezed into the stall and clumsily lowered himself onto the straw to sit with his back against the wall. He took Hattie's hand in his and Piper hid a smile.

"I'll just keep her company until she goes to sleep," he said, even though it was obvious the woman was already asleep. In a much quieter voice, he added, "I saw the thing attack her. Back in her time, at her cabin. It's like I saw it happen through the monster's eyes."

"I know." She glanced at the next stall where her friend slept. "I saw it attack Veronica."

"How? How could we see it?" He scratched the back of his head.

"Dylan's great-grandmother said the witherling touched her and gave her a fever and terrible visions. We think the creature can infect you with its touch."

"So how come Hattie didn't get infected?"

"He didn't want to infect her, I guess. It chose us. I think witherlings feed off fear as much as human flesh. I think it has to intentionally infect you. To want to torture you with visions and nightmares."

"True ones?"

"Seems like they were."

"You said the witherling has to touch you?" Willis nodded in thought. "I knew I felt something brush past me. When Raymond and I found the elk on the fence."

"Willis. Raymond—Raymond is dead."

"I know," he said bitterly. "I saw that, too." He sniffed and looked away. "I thought Dylan was going to die as well." Willis's voice broke before he cleared his throat. "In my vision, I saw the witherling eating his leg—eating Dylan alive."

"And he tried to." Dylan limped over to their stall and rested his arms on the open half-door. Snow crusted his hat and eyebrows, had piled on his shoulders. "But I'm made of tougher stuff." He winked, but there were tight lines around his mouth and eyes. He tapped his cowboy hat against the wall to dislodge the snow on its brim.

"What's wrong?" Piper asked.

"Truck won't start. Snowmobiles won't start. And now the Bobcat won't start either. Although that might be from flipping over as much as anything the witherling did. And the blizzard's worse than ever. I've never seen a storm this bad in my whole life." He scrubbed a hand over his snowy brows and shoved his hat back on. "Even if the truck would start, there's no way I could drive anywhere."

"Guess we'll just have to sit tight until it blows itself out," Willis said.

"Guess so. I wish I knew how the others are doing. I hope they're okay in their trailers."

"There's not a lot you can do about it if they aren't," Willis said.

Dylan sighed and slammed the heel of his palm into the stall door with a curse. Being helpless always made her ex-husband angry. "I'm gonna unload what I brought over in the Bobcat."

Willis gave Dylan a hopeful expression. "You didn't happen to stop by my place for cigarettes, did you?"

"I did, but I found a hell pig at your trailer. Son of a bitch was smoking the very last pack."

Piper burst out laughing. Hattie stirred in the straw. "Sorry," she whispered.

Willis rolled his eyes, but his mouth quirked. He got up, and he and Dylan left to unload the Bobcat. Osiris meowed and Piper went to check on him.

She took him out of the soiled crate and removed the catheter from his front paw. The area around his sutures looked good, with no swelling or redness. Pleased, Piper released him into the feed room with food and water and a makeshift litter tray fashioned from a cardboard box and some alfalfa pellets.

Dylan and Willis were carrying in armloads of weapons. Dylan hobbled a bit, but as usual, got on with things when they needed doing. She would do the same. Piper made her way down the aisle to Thunder's stall. The little cream-colored colt looked decidedly brighter and even had the strength to struggle against the nebulizer mask when she placed it over his muzzle. She settled herself cross-legged in the scratchy hay beside the small palomino.

To her surprise, Waylon came along and settled himself against Thunder with a heavy sigh of contentment.

Near the end of the nebulizer treatment, Dylan, who'd been speaking with Willis in hushed voices down the aisle, joined her in Thunder's stall.

Had it really been earlier this morning she'd woken up in this very spot wrapped in Dylan's arms?

He said nothing over the sound of the nebulizer's soft whirring. Piper snuck glances at him, trying to read his expression under his hat brim. Every time she looked at him, he was looking back at her, his face somber and thoughtful. In the past hours, she and Dylan had been through hell and back, people had died, reality had spun out of control into a nightmare world she couldn't begin to wrap her head around. And yet the heaviness between them now had nothing to do with any monster save the one they'd created with their divorce.

She couldn't stop herself from imagining Dylan and Allison in bed together. But what good did that do? It certainly wasn't the path to forgiveness. She didn't know if she *could* forgive him, though. How could he have slept with someone so soon after—

You left him, she reminded herself. But—

Dylan's smug face saying *I* did *enjoy it!* kept playing in her mind on a loop. Another glance at Dylan showed her he didn't look like a man enjoying himself now.

The nebulizer clicked off. Piper reared up on her knees to remove the mask. Thunder nuzzled her hand, and she stroked his velvety nose. Waylon opened one eye and returned to sleep.

"Piper."

She swallowed and slowly sank back down. They sat side-by-side, backs against the stall wall. Piper laced her hands together and looked at him to signal she was ready to listen.

"I'd do anything to go back in time and undo what happened with Allison."

The woman's name on Dylan's lips cut her to the core.

"We were married at the time," he continued. "And it was wrong. I've felt terrible for it ever since. I'm sorrier than you can ever know, and I hope you can forgive me."

"I left you." She sighed. "So of course I have to forgive you." Even if it hurt. Even if it was hard.

The silence stretched out and Piper sensed a growing tension in the air.

Dylan threw up his hands. "I give up."

"What? I said I forgive you."

"That's great, but I sort of thought I was finally going to get an apology from you." His hazel eyes sparkled with fury, a forest fire burning in their golden-green.

Piper shifted to face him. "You thought I—" Her mouth snapped shut because her first instinct was to lash out. How dare he expect an apology from her? He was the one pressuring her to have kids, pressuring her to focus her veterinary skills on large animals. He was the one who kept up the canned hunting operation. He was the one who flirted with the wranglers. He was the one who'd slept with another woman when they were still married.

After you left him, remember? She drew in a shaky breath. Was wanting kids so bad? He'd never hidden the fact he'd wanted kids any more than she'd hidden the fact she wasn't sure she did. He wanted her to be the vet on the ranch, but that stemmed from his enthusiastic belief in her skills and desire to spend time with her. He'd been disappointed she hadn't wanted to, but he hadn't insisted. And the elk hunting was something she'd always known about the ranch, and she'd moved onto it anyway.

If she'd wanted to be so principled about it, she shouldn't have moved to the ranch in the first place.

Dylan was friendly and smiled and joked with everyone and okay, sure—maybe he was flirting with the female wranglers a little. But she wasn't above friendly banter with some of her male clients either. He'd always been faithful before.

He was right. It wasn't fair for her to punish him for her dad's mistakes. He wasn't her father.

"I—I'm sorry, Dylan," she said.

He looked stunned. Despite having just said she should apologize, it was clear he never expected she would. And what did that say about her?

"I'm so very sorry."

The words unknotted something in her chest she hadn't even realized was there until it was gone. Like a tight, coiled band had been tied around her body, squeezing the life out of her, and now it had disappeared, she could draw a full breath at last.

She scooted around to face him. "I was so worried about how different we are. I thought I could change you when we married, but I should have accepted you as you were. As the man I'd always loved. And will," she added quietly.

He brushed a strand of hair from her forehead. "We have to marry someone accepting who they are, but if they never changed, it would be a piss-poor marriage. You changed me, Piper. Mostly for the better." He ducked his head to meet her gaze. "Your leaving turned me into a man that disgusted me for a while there. God, I hated you leaving."

"I hoped you'd come after me. That you'd fight for me." A fierceness crept back into her voice. Fierceness and a little temper.

"Marriage isn't a game, Piper. We weren't in high school, babe. You were my *wife*. You can't say those things about us, say you want a divorce, and take off like that without thinking there'd be consequences. My pride kept me from following you.

Maybe that was wrong, but you don't test your *husband* like that."

His chastisement angered her, but then his eyes filled with tears.

"Piper, you hurt me so bad. I've been dying inside, a little more every day since you left. And all this horror with the monsters out there? I thought I was going to die, and I didn't want to for one single reason. If I did, I'd never see you again."

Piper found that now the band around her chest was gone, she was about to fall apart without it. She climbed into Dylan's lap and hot tears slipped down her cheeks. "Dylan, we've been a couple of fools." She cried harder as he stroked a hand down her long hair. "I'm so, so sorry. When you were gone so long before, I was terrified you might be dead. I realized if you died, I didn't feel like going on without you. I don't want to go on without you anymore." She swiped a hand across her face. Salty tears had reached her mouth, and she licked them away. "I love you."

"I love you too."

She sobbed in earnest, wondering if it were possible—if *they* were possible again.

"Shh, Piper. Come on, now. It's all right." He kissed the top of her head. She eased away to look up at him. He wiped her tears away with his thumbs and took her face in his hands. "God, woman, how can you have gone through everything we just did, be crying and carrying on, and still look so beautiful?"

She sniffed and gave him a weak smile. Then he bent down and kissed her salty cheeks, kissed her nose, kissed her mouth.

It was so easy then. So familiar. Her arms came around his neck, and his mouth took hers. So familiar, but different. A new longing shot through the kiss as his tongue explored her mouth. He tasted like Dylan, but the rough hands that slid up her shirt were questioning, hesitant when they moved up her back.

Piper broke their kiss to readjust herself in his lap, wrapping her legs around his waist. Then she kissed him once more, his lips soft, but demanding on hers. He moaned into her mouth.

His arousal was obvious, pushing hard at the fly of his jeans. In response, warmth spread through her stomach and lower as she pressed herself against him there.

"Do you know how many times I've fantasized about you?" he said. His words came out as panting gasps. Piper rained down kisses on his face, down his neck, grinding herself against him. His hands were no longer questioning. They roamed up her back and slid around to cup her breasts.

"Every day," he said. "I fantasized about this every single day you've been gone. I want to rip your clothes off right now and take you. Would that be all right?"

Somehow, his hands had unhooked her bra beneath her sweater and were now on her bare breasts. She wanted to say something sexy in reply, but all that came out was a breathless, "Yes."

Willis and Hattie and Veronica were in the barn, and the stall only had a half-door, but right then, Piper didn't care in the least. Everyone else was probably sleeping anyway.

"It's not going to be anything fancy," Dylan said. "But I've been waiting a year for this and I need to be inside you now."

He grabbed her by the hips to unhook her legs from him and pushed her back into the straw. Thunder lifted his head and shot them a look from the other end of the stall, causing Waylon to let out a tired groan, but both animals returned to resting.

Dylan took his hat off and moved to set it aside.

"Put it back on. Please?"

He gave her a wicked grin and shoved the Stetson back on his head. Then Dylan reared up to unzip his jeans and wiggled them and his boxers down his thighs. The fresh scars on his right leg held her attention for all of half a second. There were bigger things to think about just then.

She remembered what he looked like, of course, but she thought maybe she'd embellished it in her memories. Exaggerated.

But if anything, she'd forgotten just how good the view was.

A desperate heat built within her. Piper clawed at her jeans. Dylan yanked them down to her ankles.

All of a sudden, he was poised between her legs, and she could feel the hard length of him brushing at her center. They were only half-naked and the lead-up had been lightning-fast, but she didn't care. Piper didn't think she'd ever wanted anything so bad as she wanted this man inside her now. Even the first time they'd slept together, the need hadn't been this intense.

Maybe because now she knew what she'd been missing. He brushed himself against her again, and she moaned.

"Say please?" he asked, with that crooked grin.

She met his eyes, locked onto them. "Please." That one word encompassed so many things. Please forgive me. Please let me come back. Please be my husband again.

She saw the answer in his hungry gaze.

And then he slid himself inside her wet heat, joining them together again.

38

Piper let out a long moan that almost made Dylan finish right then and there.

"Shh," he whispered in her ear. "We're not alone, remember? You have to be quiet."

This might be fast and hard and what had he said?—nothing fancy. But that didn't mean he couldn't make love to her all the same. This was Piper. He made himself slow down a little, to rock against her in the rhythm he knew she liked best.

Thomas Wolfe was dead wrong about saying you couldn't go home again. This, being inside Piper, was home for him more than the ranch could ever be. He should have left the place and followed her last year. She would always be his home.

God, she felt so incredible. He'd been missing this for so long. What a couple of fools, indeed.

Wolfe was right about one thing. He had to see a thing a thousand times to see it once. He would do anything to be with Piper, swallow any amount of pride, follow her to the ends of the earth to make sure she believed they were meant to be together like this forever.

Something inside him flared back to life as they moved in synchrony. This moment went beyond the physical connection between them. He felt it deep inside, a connection of their souls. Mates in every sense.

He knew Piper so well that the change in her breathing and her fingers gripping his back told him she was close. Which was lucky, because he didn't think he could have waited any longer.

Dylan thrust into her with savage freedom, saying with his body the simple summation he hadn't managed with his words.

You are mine. I am yours. I'll do anything for you.

He drove them both over the edge and he didn't care that neither of them was very quiet in the end.

—

Straw scratched his back and his foot ached, but that faded under the bliss. Piper lay beside him, her head on his chest, still panting. At this moment, they were both exactly where they belonged. After a bit, they pulled up their jeans, wrapped themselves in a blanket, and fell into a deep, contented sleep.

—

He didn't know how much later he woke, but someone was pounding on the barn door, shouting to be heard over the howling wind. Waylon was barking. Piper already stood in the stall, and even Thunder had risen on his wobbly legs.

"Someone's out there," she said. Her red-gold hair was tangled up with bits of straw. Her cheeks were red, and the newly healed scar inflicted by Veronica stood out on the left one. Blue eyes stared at him in question.

Dylan got up and opened the stall door, ignoring the pulse of pain in his foot. Somewhere down the aisle, a horse let out a disapproving whinny. Willis was standing in the open stall where Hattie lay. He was nearer the barn door but hadn't made a move to open it yet.

"Hey!" said someone on the other side of the door. It shook in its track. "Let me in!"

Piper crept beside Dylan and looked between the two men and the door.

"Sounds like Quinton," Willis said.

Dylan pictured Kyle's teenaged son standing out there in the blizzard. Quinton was a shy, smart boy who kept to himself. Kyle had told Dylan over a beer once that his son struggled to fit in anywhere, but he loved nature, and Kyle said he was thinking of becoming a forest ranger. Quinton had done some wrangling before Dylan shut down the hunting operation. The boy knew every square inch of the ranch almost as well as Dylan and though he was quiet, he was confident in his knowledge. The hunters he'd taken out had nothing but great things to say about Quinton and tipped him well. Dylan liked and trusted the kid.

But Willis wore an expression on his face that was anything but trusting. Waylon's barking grew frenzied.

"Let me in! We need help!"

Willis stood frozen in the entrance to the stall, his eyes darting back and forth as if thinking.

Dylan shot him an annoyed look. Willis had always been a cynic, but it would appear recent events had changed him into a coward. Dylan reached for the latch on the door.

"Wait."

"Willis, what's the matter with you?" But Dylan waited. "Waylon, shut up!"

The dog quieted to a low growl.

"You sure that's Quinton?" Willis said.

Piper put a hand on Dylan's forearm. "Take a minute and think. What if it's something out there trying to trick us? Make its voice sound like someone we know?"

"The witherling is dead." He looked at them both and waited for an argument. It was like they knew something he didn't, and it bugged him. "Unless hell pigs can do killer impressions, of course, I'm sure that's Quinton." Dylan refused to let fear and paranoia keep him from helping a kid in need.

He shoved open the door, and Quinton and Kyle blew into the barn with a rush of snow-laden wind and cold, Quinton propping the older man up on his shoulder. Quinton might have been trying to ease his father down, but the result was dropping Kyle onto the wood floor like a sack of grain. Waylon backed away, his hackles up, to stand beside Willis.

Dylan trusted his dog, but Kyle didn't look too dangerous just then. The man lay unmoving. Unconscious from the looks of it.

Quinton stood shivering. Both his and Kyle's faces were caked in snow, their lips blue. Piper rushed to crouch at Kyle's side and put a hand to his neck.

"I-is he d-dead?" Quinton asked.

Piper shook her head. "No. But he's got severe hypothermia. I'll get some blankets," she said. "And I'm going to need you to help me undress him."

"Quinton?" Piper looked up at the boy. "Do you think you can manage to undress yourself? I'll bring you a blanket, too. We need you both dry and warm, okay?"

The kid nodded, but in his exhaustion, or maybe relief, he slumped against a stall, shivering, and looking incapable of movement.

"I'll help him," Willis said and proceeded to do so.

Piper disappeared into the tack room to fetch horse blankets with Waylon slinking after her as if eager to be far from the scene.

When she returned, Quinton was down to boxers, and Dylan had eased Kyle out of his ice-crusted coat and was just unbuttoning his shirt.

Dylan stared at the man's chest and swallowed.

"What is it?" Piper knelt beside him, her arms full of padded, blue horse blankets.

Willis took one from her and wrapped up Quinton. Waylon

sat beside the boy and whined.

"He's been bitten." Dylan pointed at the man's torso.

Kyle's broad chest was pale under the thick, dark hair. In its center was a lurid, seeping bite wound. It was like a distorted human bite. The horseshoe shape was unnaturally large and the teeth marks narrower and deeper.

"Shit," Piper said.

"But the witherling is dead."

Dylan saw Piper and Willis exchange grim looks.

"What were you two doing out in this storm?" Piper asked Quinton. She now sounded suspicious of the boy as well, but the fact Waylon sat beside him reassured Dylan.

"I heard my dad outside calling for my mom. I got up and glanced in their room. My mom was sleeping in the bed. I opened the back door of the trailer to tell him she was inside when he took off running through the snow." Quinton looked around at the adults. "It was dumb, but I chased after him. Something about the way he was acting scared me. Like he'd gone crazy or something."

Piper and Dylan looked at each other and down at the bitten man.

"How'd you end up here?" Dylan tried to sound casual, but Piper shot him a look that told him he hadn't succeeded.

"Once I got away from the trailer, I lost my bearings. I managed to catch up with my dad. He kept going on about hearing my mom crying out in the snow. He wouldn't listen to me when I told him she was safe in bed. We kept stumbling around until we saw the lights in the barn."

"When did this happen?" Piper pointed at Kyle's chest.

Quinton clutched the blanket around him like a cloak and squatted beside his father. "When did what happen?" The boy leaned forward to peer at his dad's chest. "What *is* that?" He sounded afraid.

Piper touched the edges of the bite wound.

Dylan's throat convulsed. "Piper." Her head jerked up.

"It's not healed," they said together.

And neither were Hattie's wounds, come to think of it.

Kyle's eyes—deep, huge pools of blackness, snapped open, and Quinton screamed.

Dylan couldn't believe it, but the nightmare wasn't over.

39

There was no time for hesitation. Piper bolted over to her medical bag.

"Hold him!" she shouted over Waylon's renewed barking.

Dylan threw himself over the man, who was emitting a low hiss, but otherwise hadn't moved.

She drew up a syringe of ketamine, and unlike the situation with Veronica, Kyle was subdued enough she could find a vein. She wasn't used to finding veins on people, but it turned out to be a lot easier than dogs. The needle slid through his relatively hairless, thin skin, and within ten seconds, Kyle's disturbing black eyes closed, and he lay inert.

"Did you kill him?" Quinton asked. Willis held the teenager in place with a firm arm around his shoulders.

"He's just sleeping," Piper said. "We need to get him somewhere secure."

"The tack room," Dylan said.

"What the hell's going on around here?" In his distress, Quinton's voice cracked, belying his youth.

"I know it's scary." She traded places with Willis, who helped Dylan drag the sedated man away, and tucked her arm around him. "I'm happy to tell you all I know."

Dylan and Willis returned, both looking shaken at the ordeal of locking up their friend and colleague.

Piper gave Quinton the rundown of everything that happened during the storm. Quinton's brown eyes sparkled with anger by the time she finished. "But you say you killed the witherling. So what happened to my dad?"

Willis met Piper's gaze when she spoke. "There's a second one."

Dylan groaned and shoved his fist against his forehead.

"The Stagecoach Cannibal?" Piper said to the men. "Adam? He had a brother Amos, who was sick and laid up with pneumonia. I'd wager a guess he fed his sick brother some of the human meat."

"Turned him into a witherling," Willis said. "I saw it in my vision. His brother fed him the meat. He didn't know what it was at first, but then his brother told him. Said he had to get strong. I don't think Amos was a bad man, but he was tired of being sick, tired of being hungry. So he ate the meat. I knew Adam murdered the people. I didn't realize he ate them, too. That's why I thought Amos was the witherling. Because he is."

"And so was Adam," Piper said. "They were both cannibals."

Dylan kicked a stall door with his good foot and winced. "I have a feeling Amos is going to be pretty pissed off we killed his brother."

As if in answer, the wind screamed at the barn door, rattling it in its track.

"Why won't it just leave us alone?" Piper said. "It's like they're targeting us personally."

"That's because they are."

Everybody whirled around to Veronica, who stood rumpled and haunted-looking in the aisle. Strands of dark hair stuck to her tear-stained face.

"Is your phone working, Piper? I want to talk to Gil."

Piper grabbed her phone and it held enough charge to turn on. She handed it to Ronnie. "There're five missed calls."

"Wait." Dylan snatched the phone from Veronica's hand, and she glared at him. "What do you mean the witherlings are targeting us personally?"

Veronica snatched the phone back and muttered something in Spanish under her breath. "I want to know if my boyfriend is okay. And then I'll tell you what I know."

Dylan hung his hands on his hips and breathed through his nose in the snorting bull stance he did when he was really angry.

"Dylan." Piper cocked her head at Veronica. "She's been through enough. Let her see if she can get ahold of Gilbert." She sent him a meaningful look and hoped he got the message. Piper didn't think there was much chance Ronnie would ever talk to Gilbert again, and she saw the understanding in Dylan's eyes.

"The missed calls are from Gilbert!" Veronica held the phone up to her ear. "There's a message from him. From ten minutes ago."

Veronica's bronze skin paled to a sickly white as she listened to the message.

"What is it?" Piper took the phone from Veronica's trembling hand.

Piper put the phone on speaker and played the voicemail.

It was Gilbert's voice. But those weren't words he'd ever choose to say.

"You will die," he said. "You will pay for killing my brother." The words came halting, forced somehow from the kind and caring Gilbert in a way that clearly hurt him. "I will kill you all slowly. I will skin you alive." A pause as Gilbert took in a shuddering breath. "Peel the skin from your flesh. Eat the flesh from your bones. When my teeth snap through your bones, you will still be breathing. As I feast on your flesh, you will see your own blood running from my mouth." The line cut off.

Veronica's entire body shook. "That's Gilbert. Oh, God,

that's Gilbert. What's happened to him?"

While the words chilled Piper to her core, the fact it was Gilbert's voice cheered her. "Ronnie, this means he's still alive!" She grabbed her friend and pulled her into a tight hug, but Veronica was too shocked to reciprocate. "Which also means we have a chance at saving him if we can kill the witherling that was Amos."

Something of what Piper was saying must've sunk in. Veronica's spine stiffened as she pulled away. "You really think he's alive?"

"Well, he's talking, isn't he? The witherling forced him to say that stuff."

Dylan nodded. "I agree. We've got to kill that bastard."

"You don't happen to have another ceremonial silver dagger lying around, do you?" Piper asked, remembering how it had disintegrated in the first witherling.

He lifted a brow at her. "No. But we'll figure it out. We have to. We'll kill that monster. Save Kyle. Save Gilbert. And this blizzard will finally go."

"With any luck, that means Hattie will get returned home," Piper said.

Willis hung his head.

"So tell us what you know," Dylan said to Veronica. "You know what? Hang on."

In silence, Dylan handed out granola bars and bottles of water.

Veronica dumped out the pouch to pour a pile of granola dust into her hand. "What happened to these?"

"Crushed when my tractor got flipped by a cave bear," Dylan said as if it were obvious. He led them down the aisle near Thunder's stall, where a space heater churned out warmth.

Piper checked on Hattie as they passed. The exhausted woman slept through all the noise and commotion.

Willis and Dylan sat with Quinton huddled in his blanket between them in the aisle, backs resting against Thunder's stall.

Waylon had returned to his post of sleeping beside the little colt. Piper and Veronica sat on the other side of the aisle, their backs against a stall with a brass nameplate reading Beelzebub.

Piper caught Ronnie staring at it. "That horse can be a little cantankerous, but once you get to know him, he's sweet as pie. We call him Bub most of the time."

Veronica widened her eyes in an if-you-say-so kind of way.

"All right, that ketamine's going to wear off," Piper said. "We need a plan." She nudged Ronnie with her shoulder. "Tell us what you know."

"Okay." She twisted a strand of dark hair over her fingers as she often did when she was nervous. "When I was—I was like a—"

"A witherling," Dylan prompted.

"Yes. It was like I knew what he was thinking. Adam. You said his name was Adam. The one who turned me?"

Piper nodded.

"Well, I saw what happened here. Or could have. Or would have."

"Ronnie, what are you talking about?"

"The witherling that was once Adam—he saw something happen on the ranch here. Something I think happened in the future. And he came to stop it."

"How do you know it was the future?" Dylan said, asking the same thing Piper was wondering. "Flying cars on my ranch or something?"

Veronica, to Piper's surprise, smiled. "No. No flying cars. Something else."

And she began to tell them.

40

The thing that had once been Adam sensed his brother go out into the night and followed him, followed the shape of him outlined as a void of life. It made him as easy to track in the darkness as his human prey. Evil thrummed where a heartbeat should be.

To sense his brother as evil made him feel—not remorse— that was an emotion he'd felt rarely as a human and never as the creature he now was. But he felt something. A recognition that this evil was not what Amos would have chosen to become.

It was why his brother hunted so often in the future. They could no longer communicate as they once had, but he knew Once-Amos preferred killing those who had not yet been born in their time. Once-Adam somehow knew his brother thought this made the killing not count. He himself did not waste much time on thinking or feeling. How could he when he knew only the all-consuming hunger?

He ate whatever and whoever crossed his path with no need to travel through time unless evading capture.

Once-Adam hated the future. He did not understand it. He enjoyed hunting in the past more. He liked the times filled not with machines, but with flesh that could be either controlled or eaten. But he followed his brother wherever he went, protecting him even now as they lived as immortals.

With a crackling snap and blue sparking, Once-Adam stepped into a meadow. Stars shone from a cold, clear sky above. Dark trees surrounded the meadow. In the center of the clearing stood a large building he recognized as a barn. Inside, machinery hummed. Machines. Always machines. But he could still smell the horseflesh within and somewhere nearby, the heady scent of humans.

His brother headed not toward the barn, but the log house from where the smell of human emanated.

Once-Adam followed him with preternatural speed and crossed to the patch of grass behind the house at almost the same moment as Once-Amos. His brother looked at him with his large black eyes, unsurprised to find him there. When he tilted his head to gaze up at the house, his eyes caught enough starlight to glow green.

A dog started barking inside. Once-Adam hated dogs. The spoiled, unnatural creatures proved hard for his mind to control, having forsaken their predator past for a life of servitude.

They crept closer to the house, to crouch under the deck. Once-Adam looked up through the slats. Something scrabbled and scratched at the glass door above.

The door slid open and a dog shot onto the boards above their heads and then came to a whimpering halt. It growled, low in its throat. Once-Adam saw the dog lower his head in their direction.

"What is it, Way?" said a man's voice. "Hey, come back here, you rascal."

Once-Adam saw a small child step onto the boards and toddle after the dog. His mouth filled at once with saliva at the smell of young, tender flesh. Long ropes of it dripped from his many canines. He knew his brother would leave the child for him. Once-Amos was so foolish as to only devour the fully-grown.

The man stepped out and scooped the child in his arms. He turned and handed the small human over.

"Ma-ma," said the child.

Someone standing just inside the door held out slender arms. On the inside of the right wrist, his keen eyes made out the tiny image of a blackbird tattooed there.

"Dylan? Everything okay?" The voice sounded female.

"Waylon's acting funny," said the man.

A few beats of silence later, the woman said, "Oh, God, Dylan. I think it's going to happen tonight."

The man focused on the boards at his feet and Once-Adam shrank back. It was as if the man was looking right at him.

"Piper? If you can hear me wherever you are, use the chelated solution, all right?" The man's heavy footsteps thudded above his head. "Time paradox shit is about to get real."

Once-Adam did not listen to the words of humans much and these made less sense than usual. But he was pleased to hear the fear in the man's voice.

With a cracking, splintering heave, his brother clawed up through the deck. From inside the doorway, the woman shrieked, the child let out a lusty cry. Once-Adam climbed up beside him, eager to taste that young flesh. As he pulled himself onto the boards, the woman handed the man something that flashed silver in the moonlight.

In an instant, the man had plunged a blade into his brother's heart. Once-Amos screamed, an ungodly sound, and his body disintegrated before Once-Adam's eyes.

It was as though the knife plunged into his own heart. For the first time since he had become this creature, he felt something as powerful as the never-ending hunger. The sharp pain of grief and rage lanced through him, and he let out his *own unnatural, metallic scream.*

He turned and disappeared into the night, running miles and miles through the forest in mere seconds. As he ran, his mind twisted and turned. The grief began to recede under the hunger again. He knew what he must do.

Once-Adam need only go back in time and feast upon the bodies of Dylan and this Piper. The man would pay for what he did this night. The man and the woman named Piper. He would make them pay by filling their last days and hours with a terror and dread that would render their meat all the more tender.

They would pay and they would die.

And they would not live to kill his brother.

41

Piper wondered if she wore the same stunned look as Dylan, who was staring back from across the aisle. She figured she did. It was a lot to digest. And poor Ronnie looked exhausted to have relived these moments she'd spent inside the mind of a monster. She had told them everything Once-Adam had seen and heard and felt with incredible detail like she'd been inside him.

It was disgusting, and Veronica looked disgusted.

"Wait, so our future selves knew about the witherling coming for us? In the future?" Dylan said. "I actually said that? That time paradox shit was about to get real?"

Veronica nodded at him.

Piper laughed as Dylan moved his hat and scraped his fingers over his scalp. "Literally a head-scratcher, right?" She turned to Ronnie. "Was it a boy or a girl?"

"Don't know." Her friend shrugged with a half-smile.

"Is it really going to happen?" Piper was awe-struck at the idea of her with a kid. It was a glimpse of a future that wouldn't happen now they'd killed the witherling who'd been Adam. This future would no longer happen, right? She was surprised how upsetting the thought was that maybe the child wouldn't happen either. She ran a hand over her forearm, hidden under her sweater sleeve, and thought of her twin sister as another far more unpleasant thought occurred.

"We knew it was coming for us?" Dylan repeated slowly. "But if we killed Adam last night, how could he be under our deck in the future?"

"If we killed Adam last night," Piper said, "how could he be alive in the future to see you kill Amos and then come back in time for us to kill him last night?" Her brain hurt.

Willis groaned and put his face in his hands.

Quinton, quiet until this point, lifted his heavy lids to regard them with a face that showed he thought they were all idiots. "Witherlings can travel through time."

"Yeah?"

He sighed and sounded bored. "So this Adam witherling must have traveled into the future from a point in time before last night when you killed him."

Understanding dawned in Piper's mind. Trust the quick mind of a teenager to work it out for them.

"I'm so confused," Dylan said, scratching his head some more. "Even though we killed Adam last night, he can still come to us in the future?"

"Yes. From the past," Quinton said. "Now can we just focus on saving my dad?"

Willis, rubbing his beard in bemusement, said, "All right. Let's just look at the facts we have. Adam saw Dylan kill his brother. He got mad and came back to torture and kill you. But you killed him first. Now his brother Amos is mad and here to take revenge."

"Ironic," said Quinton, still sounding bored.

"We have to kill them both," Piper said. She shut her eyes as she puzzled it out. "Then it will be over. Except for the future where Dylan will kill Amos and finish this. That will still happen. Maybe. I think. I don't know. God, I'm not a theoretical physicist." She ran her hand over her mouth in thought. "Chelated silver," she muttered.

"Whoa, wait," Dylan said. "I have to kill a witherling again at some unknown point in the future? With our *kid* there?" His voice rose.

Piper's throat constricted at the uncertain thought flitting through her mind. In answer, her fingers closed over her forearm, as if it could stop the pain of what she'd realized. "I'm writing this all down while it's fresh," she said. "So you'll have some clues to warn you for the future. Just in case."

She jumped up and jogged through the barn to Dylan's office. A low moaning came from the tack room. The ketamine was wearing off faster than she'd hoped. If Kyle woke up full witherling, that door wouldn't hold him for long. She switched on the light and grabbed a notepad and pencil from the weathered desk.

As quickly as she could, she wrote everything Veronica had told them down on a piece of paper so nothing would be forgotten. Later, if they made it through this night, she would stick it on the fridge in Dylan's house where he could read it every day. Just in case, he'd be ready.

No, not just Dylan's house. Dylan and the woman with the bird tattoo and Dylan's child. *They* would read the note and *they* would be ready.

Piper returned to the others sitting in the aisle in front of Thunder's stall.

"Kyle's waking up. We need a plan fast."

Everyone began shouting, discussing how to defeat the Amos witherling, but she ignored them. Her mind raced.

"Chelated silver," she said. Dylan gave her a message from the future, knowing Veronica would deliver it tonight. He'd told her to use the chelated silver solution. The silver solution that came in the box with the nebulizer for Thunder.

What, was she supposed to *nebulize* the witherling to death? *Real helpful, future Dylan.* Maybe she should also write him a note to be more specific and less annoying in the future.

The sound of raised voices pulled her from her thoughts.

"Right. Shoot him with silver bullets," Willis was saying sarcastically, in the middle of an argument with Dylan. "Why don't we melt down my buckle here and make our own right now?"

"That's not silver," Quinton said seriously, as he studied the big belt buckle straining at Willis's belly.

"I know that," the older man snapped.

"Well, I don't have any more silver daggers," said Dylan. "And I'd rather not get so close next time I have to kill a witherling." He climbed to his feet with his usual easy grace, almost hiding his limp, and glowered down at Willis. "Oh yeah, that's right. Last time I checked, I'm the only one here who's actually killed a witherling. And I say we shoot the bastard somehow."

"Yes," Piper said, but nobody paid her any attention. "We shoot him." She opened Thunder's stall with a slight creak and rustled across the hay to the nebulizer box. She plucked out the large bottle of chelated silver solution and held it up triumphantly. "With this."

Willis's furry gray eyebrows shot up. "What is that?"

"Chelated silver," she said. "We can shoot the witherling with this silver solution. I can load it up in the tranquilizer gun. Did you bring it, Dylan?"

Now it was Dylan's turn to raise his eyebrows. "Uh, yeah. In case, you know, we wanted to make the witherling sleepy. I brought the tranquilizer gun."

"Sarcasm isn't helpful," Quinton said without looking up.

"No, it isn't," Piper agreed. "So is it here or not?"

"No, the tranquilizer gun isn't here!" Dylan threw his hands up in the air in obvious frustration. "It's up at the house."

"Which is several hundred yards away." Piper's heart sank.

"Through a snowstorm," added Willis.

"Filled with a witherling, hungry hell pigs, giant lions, and prehistoric bears," Dylan said. "Should be a fun trip."

"I'm in," Piper said. "As long as we have Funyuns."

"No," Dylan said.

"All the best trips include Funyuns."

Dylan didn't laugh. "You're not going out there."

She leveled a look at him. They stared one another down for several fraught, tense moments as Willis, Quinton, and Veronica looked on.

At last, she lifted her chin and said, "I'm not letting you go anywhere without me, Dylan Kincaid."

His Adam's apple moved up and down as he swallowed hard. Then he blew out a breath. "Fine. But I don't have any Funyuns. Would you settle for another atomized granola bar?"

Then he crushed her mouth with his.

Willis muttered, "About time you two got some sense."

42

Dylan hated to put Piper in danger by letting her outside the barn, but he had to admit he liked the idea of her being with him. And he wasn't feeling all that great about the barn being safe anyway. The apartment upstairs sported a huge hole in the roof. The witherling could as easily crash through the barn as hunt them in the storm. He wouldn't expect them to go out in the storm, either, which might work to their advantage.

Which meant Dylan wanted to secure the barn as much as possible before leaving Willis and the others on their own.

"Most monsters are supposed to hate fire, right?" he asked Piper, who nodded.

Together, he and Willis set out the tiki torches that hadn't been broken in the Bobcat and lit them near the barn door and the more vulnerable windows. The wind blew and snow gusted, but the little torches, sheltered somewhat by the barn itself, remained alight. A feeling of unease tightened in his gut, like a coiling snake, looking at all those burning torches. Like a scene from Frankenstein.

His nervousness must have shown because Willis said, "We'll be armed, D."

He went through the barn one last time to double-check all the shuttered windows were locked. His foot pained him at every step, but he didn't have time for it. Waylon lay snuggled against Thunder in his stall. Dylan bent and gave them both a farewell pat. He didn't blame his dog for only trusting a horse right about now.

Piper was kneeling in the stall with Hattie as he returned to the front door. She tucked the blanket around the sleeping woman. "Keep an eye on her Willis, okay?"

The foreman gave a gruff nod, and his eyes lingered on the nineteenth-century woman.

Dylan helped Willis and a visibly shaken Quinton roll a heavy feed hopper in front of the tack room. The teenager settled himself cross-legged on the floor in the hall across from the tack room. His father hissed behind it and the poor boy paled. Dylan squeezed his shoulder and then returned to Piper, who stood in front of the barn door. She was securing a bottle of the chelated silver solution inside her coat and putting on her snowshoes.

"I don't have any more ketamine," Piper told Willis in a low voice. "If Kyle wakes up—" She glanced at Quinton. Veronica sat herself down beside the boy and slung an arm around his shoulders to murmur something Dylan couldn't hear.

Willis held the shotgun in his hand and gave Piper and Dylan a grim look. "I'll keep everybody safe here. You just go get that tranquilizer gun."

Dylan strapped on his snowshoes, his injured foot protesting at the assault. Willis handed him a lead line and he tied it around his waist and then Piper's. About four feet of rope connected them. They might get lost in the snow, but they'd get lost together.

"That gun won't kill the witherling." Piper nodded toward the shotgun.

"Thus me telling you to go get the tranquilizer gun," Willis said. "The shotgun will buy us time, at least. So you two better hustle your asses."

Willis caught Dylan's gaze and held it with a small nod of determination. Dylan nodded back.

"Stay safe," Dylan said to his foreman.

"You too."

Dylan tucked his gun into his shoulder holster, wondering if it could buy *them* enough time out there to escape whatever awaited.

Willis clapped him hard on the back. A loud rattle came from the tack room and spurred Dylan to open the barn door. It rolled back to reveal a scene that made him say, "Looks like hell's frozen over."

Because in that moment, in his mind, hell was not a fiery lake. Hell was unrelenting cold. Outside, the wind howled like a hungry beast through a landscape of pure white on black. These were not the fluffy snowflakes of a Christmas card, but icy missiles being launched at his face. Like someone was doing it on purpose. Somebody who was pissed off. Which was true. He shivered and hesitated for a moment. Piper bumped into his back, forcing him to take the first step out.

Willis, his face grim and full of regret, pushed the door closed on them.

The second the door closed, the wind and snow stopped.

"Whoa." Piper stared around in the sudden, eerie silence.

"It's like somebody threw a switch," he said. The cold air in his lungs made him cough.

Even though it was afternoon, it was dark. A sliver of moon reflected a soft, white light off the snowy landscape. Behind him, Piper tugged up one of the lit tiki torches from the ground and held it high.

At the corner of the barn, snow piled up almost to the roof, but what he saw next sent a chill straight to the marrow of his bones. A path, wide enough to walk single-file, carved its way perfectly through the snow in the direction of the house.

An invitation if he'd ever seen one. And not one he cared to answer. Ravens and crows lined the snowy banks on either side.

"What do we do?" Piper asked, her hand on his back.

Piper was a strong and independent woman, with feminist ideals he'd grown to appreciate, but he sensed she wanted his direction and would follow it. And as the man who hoped to be her husband again soon, he'd give it to her.

"I think we need to get to the house and get that tranquilizer gun. It's our best shot at finishing this."

"You know he can summon predators. Control them. Like with Waylon. Whatever's out there is going to come for us."

Dylan put an arm around her shoulder. "I'm not going to let anything hurt us." He pulled her hard against his side. "Don't forget. We saw our future, Pie. We're going to get through this okay."

She didn't say anything as she eased away.

"Come on." He reached down and squeezed her gloved hand. They were like astronauts on a spacewalk, outfitted in heavy, clumsy gear and tethered to each other. "The sooner we get there, the sooner we can end this. Stick right behind me, all right?"

He stepped forward on the path, trying his best not to limp. Despite walls of snow five feet high on either side to create the path, the snow under his feet was still deep. He avoided looking at all those birds lined up like pigeons on a telephone wire. Black eyes stared down at them from either side.

"Ignore them," he said. "He's just trying to scare us."

"I know. And it's not their fault." Piper struggled with her snowshoes, which were too big.

"Walk in my steps," he told her in a hushed voice.

It was tempting to untie the ropes from their waists and move a little easier, but he knew the witherling could bring back the howling winds and blinding snow in an instant. His breath puffed out in clouds sparkling in the light of the tiki torch. The only sound was the shushing lift and fall of their snowshoes.

Deep darkness lay ahead on the snowy path, and a glance up showed him a night sky with cold, sharp stars that provided no light.

"I don't like that I can't see over," Piper said. She craned her neck, but the thick walls of snow, topped with so many black birds, hid everything from view.

"If it's any consolation, I can't see either."

"It's not, actually."

He laughed, but a terrifying noise cut him off.

Strange laughter, like a hyena or yipping coyote, sounded in the distance to his left. All at once, the ravens and crows rose into the air with raucous cries and disappeared into the night. Piper pressed herself against his back.

"It's him," she whispered.

The sound shifted with breakneck speed, coming from their right now. He turned toward it and shoved Piper further behind him. At the same time, he pulled the gun from his shoulder holster. All sense of security it might have provided in the past had evaporated. The .357 was no more than a flyswatter to a witherling, or whatever prehistoric carnivore it might call to his aid.

Dylan was already colder than he'd ever been in his life, but the creepy laughter made his blood freeze. The sound surrounded them, coming from every direction and then cut off.

The relief was short-lived as he wondered what that meant. He was so vulnerable standing in a near-tunnel of snow in arctic air, unable to see a damn thing while being hunted by an evil monster. His heart beat somewhere in the vicinity of his throat.

But they had to keep moving. The barn was an uncomfortable distance away now even if they chose to turn back. One good thing about the numbing cold was he no longer felt any pain in his foot.

"We're going to be all right." He just had to remember what Veronica described. He and Piper in the future with a child. "We already know we survive. Don't forget that, okay?"

Piper again said nothing, only trudged along in his footsteps. He stopped and faced her and with her head bowed, she plowed straight into him. She wobbled in her snowshoes, and he caught her arms in his hands. She was trembling—from cold or fear or both.

"Pie, what is it? It's like you don't believe that vision or something."

"I do." She wouldn't meet his eye.

The ice crystals in his veins coalesced into a frozen dagger, which lodged in his heart. What if she knew something from her visions? Something she didn't want to tell him? "Piper."

"I do believe it, okay, Dylan? Keep going. We need to get to the house."

"Not until you tell me what you're thinking."

"Go!" A note of hysteria entered the word. Terror flared in her eyes. It reminded him of the gleam in the eye of an elk bull when it turned to see a hunter had him in its sights. It was the knowledge of impending death. "Go, Dylan!"

"No."

She sighed. "At least keep moving while I tell you." She shoved him around. "Go, all right?"

"Fine, but if you stop talking, I stop moving."

For a few steps, there was nothing but the rhythmic crunch of their snowshoes.

Then, in a soft voice, "Ronnie's vision. It was you on the deck. She said as much. And your child, most likely."

"Most likely?" He let the skepticism bleed through, to bolster himself as much as her.

She ignored it. "Ronnie saw a woman's arms, remember? A woman. Not necessarily me."

"Of course it's necessarily you." He forced himself to keep moving forward rather than spin around and confront her. "There's no other woman on this planet I want to be with."

"Yeah, well, you know as well as anybody you don't always get what you want."

"What's that supposed to mean?"

"That you might want to be with me, but you can't if I'm dead."

Now he did stop in his tracks and whirled around. "No, Piper. I refuse to believe it. Why would you think that?"

"The tattoo," she whispered and gave him another shove. "The blackbird on the woman's wrist."

It was true Piper wasn't a tattoo kind of woman, but people changed. They changed, damn it.

"Why can't you get a tattoo in the future?" he said. Reluctantly, he turned around, but only because rustling came from behind them, on the left. He wasn't sure if Piper had heard it. He wasn't even sure *he'd* heard it. There was no point alarming her until he was.

"Do you remember my sister got a tattoo when she was in college?"

And he did, with dawning horror. "Yeah."

"So, you remember what happened?"

Dylan's feet felt like they walked through molten lead rather than snow. Piper's twin—her identical twin sister—had experienced a terrible allergic reaction to a small butterfly tattoo on her ankle. In the end, the doctor prescribed laser removal because the reaction was so bad and wouldn't stop.

"Besides the fact I have no special affinity to birds, I would never risk getting a tattoo," she said quietly. "And that means that woman in Ronnie's vision—in your future—wasn't me."

"A babysitter."

"Ronnie said the child said *mama*."

"Maybe we decided not to get back together after all," he said, too quickly. Right then, he'd take any reason other than Piper's death for that vision to be of another woman.

She laughed, a strangled sound holding no amusement. "I guess that's the best we can hope for. Either I die tonight or we don't get back together, and you end up with another woman."

"I hate both of those," he said.

"You think?"

A growl rolled in from behind them, as deep and throaty as a tractor engine. It was something big.

43

Piper, already in the grips of panic over her impending death or her impending heartbreak, felt her galloping pulse ratchet even higher. It throbbed relentlessly in her ears. She refused to accept she wouldn't come out of this ordeal alive. But to survive all of this and still lose Dylan?

Her stomach dropped down an icy slide into her frozen feet until all sensation coalesced into only the heavy, rapid drumbeat of her heart. How many times in the space of a few days could she feel this terrified before her heart gave out altogether?

Dylan shoved her behind him again. He kept doing that, and she hated that she wanted him to. She couldn't hide behind a man and cower while he faced danger alone. She made herself step away from the shelter of his broad back and hold the tiki torch aloft.

In an instant, she wished she hadn't.

"This is something new," Dylan breathed.

A wolf, larger than any she'd ever seen, crept to the edge of the wall of snow and peered down at them with yellow eyes. His lips—or hers—it could be a female, Piper thought with a sudden sense of giddiness—those lips curled back to reveal sharp, white canines. The wolf was a little bigger than a Newfoundland, which was frightening enough. But those teeth! They were larger than any she'd seen on any dog or modern wolf. It was like a wolf that had grown the teeth of a lion.

Was this what would kill her?

"A dire wolf," she whispered.

"*Game of Thrones* exaggerated a tad," Dylan said, conversationally. "But it's still scary as shit."

The wolf dropped into a crouch, muscles bunched for the leap, but before it could do so, Piper waved her torch in its face. The wolf shied away, but then it made a weird jerky movement and came close enough its whiskers burned in the flame.

And that pissed off Piper. Sure, the dire wolf might still have elected to eat her of its own volition, but the witherling was forcing this dire wolf to burn itself in obedience to him.

The wolf whimpered and Piper whipped the tiki torch away.

"Amos!" she shouted on impulse. Ringing silence answered her, but it turned out naming a fear *did* diminish it. "Amos! Let it go! This is between you and us. Leave this animal alone!"

Abruptly, the wolf sat on its haunches on the crest of the wall causing a mini-avalanche to tumble onto the path. It whimpered, either at not being able to run away or not being allowed to attack, but it didn't budge.

"Let's go." Piper let Dylan pull her along, the rope tugging at her waist. They walked backward so they could watch the wolf, still as a statue. Its golden eyes glittered, watching their slow escape.

"He's not going to let any animal eat us," Dylan said. "He wants to skin us alive himself. Just wants to scare us in the meantime."

"Well, it's working. Where do you think he is?"

"Don't know. But I know where he's going to be."

"The house?"

"Yep."

She dropped her voice to the barest whisper. "I don't think he could know why we're going there though. That's our only hope." The bottle of chelated silver bumped reassuringly inside her jacket.

The path curved and dipped until they lost sight of the dire wolf. Their terror receded enough that they faced forward. No sound of footsteps followed them, but Piper sensed the wolf followed, a hunter familiar with moving in silence through the snow.

The cold numbed her body and mind alike, her thoughts drifting to the Ice Age. Jealousy filled her that the witherling could travel through time and see such distant things as dire wolves and mastodons. Even the American Revolution or King Tut himself. Her legs moved up and down like pistons, heavy as machinery and just as unfeeling. She lost herself in a daydream where she traveled to the future and punched the woman with Dylan in Veronica's vision. Right in the face. And then, for good measure, traveled to the past and punched Allison in the face before she could sleep with her husband.

She shook herself, more afraid at having stopped being afraid than anything that had come before. Was this the start of hypothermia? Her teeth chattered hard. That was a good sign, right? She was still shivering. Her body was trying to keep her warm. It was just her mind that was failing. She couldn't let the cold and exhaustion and despair anesthetize her brain. Piper needed to stay alert. But she was so tired of being terrified out of her mind.

She poked Dylan in the back. "You all right?"

"Yeah." He, at least, sounded alert as ever. His gloved hand still gripped the gun at his side. "Not long now."

The path began to rise, and the walls of snow appeared to shrink until they walked on top of the deep, deep snow. A new fear consumed her of sinking into its depths to be smothered alive.

"Don't stop moving," Dylan said, reading her thoughts.

She focused on the house, so close now. Snow buried the yard and bushes. The deck itself had disappeared and only the top of the railing showed. The snow rose halfway up the slider.

The house lay waiting for them. Dark, yes. But empty? Not likely.

44

Dylan didn't like that it had been all too easy to reach the house. Sure, the dire wolf had come along, but it hadn't attacked. The witherling was taunting them. As if to confirm that, the wind swirled and built, extinguishing the torch and plunging them into darkness.

He held up an arm to shield his face from the onslaught. The snow whipped around them like a tornado, and he pulled Piper into a crouch beside him and wrapped his arms around her, the gun still gripped in his hand. With his other hand, he hung onto his hat, using it to shield Piper's face as he bent his head over hers.

Dylan clung to Piper in the building vacuum the wind created. She wouldn't die. He wouldn't let her. She *had* to be the woman in the vision, or he didn't want any part of that future.

He lifted his head to shout, his eyes squeezed tight as he tucked her close against him. "You can't have her, you bastard! Do you hear me? I won't let you kill her."

The wind sucked his words away, and with it, his breath. His lungs burned, the only warm part of him. They would suffocate in the snow. But at least they'd die together.

In an instant, the wind disappeared. They huddled for a moment as he gasped for the icy cold air that seared his lungs. Dylan unfolded himself and pulled Piper to her feet. They stared at the sight before them.

Even in the darkness, he could see all the snow had blown off the deck and stairs. No sign of the dead hell pig remained. Their way into the house was made clear.

"I don't want you going in there," he said.

"Well, I sure as heck don't want you leaving me out here." Piper squeezed his hand. "We go in together, all right?"

He squeezed her hand back. "I guess that's what love is all about. Facing the monsters side-by-side."

"I was hoping the monsters would be more metaphorical."

He laughed, releasing clouds of vapor around his face.

And then they climbed the stairs, hand-in-hand, awkward in their snowshoes. The sliding door was unlocked, and he opened it wide. He paused a moment to untie the rope around their waists.

"Don't take off your snowshoes," he told Piper. "We need to be able to get back across the snow quickly." An overpowering stench of rotting flesh hit him like a punch in the nose and underneath, another stronger smell he couldn't identify. They stepped into the living room together. A wet trail led into the kitchen.

He squinted at it in the dark. It wasn't red like blood. Piper held up her phone light to reveal a flash of iridescence in the liquid trail.

"Is that—"

"Dylan."

She pointed to where the trail led to Gilbert. In the entrance to the kitchen, he sat tied to a chair by thick coils of rope, his head lolling back to reveal a huge bite wound in his throat. For a second, Dylan thought the man was dead and the source of the smell, but then Gilbert's chest rose with a deep breath. His head snapped up.

"He's still alive!" Piper rushed forward, but Dylan grabbed her by the arm to stop her just in time.

Gilbert's eyes popped open. Just like the others—nothing but blackness. He snarled, revealing rows of sharp teeth. Thank the good Lord the man was tied up, though it was puzzling why.

"Let's focus on getting what we came for," he said, reluctant to say out loud what that was. "We'll get Gilbert back to his old self once we kill the monster. Same as Veronica."

Then a rasping click drew his attention to Gilbert's hand, trapped at his side by the rope around his chest. Dylan realized in an instant. "Get out of here, Piper! Get what we need!"

To her credit, Piper didn't question him. She clomped as fast as she could toward the entry hall where the gun cabinet stood.

The clicking noise repeated and Dylan rushed forward just as a small flame leaped to life from the lighter in Gilbert's fist. Like a fiery zipper, the spark shot down the line of what must be gasoline on the chair leg. The floor under the chair erupted into flames, and fire rolled out the kitchen toward him.

"Dylan!" Piper's voice shouted through the sudden roar.

"Get out!" he shouted back.

Dylan fought every instinct to run because to do so would mean following the trail of gasoline back into the living room. The kitchen, with Gilbert's flaming chair, was safer.

Gilbert.

Dylan, clumsy in his snowshoes, ripped down a curtain—one Piper had insisted on hanging—from the kitchen window. He beat out the flames under the chair before they could consume the man. Behind him, heat rolled off the fire gaining ground in the living room.

He glanced over his shoulder when Piper opened the front door on a gust. The flames leaped up like living things and raced over the couch. His house was being destroyed. His anger burned like the flames.

But he forced himself to focus on Gilbert. If Dylan could free him, he'd be releasing a monster. If he left the man tied up, Gilbert would die in the fire, making Dylan the monster.

It wasn't a choice in his book. Dylan used his teeth to pull off the glove of his right hand and yanked a butcher knife from the wooden block on the counter. He sawed at the ropes on the back of the chair. Gilbert snarled and thrashed, rocking the chair on its legs, but Dylan did his best to ignore him. Smoke billowed in from the living room. He considered opening the kitchen window but was afraid the fresh air would feed the fire. From the back yard, he could hear Piper screaming for him to get out.

The ropes were tough. He sawed and cut and slashed and sawed while tears streamed from his eyes, and his lungs burned. Gilbert gave another hard thrash. The ropes fell to the blackened floor. The man leaped out of the chair and faced Dylan.

Dylan held the knife in front of him. He'd be plenty pissed to have risked his life to save the man from the fire only to have to stab him to death. Well, it wasn't a silver knife, so maybe not to death, exactly.

Gilbert's black eyes fixed on him. For the briefest moment, a human expression crossed his features. One of turmoil and conflict, like something battled inside him. Whichever side won, Dylan wasn't sure, but the man threw himself through the kitchen window and into the backyard with a crash of shattering glass.

Dylan wasted no time in following. Piper was out there. He used one precious second to retrieve his glove from the kitchen counter and pull it back on. Then he knocked aside jagged pieces of glass and pulled himself through the broken window.

He caught a glimpse of Gilbert bounding over the snow, animal-like, toward the barn. To his horror, the barn was engulfed in flames as well, thick clouds of gray smoke appearing light against the black sky.

"Oh no," he breathed. Willis and Veronica and Quinton and Hattie. Kyle. Waylon. All the horses.

"Dylan!" Piper shouted up at him, relief visible on her pale face.

Normally, it would be a long drop from the kitchen to the yard, with the walkout basement below. But with all the snow, he threw a leg over the sill and stepped out. Pain lanced from his foot up his shin. *Too bad, foot.* He gingerly navigated the deep snow to join Piper on the path the witherling had created.

"We need to get to the barn," he said. "We need to save them."

45

Piper pulled Dylan against her with a sob of gratitude. "I thought I lost you. Again."

He patted her back. "I'm fine, Piper. We gotta go. The others could be trapped."

"I know." Her heart clenched at the thought of all the people and animals that might even now be burning. "Go help them. I need to load up the darts."

He glanced down at the case at their feet. Opening it was as far as Piper had gotten before she'd been too distracted by Dylan's fate to continue.

"I'll wait," he said.

"No. Like you said, they could be trapped in the fire. You have a job to do and so do I."

She could see the internal struggle as he looked from her to the burning barn and back to her. Behind them, the house crackled and roared with flames.

She put her gloved hand on his chest. "These darts our only chance at ending this. I need you to save Ronnie. And Willis and

Hattie and that boy. Go." She gave a little shove to goad him into action.

Dylan kissed her hard. "Once I know they're out of the barn safe, I'm coming back for you."

"Then we'll meet in the middle." Tears sprang to her eyes, wishing they could have done that a year ago.

His broad back turned, and he tromped through the snow, making the trek back to the barn. She hated to see him limp.

Piper ripped off her gloves. She would have to work fast. The witherling might appear at any moment, and her fingers would soon become too numb for delicate work. She rushed to assemble the pieces. The syringe, the dart case, the needle cover. The fire was at least illuminating her work. A lump formed in her throat thinking of Dylan's childhood home going up in flames.

His parents were gone forever, and now everything they'd built would soon be as well. Dylan would have nothing.

No, she thought fiercely. He'd have her. And they'd make a new family. A new home.

In the distance, the odd hyena laugh echoed. Cold dread pooled in her stomach at the thought of Dylan alone.

She blew on her hands and rubbed them together. One by one, she laid out the empty darts in front of her. Five in total. She'd have five shots. It wasn't much against the lightning speed of a witherling, but it was all she'd have.

She took each one in turn and pressurized them, readying the darts to be filled with the chelated silver solution.

Too fast. The cold was setting in too fast. Even in that short time, her fingers were clumsy with cold. She struggled to unscrew the bottle of solution, to draw up the liquid into a syringe. She emptied the syringe into the chamber of the dart, giving herself a weapon. A shot of silver that could destroy the witherling. She hoped.

The laugh came again in the distance. She said a prayer for Dylan and returned her focus to finishing this task. She reached for the bottle of solution to fill another syringe but knocked it over to send it spinning down the icy slope of the yard.

"No!"

She jumped up and snatched the bottle. Empty. The silver solution dissolved into the snow around her. Piper buried her head in her hands and fought the urge to cry. One shot. She'd get one shot at slaying the monster. No time for lamenting. Piper loaded the precious dart into the gun. The only thing left to do was put one foot in front of the other.

The laugh sounded again. The witherling was close. Good. She gripped the tranquilizer gun hard and smiled grimly. She would not miss her one shot. At last, she was on more even footing with her enemy. Let him come and find her.

But as she made her slow, laborious way, it became clear the witherling had no such plan to seek her out. It was a solitary journey, for which she was thankful. Her shot of silver solution could neither be wasted on a primeval predator nor would it be any use against a hell pig or dire wolf. Acrid smoke drifted in the air above her to blot out the stars. She followed in Dylan's tracks, relieved with every step that they didn't come to an end. If possible, the trip back to the barn felt even longer than the trip to the house.

At last, an orange glow from the burning barn spilled over the banks of snow like a false dawn. Flames crackled and heat poured from the fire. To her horror, a horse screamed. She pushed herself forward faster.

Had Dylan not released them? Were their friends still trapped inside?

Piper jogged on numb legs and clumsy snowshoes as best she could, her breath ragged. The screams intensified, sickening, and terrible. What was happening? With a grunt, she kicked her leg to dig her snowshoe into the wall of snow. She clawed and heaved her way up out of the path. Her arms and legs were no more than quivering, over-stretched rubber bands, but she managed to pull herself over the crest of the snowbank to stand atop it.

Before her, behind her, all around her, a terrifying scene awaited. The barn stood burning not thirty yards away. In an arc around the barn stood dark figures, grotesquely lit in the fire. A huge circle of meadow, the snow was gone so the grass was visible, stretched in front of the barn. A snowy bank encircled the scene, row upon row of ravens and crows assembled atop it. The battleground had been drawn.

A prehistoric lion stood cheek-to-jowl with a mountain lion. A coyote paced next to a dire wolf. To her shock, Foxy sat on her haunches between the dire wolf's front legs. A short-faced bear dwarfed the black bears on either side of it. A trio of entelodonts sat together like a nightmare version of the three little pigs. And interspersed between all the animals were at least two dozen men-turned-witherling spawn.

Piper recognized a Union soldier's uniform. A Native American man wore buckskin. She spotted a tattered pinstripe suit on another that might have come from the Roaring Twenties. Another man wore a form-fitted bodysuit, lined with lights and sensors she couldn't begin to understand.

Not one of the wither-men wore contemporary clothes with the notable exception of Gilbert and Kyle. Her heart sunk at the sight of them. The rest appeared to have been plucked from other times—past and future—bitten and turned, and brought to this place and time with the sole purpose of terrorizing and killing.

At the center of this hellish half-circle huddled Dylan, Willis, Ronnie, Hattie, Quinton, and Waylon silhouetted against the orange flames shooting up from the barn. They stood with their backs together, clutching tiki torches no better than matchsticks. The horses, even little Thunder, nervously trotted around the cluster of humans in the middle.

But where the hell was her target?

She drew in a deep breath of frigid air and yelled as loud as she could. "Amos! You coward! Do you really need all this help? Come out here and face me alone!"

In response, dozens of glowing eyes turned in her direction from both animals and once-humans. A crow cawed. The short-faced bear stood on its haunches and roared. With a screaming whinny, Bub, the horse nearest the bear, shied away, edging too close to the giant lion. One massive paw swiped out and caught the horse's rear leg. Bub's legs crumpled under him as he fell to the ground to land on his side. The lion pounced.

The effect was like a cracked whip on the circle of monsters. The two closest wither-men fell upon the horse and ripped at his stomach with their bare hands. The dire wolf leaped onto the horse's hindquarters even as the lion took a savage bite from Bub's long neck.

The horse screamed, heart-rending and near human in its cries. Legs flailed, and by the light of the fire, she saw sprays of blood mist the air as the poor creature was eaten alive. Piper watched with dread as Dylan stumbled forward, a rifle clutched in his hand.

"No!" she yelled, but she was too far away to stop him.

Willis tried though, reached out only to have Dylan shake him off.

"Dylan, no!" she said again, over the horse's continued screams.

The rest of the wither-men's heads swiveled in her direction along with one curious coyote. They all looked so hungry.

Dylan headed straight toward Bub and to her astonishment, the lion, wolf, and wither-men fell back as one.

Amos controlled them all, of course. Dylan was right. The witherling had no intention of letting anything else kill what he wanted for himself.

Looking more confident, Dylan marched forward. If his foot hurt, he no longer limped. But adrenaline was also a hell of a thing. He placed the barrel of the rifle against the horse's forehead and pulled the trigger. The screams cut off at once.

For the briefest moment, a collective sigh of relief pulsed through the circle in the heavy silence.

Then all hell broke loose.

46

Suddenly snarls, growls, roars, and shrieks filled Dylan's ears. He turned away from the pathetic sight of Bub, so reminiscent of poor Lightning, and saw Piper tumbling down a hill of snow into the cleared meadow. He had to get to her. But then movement turned his attention to his friends. Piper wasn't in any immediate danger, which was more than he could say for the others.

The half-circle of space around them was shrinking as animals and monsters alike drew closer, tightening the noose. Waylon nipped at Thunder's heels, herding him behind the humans, and in the nick of time too because all at once the other horses broke through the line. They pounded over the clearing and hit deep snow at the edges.

A few carnivores peeled away to pursue the struggling horses. It wasn't enough to shrink the line of monsters encroaching on his friends. A horse screamed, but Dylan couldn't help that one. He had to save the others. The little group couldn't back up any farther without risking injury from the flames licking out the barn door.

The fire also held the monsters at bay. Willis thrust his torch at a coyote creeping forward with raised hackles. Quinton, his young face looking vicious in the firelight, slashed his torch around like a sword. Too much, as luck would have it, and the flame blew out. The coyote, emboldened at this turn of events, lunged forward and snapped at the boy's leg.

Dylan ran toward the group, accepting his foot would hurt for the foreseeable future. The beasts and wither-men fell back from him with frustrated snarls. He was untouchable. For now. Dylan stretched out his arms to protect Willis, Veronica, Hattie, and Quinton. But it wasn't enough. He couldn't encircle them all. They were too close to the fire as it was, and they couldn't stand behind him single-file.

His gaze roved over the group of hungry predators. Behind them, Piper, her snowshoes gone, was approaching, bringing herself closer to danger.

A black-eyed wither-man leaped through the air with an inhuman cry and tumbled into Willis's shoulder. A shotgun blast sent the creature rocketing backward, a mess for the moment.

A hell pig barreled toward the left side of their group, where Quinton and Veronica clutched at one another. The beast gave a porcine squeal and the group scattered like bowling pins, separating Dylan off with Willis and Hattie, leaving the other two vulnerable.

Before the pig could do any damage, Piper ran and pushed herself in front of Quinton and Veronica. As with Dylan, the animal wheeled away to avoid colliding with Piper. His hopes soared. So long as he and Piper stood in front of the others, they'd be safe. She clutched the tranquilizer gun in her hand.

The hungry horde paced in front of them, looking for a weak spot. The dire wolf whined, perhaps in frustration. The hell pigs trotted with tails erect, like some sort of overgrown warthogs. The short-faced bear rocked back and forth on its front legs. But nothing was so terrifying as the ones who had been men. Their lips peeled back, their sharp teeth catching the firelight. Clawed hands hung at their sides, ready and waiting for the command from their master.

Wherever he might be hiding.

"We appear to be at a stalemate," Piper said, raising her voice over the sound of the fire, of timbers crashing down inside the barn.

Sparks flew into the air, stoking hot anger in Dylan's chest. His house *and* his new barn. Rage clogged his throat to see his ranch destroyed.

One of the wither-men unhinged his jaw and screamed at them. Its pacing grew frenetic. The control held on that one was about to snap. Or maybe Amos had decided he didn't care how they died after all.

Behind him, Quinton gasped, and Dylan's stomach did a flip. The monster pacing before him was Kyle.

The moments stretched into fraught minutes. The muscles in Dylan's shoulders bunched as he held the rifle at the ready. The tendons in his neck were tight and aching. Sweat trickled down his back from the heat of the fire behind him.

They'd all be barbequed alive if something didn't change soon.

And then something did.

Piper broke from their group and marched toward the line of carnivores. "Come and get me, Amos! Let's finish this."

"Piper, no!" Dylan stepped toward her, and the wither-men hissed and moved closer to the others.

"Take care of them," she said. "I've got to end this, Dylan. We know it's got to be me."

He didn't like what she implied. That she thought the future revealed she was dead and so she must have been the one to face down the witherling.

She turned back to give him one last look, and he'd never seen her so beautiful. The fire gleamed red in her strawberry blonde hair and her blue eyes glowed in her flushed face. She mouthed the words.

I love you.

Then she shouldered past the short-faced bear, so audacious as to trail a hand down the great beast's side as she passed it. He suspected she felt awe and admiration for the prehistoric animal and even pity for the creature. It snorted when she touched it, but let her by unharmed.

How could she do this to him? Leave him so he had to choose between protecting the others and helping her? As the distance between them grew, his fingers curled around the rifle, and he bared his teeth with a shout of frustration.

Piper was now about twenty yards away. She stood ramrod straight, all alone in the clearing. Out there, away from the burning barn, the details of her disappeared into the darkness.

From the nearby forest, a form materialized. So dark at first as to be no more than a shadow. But as it approached, Dylan's heart hammered even harder. Large, sprawling antlers became clear. It might have been his imagination, but he caught the whiff of rotting meat all the way over here.

The witherling headed straight toward Piper.

She looked very small as she held her ground.

He thought nothing would ever force him to look away from that scene, but to his right, footsteps crunched in snow, dozens of flapping wings took flight, and someone shouted in alarm.

He turned to see the rest of his ranch hands from the trailers making their way over the hill of snow and into the clearing, sending corvid birds scattering into the air. Michael and Randy. And to his dismay, Kyle's and Raymond's wives, Michael's girlfriend Tanya, and Raymond's two little kids.

The seven of them stood on a patch of yellowed grass, a hill of snow behind them, the meadow and burning barn before them. The adults held guns, while Raymond's kids hid their faces in their mother's coat.

Dylan wasn't the only one to notice their approach. In unison, every carnivore and monstrous man's head swiveled in the newcomers' direction.

The first animal, a mountain lion, sprang at them, and Kyle's wife screamed.

47

Someone screamed behind Piper, but she couldn't break focus. The witherling strode toward her, his smooth movements at odds with his rotting, broken body. White ribs gleamed in the darkness. Something wet inside his torso reflected light. And those antlers. Huge and sharp and menacing. Ropes of putrid velvet hung in silhouette.

The smell made her gag. She'd ripped off her glove to hold the trigger of the dart gun better and now her finger was frozen to it, fused with the gun.

One shot. She had just one shot. It had to be right in the monster's heart. She waited for him to come nearer.

Behind her, gunshots blasted, people shouted, animals snarled, and wither-men shrieked.

You will pay! It was a whisper, but louder than anything Piper had ever heard. *You will die!* The noise grew in her brain, threatening to tear apart each synapse as it reverberated down her neurons.

YOU WILL DIE! DIE! DIE!

Her hands convulsed to fly up and cover her ears. The tranquilizer gun fell at her feet, and still, she heard the evil voice in her mind. Piper doubled over and collapsed on her knees in the grass, her hands clapped to the sides of her head.

The witherling could have sped to her in an instant, but he made his slow and steady way over the stubbled field. She knew he relished each terrified breath she struggled to draw. The tranquilizer gun glimmered nearby, but she couldn't pull her hands from her head to grab it.

Then he was there, looming above, the giant rack of antlers outlined against the sky. She looked up and up and up into those bottomless pools of pure black.

DIE. DIE. DIE. DIE. DIE.

The words cut off. A paralyzing terror gripped Piper's body. The witherling was manipulating her with fear, making it impossible for her to move.

Thick strands of viscous saliva hung from his canine-filled mouth of decay. His face, a skull with tattered strips of flesh, tipped down toward her. A long intake of breath hissed through the holes where nostrils should be.

Piper struggled to think coherent thoughts. Her brain was encased in a cloying, heavy layer of dread that made her long to die. Death would be better than this agony of fear invading her mind. She'd never known fear could hurt before. She should let herself die and then she could—

"Piper!"

The witherling's head whipped in the direction of the voice, releasing the hold on Piper's mind and body. Dylan was running toward her, a scene of carnage lit up behind him by the blazing barn. Gunshots fired and creatures howled as animal and human shapes fought and twisted.

The witherling ran at Dylan, and she screamed as the monster slashed out a clawed hand. Dylan turned and ducked. The fabric of his coat ripped and he yelped, tumbling to the ground.

Piper scrabbled in the grass at her feet for the tranquilizer gun.

"Dad, no!" came Quinton's voice from far away. Rifles fired, shotguns boomed. But she made herself shut it out.

The witherling fell upon Dylan, and she ran toward them both. Ran as fast as she'd ever run in her life, the tranquilizer gun outstretched in her hand.

The witherling's back was to her as he curled over Dylan, ready to devour him. She needed a clear shot at his chest if she wanted to hit his heart. Oh God, she didn't even know for sure the silver solution would be enough—if it would work.

"Hey, Amos! Look at me. It's me you want."

But the witherling didn't turn her way. His antlers bent over Dylan's head, and he screamed. Did he even now bite Dylan?

"Help me!" She didn't know who she was asking, crying out a desperate plea, a prayer.

From out of the night sky, a raven rocketed down toward the witherling, cawing and screeching. The antlers rose up as the witherling lifted his head. The raven beats its wings, one of them with two white feathers, around the creature's face, until he reared up with a rusty-gate scream, unfolding himself from his crouch over Dylan.

Long, clawed hands swiped at the raven. It bobbed and weaved and circled him until the witherling turned.

He faced Piper and the raven flew away. She'd recognized the bird, the one she'd saved on her porch. It had repaid the favor, buying her this one moment of time.

By the stingy light of the moon, she caught sight of the witherling's slippery, beating heart visible through the jagged ribs.

She drew a deep breath, sighted down the tranquilizer gun, and squeezed the trigger.

With a pop of pressurized air, the dart flew through the darkness and found its home deep inside the monster's heart.

The reaction was instantaneous. Amos—the witherling—let

out an unearthly scream just as his brother had done. His hands clutched at his chest, but it was too late. The chelated silver solution was working.

From nearer the barn, Quinton gave an anguished cry and Veronica screamed. She glanced over to see the wither-men falling to the ground. What prehistoric predators remained were scattering away from the burning fire to disappear into the dark.

The witherling shrieked. Piper looked back to watch the massive rack of antlers recede into his skull. His body knitted itself back into the human he'd been before, one who resembled his brother. She felt a tremor of pity as she watched the man die and decompose before her eyes.

She ran forward in time to glance the sizzling pile of ashes singeing the grass.

But that was not what concerned her.

To her relief, Dylan was sitting up, rubbing a hand over his face.

"Are you all right?" she gasped.

"Yeah. He—he scratched me good across my back and it hurt like a mother." Dylan reached for his left shoulder blade. "But I think it's healing already."

Dylan rose to his feet and wrapped Piper in a tight hug, tucking her head against his chest. "It's over. You did it, babe. It's over."

"It was that raven. A bird saved us." She knew she sounded a bit hysterical. "Allergies or not, I think I might be getting a raven tattoo."

He laughed, a rumble under her ear.

They turned to the burning barn and the ragged group of people standing in the clearing. They included not only Dylan's group, but the shapes of dozens of wither-men returned to human.

"Piper!" came a shout from Willis. "Dylan! Get over here!"

Someone was sobbing.

Piper broke into a run, as did Dylan beside her.

The confused men milling around parted to let them through.

Quinton's mother had an arm around him as the pair sobbed over the prone body of Kyle.

"Hell of an unlucky thing." Willis glanced at Randy, who stood a short distance away, wringing his hands. "Kyle got shot just as he turned back human."

"Quinton, I'm so sorry," Randy burst out.

"He—he's dead?" Dylan asked.

Willis gave a grim nod. "Veronica's over there." He lifted his chin to point.

Piper's stomach went into a free fall as she stumbled to where Ronnie lay. Gilbert knelt beside her, crying.

"What happened?" she asked.

Gilbert looked up, his eyes red-rimmed. "A giant lion. Piper, it was huge."

She gazed down at the pool of blood, in which lay what remained of her best friend.

"Oh, God." Piper covered her mouth. "It wasn't supposed to end this way." She felt for a pulse.

Epilogue

"Thanks, Jeb." Piper pulled off her white coat and hung it on the hook by her office door. "I appreciate you closing up."

"No problem, ma'am." The shy man smiled, dressed in his tech scrubs. All traces of the young Civil War soldier, haunted by his experiences helping a surgeon on the battlefield, had disappeared. He'd blossomed into quite the competent animal nurse.

Destroying the witherlings hadn't returned their victims to their correct times.

"You'll keep an eye on the relief vet for me, right?" Piper put a hand on her swollen belly.

"Of course. You can count on me."

"Um, hello, what do you think I'll be doing?" Veronica came up beside her with a present wrapped in pink and white paper. As usual, she let the diamond ring sparkle as her left hand lingered on the gift.

It made Piper smile to think of Ronnie's and Gilbert's

upcoming spring wedding.

Piper caught the slight limp as her best friend moved, but she doubted anyone who wasn't looking for it would see it now. From Veronica's right knee down, she moved confidently on the last and final in a series of prosthetic limbs she'd used doing her recovery.

"You already threw me a baby shower, Ronnie. You don't have to give me any more presents."

"Of course I do. My honorary niece can't rely on you for her fashion sense. And it's your last day of work."

"Not forever."

"I know. But I'll miss you."

"Ronnie. You and Gilbert live on the ranch now."

Veronica laughed. "But I won't see you every day."

"Not at work. But I'll still see you just about every day. It's kind of impossible to get rid of you. Shall we drive home together?"

She and Veronica walked out the front of her practice. Jeb lived in her old apartment now so she could no longer exit out the back. Veronica drove them home—she was quite amazing at driving with that prosthetic foot of hers.

On the drive, Ronnie talked on and on about bridesmaid dresses and flowers. "Do you think Foxy should be the ring bearer?"

"Sure." Piper smiled, remembering how the little Shiba Inu had returned to her owner's side after the battle, whining to find Veronica so injured. The dog had visited Ronnie many times at the hospital throughout her recovery and deserved a place in the wedding.

Piper let Ronnie's chatter wash over her. Her thoughts were too focused on the Crazy K spread out below. She spotted Randy's old trailer where Ronnie and Gilbert now lived. The poor man had moved away to another ranch, too ashamed to face Quinton and his mom, who'd stayed on. No one blamed him, but it was a tough thing.

It had also been a real tough thing explaining everything to the police. The bizarre fires were attributed to an arsonist, who'd perished in the old barn. Only bones survived of the stash of body parts Piper had found, and Dylan had buried them deep in the forest before the police arrived. Veronica's and Hattie's injuries were explained as the work of a bear, who'd been crazed by the fires. Poor Kyle had been shot dead on accident, in an attempt to kill the rogue animal and conveniently, there was even a dead black bear to show the authorities. Luckily, the sheriff wrote it up as an accident because he was Michael's father.

Explaining the appearance of new people from other times had proved more difficult, but they were making progress on that too, with the help of a lawyer friend of Dylan's.

Piper's gaze moved over to the trailer where Hattie now lived with Willis. Hattie had been delighted when Piper's online search turned up an old newspaper photograph of her friend Anna, one of the first women to cast her vote in Colorado in 1893. The newlyweds were out on the redwood deck, barbequing in the mild fall weather. Piper smiled to think of their happiness.

At the movement down by the new red barn, her smile widened. Thunder trotted around on a lead line, worked by one of the men left behind and out of his time. A dozen of them had elected to stay at the Crazy K. And they needed every one of them to run the popular—and highly profitable—dude ranch she and Dylan had worked so hard to create.

The hunters' cabins now accommodated family reunions, parents with children who wanted to play cowboy, and couples who desired a romantic adventure. A large dining hall stood near the cabins. At this moment, a family of five peered into one of the elk pens, where the remains of Dylan's elk stock would live out their days in peace.

The shining jewel in the center of the ranch, at least from Piper's viewpoint, was the new house. It had much the same layout as before—river rock and split logs and a wrap-around deck—but all the memories inside this house were new and fresh and happy.

Ronnie pulled her little car around to the front door and dropped Piper off. She went inside to be greeted by the heavenly scent of cooking pot roast.

"Hey, wife of mine!" Dylan came out of the kitchen wearing an apron, Waylon following behind with his tail wagging high. He pulled the apron over his head and came over to grab her hand. He planted a kiss on the raven tattoo on the inside of her wrist, right on her pulse.

Piper had tracked down an artist who used an unusual hypoallergenic tattoo ink, and she'd had no reaction.

"Wife," he said again. "Don't think I'll ever get tired of calling you that."

"I know what you mean, husband." She kissed him on the mouth.

"Dinner should be ready in a half-hour or so. Celebratory drink?"

"Sure." Piper's heart filled with joy. She couldn't believe her good fortune. She had found the love of her life, lost him, and found him again. Their love was richer and deeper for it. And they had created a new love between them. Her hand went to her stomach once more.

Piper settled herself on the couch, and Waylon lay on the floor, putting his head on her feet. Osiris curled up against the hound. A moment later, Dylan handed her a glass of sparkling apple cider and sat down. "To maternity leave."

They clinked their glasses together and drank.

A few minutes later, Dylan turned on the evening news.

"—been dozens of sightings of a large bear, described as bigger than any grizzly. Employees working in the Gunnison National Forest say they have been plagued with such reports and claim they are part of a mass prank."

Piper snorted. "It ain't a prank, guys." Her laugh faded into a pensive silence. "You ever worry about the future?"

"Not really. We killed the witherlings."

"But time travel paradoxes are tricky."

"It's true, but we killed them before. If we have to, we can do it again. In fact, the only thing I worry about for the future is that I'll run out of ideas on how to make you happy."

She sighed and rested her head on his shoulder. "Don't worry about that, Dylan. I only need you. You make me happier than I could ever imagine."

They sat together like that for a long time. Somewhere off in the forest, a creature roared, but with Dylan at her side, she wasn't scared. Together, they could face anything.

Acknowledgements

I'm going to try to fit this all in before they cue the orchestra to play me off. First, thank you to Literary Wanderlust, and my kind and gracious editor, Susan Brooks, for creating a space to publish unique books. Lisa Guire, I apologize for my love/hate relationship with commas. Thanks for your copy editor's keen eye. Pozu Mitsuma, many thanks for creating my cover.

To my mother, Sherrie, my first cheerleader, I haven't found a narrator who can captivate me like you did reading me library books as a child. You introduced me to the magic of books that sent me down this road. My father, David, showed me the power of books when I found him—big, burly man that he was—crying over Where the Red Fern Grows. He always believed in me. Dad, I hope you're reading my book in heaven with a bag of mini Butterfingers.

Speaking of, I once heard a quote along the lines that all writers go to heaven because they already lived their hell on earth. I'd never survive it without some incredible fellow writers. Amy Wilson and Amanda Nay, you have no idea how much our critique group has meant to me. Thank you for all your insight—you're always right. To so many people at RMFW and the Southwest Littleton Critique Group, I wouldn't be a writer without you. It would be a long list to name you all, but you know who you are, and you're pretty darn special.

Danielle and Patrick Greenleaf, thanks for reading and cheering me on. Dannie, for the last time, they're only kind of like zombies. Thanks for always being there and having the courage to ask me how my writing's been going. Special thanks to my mother-in-law, Jenny, and my sister-in-law, Caroline, for enthusiastically reading my books over the years. All my in-laws are a top-notch group. Suzy, I'll never forget my Casio electronic typewriter, and Martha, your unwavering belief that I would one day be an author. Thank you both.

I'm so grateful to the readers. If you're anything like me, I imagine you read to find a fun escape from everyday life. I hope I gave you that. Thanks for reading.

Finally, to my family, you are my reason, full stop. This writer is stumped to find the words to say how much I love you. Thank you to my best friend—and best husband ever, Jon. You've made every worthwhile dream of mine come true. To my three wonderful kids, Isabelle, Zoe, and Luke, you made me the winner of the best children sweepstakes. You're the bravest beta readers to give your own mom honest and perceptive critiques. I love our brainstorming walks. To my cats, Delilah and Wanda, your ability to help me procrastinate is second to none. And of course, thank you to Aubie and George, my pugs. Their not-so-gentle snoring is the happy soundtrack for my writing.